GRIMOIRE

ALLAN LEVERONE

For Wesley: I can't wait to meet you

PART ONE
HISTORY

1

October 12, 1798
The forest outside Paskagankee, Massachusetts
Province of Maine

The nighttime breeze threatened winter's chill as Samuel Beebe hiked through the forest. The temperature had been steadily dropping since this afternoon and now the cold chewed through Samuel's clothing with grim relentlessness. He stopped several times to refasten his leather bootlaces, pulling them tight with fingers turning numb.

It didn't help.

Midnight was approaching and Samuel knew that by morning a thick layer of frost would have stiffened the field grass. The leaves littering the forest floor, fiery shades of red and yellow, would be crinkly and delicate, like the skin of a dying old man.

Samuel's breath condensed in front of his face and then floated away in the uneven light of his lantern. He slogged along, weighted down by the materials he'd spirited out of the family's farmhouse, his goal a secret location deep in the primeval forest surrounding the village of Paskagankee.

It was more than a two-mile hike. Normally, walking that distance would be child's play for a boy well used to working long hours on the family farm. But in the dark, and with his rising sense of anticipation, the journey seemed to take forever.

He didn't care.

He shifted the bag's strap on his shoulder. The leather dug through his sheepskin coat and into the skin with every step. It seemed he was destined to be uncomfortable as he completed this sacred ritual.

He didn't care about that, either.

What was a little discomfort when compared with the opportunity to experience wondrous, illicit, forbidden things? What did a few bruises matter when he would soon be afforded insights far deeper and more valuable than anything he'd ever learned in Paskagankee's little one-room schoolhouse?

He was excited and, he had to admit to himself, a little frightened. He'd stumbled upon the combination to Pa's home safe last week snooping through Ma's dresser, and after a nervous few days trying to decide what to do with that information, had finally used it.

Opening the safe had really been nothing but a lark. He didn't really expect to find anything of interest, but boy was he wrong on *that* count.

He'd waited to dig into the safe until he was certain everyone in the family was otherwise occupied. Three long days of anticipation, when all he'd wanted was to scream at everyone to leave the house for a while so he could tend to his business. It was an eternity for an inquisitive thirteen-year-old.

And then, when he was finally able to sate his curiosity, the stuff he found inside at first was a disappointment.

It was boring as hell, in fact.

The Last Will and Testament of Thaddeus and Catherine Beebe.

The official-looking document called the Property Deed, printed on thick, stiff paper and decorated with a fancy seal. Samuel didn't have a lot of school-smarts but he assumed that paper was important because it gave the Beebes permission to live where they lived and farm the land under their boots.

A series of other official-looking documents—like Certificates of Live Birth issued by the Province of Maine for the Beebe children—and similar stuff, none of which Samuel gave a damn about.

He'd almost tossed everything back inside the safe and closed it in disgust.

But then he'd found something that rendered everything else irrelevant, tucked away behind and beneath all the other official looking and thus boring junk. It was an item he didn't exactly understand at first, but one he immediately recognized held significance based solely on the fact that he *didn't* understand it.

The item was a book. The book was leather bound. It was written partly in a weird kind of stilted old English and partly in what he thought might be Latin. And it was confusing to read. Some of the English portions were nearly as indecipherable as the Latin.

The book was old.

It was ancient.

Samuel recognized that much immediately.

It was also forbidden, and thus scary, and thus desirable.

It resembled in appearance the Holy Bible Ma kept in a special place in the sitting room: atop a small reading table in the corner.

But it was definitely *not* a bible. Its cover depicted a horned goat standing on its hind legs like a man, performing some kind of bizarre-looking dance, capering in a forest that looked a lot like that surrounding Paskagankee.

The design was somehow unnatural. Perverse. Obscene, even.

Samuel gazed at the book for a while inside the safe and then eventually picked it up. When he did he felt a sensation of power radiating out of it, at once thrilling and sickening. The sensation flooded his body, racing through his fingers where they clutched the book, traveling up his arms like fire consuming kindling-wood, and then spreading throughout his body, warming it and filling it with dread.

He panicked. He tossed the book back into the safe where it fell among the boring documents with a muffled thump. He swore never to touch the clearly accursed volume ever again, even as he was reaching for it with shaking hands. He hesitated only a moment and then lifted it out of the safe once more, eyeing it with equal parts revulsion and fascination.

The strange feelings flooded his body again, but this time he was prepared for them, and so the terror was lessened.

Slightly.

This time Samuel held onto the book instead of tossing it away like a frightened child, and as the seconds passed and the feelings inside him did not intensify, he began to understand that this book was special. It held the promise of wonder and adventure, two things sorely lacking in the existence of a thirteen-year-old farmer's son in 1798 Paskagankee.

He sat motionless in front of Pa's safe, the bible-that-wasn't-a-bible clutched in his hands, heart beating wildly as he considered his alternatives.

He could put the book away and pretend he'd never filched the combination and investigated what was clearly none of his business. Ma and Pa had never expressly forbidden him from opening the safe, but that was only because they'd never felt it necessary. The fact that the safe was kept locked and the combination hidden away was evidence enough that he should have left it alone.

Returning the book to the safe was what he should do. He knew as much.

He also knew he could not. He simply didn't have it in him. The book was too valuable, its contents too alluring, to remain unexplored.

So he kept it.

He returned the documents and the remaining contents of the safe back the way he'd found them, as best he could recall. Then he closed the heavy door and spun the combination dial, wondering on the likelihood of his getting caught "borrowing" the strange book with the obscene-looking goat on the front cover.

He'd never seen Ma or Pa open the safe. Not once, for as long as he could remember. But that didn't mean much. Maybe they dug through it every night after the children were sleeping. Or maybe once a week, or once a month. If any of those things were the case, Samuel knew the book's disappearance would not go unnoticed.

But he took it anyway.

Over the next few days and nights, Samuel examined the book every chance he could. It wasn't easy, either. Working a farm was strenuous, even for a strapping thirteen-year-old, and finding a location to read where he would not be disturbed by one of his brothers was a very real problem.

But Samuel was nothing if not determined. He settled on hiding the book in the barn, stealing away after dinner each night and managing thirty minutes or so of time by himself before sneaking back to the family. He kept his disappearances short enough that no one noticed his absence or thought it odd.

And the more he read, the more fascinated he became. Obsessed, even. The feeling of dread lessened each time he lifted the book. Perhaps he was building up a tolerance to it, like someone could become immune to the effects of certain diseases by being around them.

After three days of reading he knew he wanted to attempt one of the "experiments" outlined in the book.

After four days he'd developed a plan.

And now here he was, miles from the farmhouse after sneaking out of his bedroom while everyone else slumbered. He'd finally arrived at his destination and set to work in the darkness inside a small clearing in an area of the forest that had likely never been trod by human feet.

Samuel shivered as the temperature continued to fall. He knew the chill was only partly due to the temperature. There was also a healthy fear.

Now that he was here he wanted to stop.

He knew he should stop.

He could not stop.

He began whistling as he worked, not because he felt cheerful but as a way to calm his nerves and ward off the increasing certainty that he was doing something wrong, something bad, that he was giving in to a darkness dropping like a woolen blanket over his soul.

He stopped whistling mere moments after starting. Rather than lifting his spirits, the sound had the opposite effect. It burst from his lips only to be swallowed up whole by the forest crowding in on Samuel. The trees were thick and menacing.

Still he kept working.

Samuel ignored his shaking limbs and his wavering will and made an agreement with himself. He would see this experiment through and then return the book to its rightful place inside Pa's safe tomorrow.

It was a fair compromise. He could sate his curiosity tonight and still wash his hands of the book's dark promise.

He remained frightened but felt marginally better now that he had a plan.

It was only one night. Only one experiment.

What was the worst that could happen?

2

Samuel opened the special book and placed it on the ground next to his lantern so he could refer to it as he worked.

He'd spent virtually all his spare time over the last few days studying the experiment, so he felt familiar with the steps, more or less. They were complicated, though, and he knew it would be impossible to perform them properly and in the correct order without checking the text regularly.

The book lay open to his chosen experiment, its pages flat. Shadows cast by the lantern skittered and danced across its surface. It was a large book, maybe close to five hundred pages long, and the night breeze was blowing steadily, so Samuel stepped away to find a pair of stones large enough to hold the pages still.

He made it three steps before he stopped.

Eyed the book suspiciously.

The breeze ruffled his hair against his skull, causing it to drop down his forehead and over his eyes, and yet the pages remained flat.

They didn't riffle.

They didn't flap.

They didn't move at all. They remained utterly immobile, as if someone had taken the time to glue the book's pages together, one by one, on either side of the experiment Samuel had selected. It was the sort of thing one of his brothers might do to annoy Samuel.

But of course that was silly, not to mention impossible. Samuel would certainly have noticed the pages sticking together when he opened the book upon his arrival in this desolate clearing. In fact, he recalled with crystal clarity riffling the pages just moments ago.

Clearly no one had followed Samuel out here and glued the pages together. The book had never left his sight.

Still. The pages. How could the pages lay so flat against the still-freshening breeze, as if made of stone themselves?

Samuel swallowed heavily.

His stomach felt queasy, like he might need to use the outhouse.

He ignored the chill that suddenly seemed to have gotten much worse and stepped forward. Knelt and riffled the pages. They rustled softly, exactly as he'd known they would, and then dropped and remained stationary again.

As still as death.

Samuel took a deep breath and blew it out forcefully. He ignored that thought as best he could and pushed to his feet. He knew if he hesitated any longer he would slam the book closed and gather his supplies and slink home like a frightened child.

And he was no frightened child. He was damned near an adult, working fourteen hours a day on the farm and doing every last chore his pa and his older brothers did, and doing them every bit as well as them, too.

He pushed his misgivings aside and got to work.

* * *

Samuel Beebe's family had lived in Paskagankee for generations. They were among the village's earliest settlers, journeying north from Providence way back in the mid-1600s and carving the family farm out of the wilderness over the course of many decades.

Samuel's father had served in the Colonial Army during the War for Independence, participating in some of its bloodiest campaigns, including Camden and Germantown. Somehow, against all odds, Thaddeus Beebe not only returned alive, but he did so uninjured and whole. And he did so bearing numerous trophies won on the battlefield, including a Redcoat officer's sword he'd taken from the man after shooting him right off his horse.

It was Pa's most prized possession, and Samuel now held that sword in his hands. He'd taken it from Pa's closet in preparation for tonight's ceremony and hidden it—riskily—under his bed for two days, during which time he'd sweated every moment, knowing his punishment would be severe were it to be found.

The first step in the ceremony was simple, so simple Samuel didn't even bother referring to the book before starting. He stood roughly in the middle of the clearing and measured two sword-lengths in the four cardinal directions, marking a point on the ground for each. He placed the tip of the sword in the dirt and connected the points, working carefully, constructing as perfectly round a circle as he could manage.

He moved to the book and double-checked the next step, though he knew perfectly well what that one was as well. The pages remained unaffected by the breeze, which had continued to increase in intensity under the glittering, starlit skies.

Samuel gazed at the open book, committing the design to memory, as if he hadn't already done so. His body quivered with the thrill of the forbidden. He returned to the circle and again placed the tip of his father's sword into the ground.

He began dragging the sword through the dirt, as he'd done to construct the circle, but remaining inside it at all times. Without lifting the sword, Samuel began at due north and replicated the pattern taken from the pages of the book. It consisted of five straight-line segments inside the circle.

He took his time and worked carefully. He suspected if the design filling the circle was constructed improperly the ceremony would be a failure and all of his time would be wasted.

Upon completion, he lifted the sword from the ground and stepped out of the circle, careful not to disturb what he'd just drawn. It was a five-pointed star, the tip of each point piercing the circle and thrusting slightly through the outer edge.

This time when he stepped to the book, Samuel realized that not only was he still shaking, he was sweating heavily despite the chill in the air.

Stop now. This is your last chance.

The thought flitted through his brain and he ignored it. He

hadn't taken all these chances, risking a beating from Pa and sneaking out of the house while the family slept, only to get this close to finishing the ceremony and then quit like a baby.

He was no baby.

He was practically an adult and he would see this thing through to the end.

He breathed deeply—and shakily—and continued. Just outside the circle, adjacent to each of the marks he'd made corresponding to the four cardinal direction points—north, east, south and west—he recreated the drawing of the capering horned goat.

It was painstaking work.

The breeze blew and the temperature continued to fall, and by the time he finished drawing his four horned goats, Samuel guessed at least an hour had passed. He couldn't be sure because he'd left his pocket watch at home, and he'd been so wrapped up in recreating the intricacies of the drawing that the time had passed quickly.

At last he stepped back and examined his work, his gaze flitting from the drawing inside the ancient, leather-bound book to the representations he'd made with the tip of his father's sword in the Paskagankee dirt. Samuel was impressed with the quality of his work and hoped it would be good enough. In any event, it was the best he could manage.

It was time to continue.

The sword had carved narrow, shallow grooves in the dirt, and now Samuel bent over those grooves, squinting against the lantern's flickering light. In his hands was a small jar of lamp oil he'd filched from Ma's larder.

Starting at the northernmost point, he held the jar over the grooves and began pouring lamp oil into the dirt. He circled the design and continued pouring until arriving back at the starting point. Then he entered the circle and repeated the procedure for the five straight lines filling its interior.

It was slow work, and tiring, even for a thirteen–year-old toughened by farm life. By the time he'd finished, Samuel's back was aching. It cracked loudly in the desolate forest as he straightened.

He barely noticed. His excitement had begun to build as he poured the oil, until now it overshadowed even the dread he'd been feeling almost nonstop since finding the book inside Pa's safe.

He bent and lifted the ancient manuscript off the ground. The familiar sense of foreboding filled him but he ignored it, as he now always did.

Samuel fumbled in the pocket of his trousers and removed a box of matches. He held the special book against his body with his left elbow, careful not to lose his place, and then slid a match across the side of the matchbox. When it flared, he squatted at the edge of the circle and dropped it into one of the oil-filled grooves.

The oil ignited and the flames raced around the circle, simultaneously filling in the five lines of its interior. In seconds the design was ablaze, yellow flames accentuating the surprisingly well-drawn pentagram inside the surprisingly well-drawn circle in the middle of the isolated forest, the fiery construction ringed by the surprisingly well-drawn capering horned goats.

Samuel admired his work for a moment. His time was limited, but not so limited that he could not spare a few seconds to gaze at his creation with well-justified pride. The lamp oil was thick and he knew it would burn plenty long enough to complete the ceremony.

The fear he'd been feeling intensified, the certainty that what he was doing was unnatural and obscene, and for a moment he considered extinguishing the flames and returning home. He could sneak the book back into the safe tomorrow or the next day and no one would be the wiser.

It was what he should do.

He stood and gazed at the flaming pentagram under the moonlit sky and knew he would do nothing of the kind.

He'd come too far to back out now.

3

Samuel dropped the matchbox back into his pocket and knelt before the drawing of the capering horned goat on the south side of the circle. Then he turned and faced east. He angled the book so that its pages would be illuminated by the flames and began to read, chanting in a voice surprising in its steadiness:

"O Lautrayth, Feremin, and Oliroomim, spirits who attend upon sinners, I, Samuel Beebe, trusting in your power, conjure you by Him who spoke and all things were made, and who knows all things even before they come to pass, and by heaven and earth, fire and air and water, Sun and Moon and stars, to send me one spirit, who should come to me gently, without causing me fear, and you should fulfill entirely whatever I command you, and bring it effectively to pass. By this flaming circle with which you are effectively invoked, you must be compelled to come here without delay and humbly fulfill my commands."

He paused a moment and repeated the entire passage.

Then he paused a few more seconds and chanted the words a third time.

And then he sat back on his haunches and waited.

The wind moaned in the trees and the flames danced inside the pentagram and for some time nothing happened. Samuel felt his confidence—and his terror—begin to ebb. His fear that he would do something wrong had apparently been well founded. Either he'd failed in reproducing the drawings properly, or he'd mispronounced something in the incantation, or he—

The flames began to change color.

The yellow and green tints began to fade, changes that were initially subtle but then impossible to miss. The fire's reddish hue became more pronounced, and then more pronounced still, until within sixty seconds they had turned the bright crimson of arterial flow, every bit as thick and lush as the blood of a slaughtered calf.

The flames rose in height as they changed color. It was impossible but it was happening. They reached for the sky in undulating, ropy lengths that precisely resembled the picture Samuel had seen once in a book, of snakes being charmed by an Indian *fakir.*

He was spellbound. He stared, eyes wide, at what he had wrought. The flames continued to redden, brightening and lengthening, until Samuel thought he would have to avert his eyes.

Their intensity was stunning.

It was entrancing.

It was...*unnatural.*

Samuel's awe began to turn to back to fear as the realization struck that he hadn't the slightest clue how to put a stop to this unnatural occurrence if he decided it had gone too far. The flames continued to redden and lengthen and the wind whistled through the trees above his head and—

In his peripheral vision Samuel thought he saw movement.

He swung his head to the left, peering through the flames and the smoke.

Nothing.

The wind whipped, now a frenzied howl, but somehow the flames were unaffected, licking straight up as if drawn by some unseen force. The intensity of the fire made it difficult to see, and if not for his fear Samuel might have given up looking.

But he *was* afraid and so he *did* keep looking, and finally he observed what must have drawn his attention in the first place. It was a black mass, amorphous and swirling, so utterly dark it stood out against the murky background of the forest trees.

The mass resembled the smoke that had initially risen from the burning lamp oil...except it didn't.

That smoke had acted exactly as the smoke always acted from every fire Samuel had ever seen: it rose from the flames and immediately began to be diffused by air currents, shifting this way and that with the changing breeze and the superheated air from the fire.

This smoke—if it was even smoke at all—was different. Much different.

It was maybe five or six feet in diameter and perhaps eight to ten feet in height, and it swirled and undulated, but in a way that seemed somehow unnatural.

Abnormal.

Aberrant.

To Samuel it resembled a funnel cloud, except it didn't extend downward from a thunderhead. It resembled a swarm of bees, except it was simply a black mass of nothingness.

Swirling, churning, the mass at the edge of the trees on the far side of the clearing at first seemed stationary, and as frightening as it was, it didn't provoke any greater fear in Samuel than had the blood-red flames or the fact that those flames seemed to be reaching for the stars of their own accord. He wasn't sure he could *get* any more afraid than he already was, in any event.

But he was wrong about that.

He discovered he was wrong at the same moment he realized the amorphous black mass wasn't stationary at all. It was moving toward the flaming circle. It was moving slowly, but *it was approaching.*

Samuel's bowels tightened and his bladder felt suddenly full and he prepared to spring to his feet and sprint toward the farm, knowing instinctively he could never outrace that...thing...but prepared to try anyway.

Except he couldn't move.

Whether from terror or some spell cast by the malevolent force on the other side of the pentagram, Samuel Beebe was frozen to the spot. He whimpered as the undulating mass approached, now moving with greater urgency as it seemed to sense Samuel's inability to escape.

In seconds the mass had progressed from the edge of the clearing to a point on the far side of the flaming circle. It paused, and then moved straight at Samuel, directly through the flames.

Samuel was horrified to see that even the flames, now such a bright crimson he could barely stand to look at them, disappeared as the black mass moved through them. They weren't smothered, Samuel could see them resuming their ropy quest to reach the sky behind the mass after it moved past, but the location containing the mass seemed so thick, and so dark, *and so evil*—Samuel was aware of the thought flitting through his brain even in its current, terror-filled state—that it simply absorbed all light, even light as intense as that cast by the flames.

In seconds the mass moved through the pentagram inside the circle, and just before it burst out the other side, Samuel realized with the clarity wrought by extreme terror that he was no longer frozen in place. He could move, which meant he could run.

So he did.

He made it less than ten feet before the mass of inky blackness enveloped him. It surrounded Samuel, choking out the light from the flaming pentagram, and the light from the lantern, and the ambient light cast by the moon and stars.

There *was* no light in the space occupied by the awful black mass.

Samuel stumbled, confused and afraid. He fell to his knees and cracked one open on a rock. He could feel the blood begin to flow from the gash, the wound was deep and painful, but he barely noticed and paid it little mind as his entire focus was on escape.

But there was to be no escape.

The darkness inside the void was complete, and eternal, and unrelenting, and despite Samuel's body having fallen to the ground, within seconds he could no longer discern up from down or right from left. He flailed his arms and legs in panic, punching and kicking, but against what he did not know. The mass was solid but insubstantial and his attempted blows accomplished nothing.

A faraway buzzing sound began to fill Samuel's consciousness. It began as an addendum to his terror, a corollary that started almost unnoticeably but then began to grow in volume and intensity, and then the buzzing sound entered the void that had enveloped Samuel, and it became loud and insistent and soon it overwhelmed his senses, and then it was inside his head, it had entered his body through his nose or his mouth or perhaps his ears, he didn't know and didn't care, and the buzzing was nowhere but everywhere and it was relentless and loud and eating away at Samuel's brain until he could no longer stand it and he knew he was about to die, and he wished he *would* die, anything to end the torment of the void and the buzzing, and in his tortured mind he apologized to God for the abomination his carelessness and stupidity had called into the world, and he apologized and he begged to die, begged to be released from this terror and misery, and then the blackness granted his request, it strangled him and choked him and he could feel his life leaching away, and at last Samuel was released from his pain and his terror and his misery, and as consciousness left him he was thankful it was all finally over.

4

Samuel was cold. He discovered he was shivering violently as his eyes blinked open. He pushed himself to a sitting position and took a moment to survey his surroundings.

The flames had burned themselves out inside the grooves of the pentagram, and his first thought was to wonder how long he'd been unconscious. That the fire had consumed the entirety of the lamp oil would seem to indicate it had been a considerable amount of time, as would the fact that a thin layer of dew—well on its way to becoming frost—had covered his clothing and even made headway onto his exposed skin.

That would explain the shivering.

His second thought was to wonder what had happened to the void, to the inky black mass that so resembled a huge swarm of bees but was most certainly *not* a swarm of bees. The void was nowhere to be seen.

Samuel knew he should be glad. He should be grateful it was gone and terrified that it might return, but to his surprise, he couldn't manage either one.

He didn't feel any gratitude or fear because he couldn't feel anything at all. Samuel realized with surprise but no concern that he had become merely a husk, a shell of a human being not substantially different from the inky black mass itself.

He was a void, dark and empty and eternal.

And he realized something surprising: he wished the void would return. He missed it. He missed it with an intensity of feeling he'd never before experienced.

His initial fear had been based on the unknown. On the void's unfamiliarity. On the fact it was utterly unlike anything Samuel had ever experienced, or ever *heard* of anyone experiencing.

But now that he had experienced the void he'd gotten past his unreasoning fear. During the void's presence Samuel recalled that he'd been filled with knowledge and confidence and desire, a throbbing desire that was only partly sexual, and that had been as intensely scarlet as the flames burning inside the circle.

He recalled that his soul had been full and empty at the same time, a logical contradiction whose truth was every bit as accurate as its impossibility. His soul had contained terrible knowledge, and awful desire, and need, oh, a need that had been excruciating in its intensity.

And now he was just empty.

He glanced down at his knee, the one that he remembered splitting open on a rock as he lost his balance during the void's initial onslaught. It had been a painful injury, and should be still, but it was not. The lack of feeling inside Samuel apparently extended to his human shell, because although blood had soaked his trousers at the knee and begun wicking along the material in both directions, he felt no pain.

Wait. That's not entirely true.

There was pain. He could feel it and it was strong. He just didn't care. He was entirely unaffected by the physical trauma he'd suffered.

It made no sense.

He bent his knee slowly, experimentally, wincing as he prepared for the wave of agony he knew would follow.

The wave came but he was unaffected.

He bent the knee again, this time quickly, extending the joint as far as he could, and the pain was immense and he still didn't care. Blood rushed from the wound and he didn't care.

Nothing mattered.

But that's not true, either.

Some things did matter, and the more Samuel considered those things, the more he realized he'd let those things go unattended for far too long. People had sinned against him, had caused him grievous harm, and he'd been too weak to respond appropriately.

He'd been too intimidated.

Too afraid.

The time for reckoning was overdue, and the list of those to suffer for their transgressions was long.

Samuel's ma and pa, who had ignored his wishes to stay in school, forcing him to quit and work day after day on the farm, would be an excellent place to start. They had stolen his childhood and sapped him of his inquisitiveness, and for that they must pay.

Samuel's brothers, Joshua and Henry, who had teased him relentlessly under the guise of "turning you into a man," torturing him with their words and their deeds, also. They were older and bigger, but certainly not wiser, and they too must suffer for their sins.

And then there were the townspeople. It had never occurred to Samuel until just now how many Paskagankee residents needed to be held to an accounting for the stains on their souls. The more he considered the subject, the clearer it became that all of them must pay.

Samuel had a lot of work to do. Calling the guilty to account for their sins would not be easy, and it would not be pretty. But it was necessary, and someone had to do it, and Samuel now realized *he* had been chosen to do it.

He climbed to his feet, still shivering violently from the cold and the dew that was turning to frost, and he didn't care. Being cold didn't bother him, so he ignored the sensation.

He took a step in the direction of the Beebe family farm and his injured knee nearly buckled and a wave of pain came like a bolt of lightning striking his kneecap and radiating outward in both directions, and he still didn't care. He ignored the pain and kept walking.

Or perhaps staggering.

Most of the supplies he'd lugged to the clearing were irrelevant to him now, so he left them.

There were two exceptions, however. The sword he'd taken from his father might be useful in extracting vengeance from those against whom it was long overdue, and so Samuel picked it up off the ground and dusted it off and prepared to carry it home and put it to the use for which it had been intended.

And then there was the book whose inadvertent discovery by Samuel had set his epiphany in motion. The book that just hours ago had been the subject of his boyish curiosity, but which now had become the focus of his entire soulless existence.

He would cherish the book and protect it at all costs. He *must* cherish the book and protect. That was now the focus of his life, even more so than calling others to account for their failings.

The book remained on the ground, its pages open to the drawing of the capering horned goat and the mystical incantations. Samuel lifted it reverentially. He closed it and carefully brushed off its leather binding.

When he'd cleaned the book as thoroughly as he could manage, he wrapped his coat tightly around it and secured it under his arm. The sensation of evil he'd felt every time he made contact it prior to the void's appearance was gone, replaced by a feeling of warmth, an intense crimson heat that reminded him exactly of the deep red emitted by the fiery pentagram earlier in the evening.

His preparations complete, Samuel fixed his eyes on the distance and began marching toward his home, the farmhouse where those who most deserved retribution slept, unaware and unprotected.

And soon to face his wrath.

PART TWO
POSSESSION

1

Friday, October 13, 2017
Paskagankee, Maine

The attic was cool but not uncomfortable.

Julie Beebe had managed to sneak three bottles of wine past her parents—the illicit act wasn't difficult, they rarely paid much attention to Julie or her sixteen-year-old twin Jake, anyway—and a warm alcohol buzz served more than adequately to keep the chill at bay for Julie and her three best friends. She could see the flush on their faces and had begun to feel the effects of the wine as well.

She'd pulled out all the stops for this sleepover party. With summer long-since relegated to the realm of happy memory in northern Maine, Julie wanted the sleepover to be as exciting—and scary—as possible, even if Halloween was still a couple of weeks away.

She'd instructed her friends to bring sleeping bags and their heaviest flannel pajamas. They would be spending the entire night in the attic. Alone.

To prepare, Julie had strung one of her father's heavy orange extension cords from the second floor hallway, up the pull-down stairs and into the attic. She'd then plugged a multiple-outlet power strip into the extension, giving her the opportunity to transform the dreary attic into a party room.

Or close enough for bored teenagers, anyway.

Two of the outlets she'd used to power a pair of portable electric heaters, placing one at each end of the attic beneath the vented peaks. The rest had been used for two lamps plus her stereo.

The result was a more-or-less cozy nook that would offer privacy from her parents—not to mention Jake—as well as plenty of spooky ambience for a pre-Halloween sleepover party.

The first couple of hours were spent listening to music and gossiping and, of course, drinking wine. The girls had been best friends since their first day in Paskagankee's only preschool more than ten years ago, and were rarely at a loss for conversation when together.

The fact that they'd spent all day in each other's company at school this afternoon changed nothing. They discussed boys, and their plans for Halloween, and boys, and which school subjects were becoming a pain in the ass less than two months into the school year, and boys, and music, and boys, and they giggled and laughed and danced and drank wine.

Julie had initially retracted the collapsible attic stairs following her friends' arrival. A couple of hours after opening the first bottle of wine, however, she was forced to raise the white flag on her plan for keeping parents and brother away. The wine was doing what wine did, and the girls' near-constant trips downstairs to use the bathroom finally wore her down.

She left the stairs extended to the hallway below.

Julie had begged Jake to leave her and her friends alone, and thus far he'd obliged, even with the stairs lowered. But Jake had a massive crush on her best friend, Brittany Carson, and seriously doubted he would be able to resist the temptation to join them at some point in the evening.

She hoped he would, but Jake wasn't exactly a model of reliability, especially where Britt was involved.

In the meantime, Julie and enjoyed the evening and each other's company. As midnight approached, she could feel the party winding down. The opening bell at Paskagankee High School rang at the ungodly hour of seven-ten a.m., which meant the girls had all been up since around six a.m.

They were tired, and the wine wasn't helping keep anyone awake.

Brittany yawned, and then Kara Newton yawned.

Chelsea Grove looked from one to the other and said, "You can't be serious. You're tired already? What a bunch of wusses!" She started laughing at them but then covered her mouth with her own hand and tried to turn away, unable to suppress a yawn.

Julie smiled but knew she needed to take action quickly or the girls would be burrowed into sleeping bags and snoring softly within minutes.

She was glad she'd saved the best part of the get-together for exactly this situation.

She pushed to her feet and walked to a jumble of old junk piled in one corner of the attic. Some of the stuff had been here as long as Julie could remember, but the pile grew a little each year as old lamps, spare chairs and other things the family no longer used but didn't want to toss out were added.

Standing to one side of the pile was an old dresser that had once belonged to Julie's grandmother or great-grandmother, or maybe it was even older than that. She pulled open one of the drawers and retrieved a beat-up old box she'd placed inside it while preparing for her party.

Then she returned to the circle of light in the middle of the attic, conscious of six eyes watching curiously. She dropped the box onto the floor and lowered her voice, hoping to affect a spooky tone.

"And now," she said, "it's time to get down to the real reason I called you all here tonight."

She opened the crumbling cardboard carton and withdrew a Ouija board and a scuffed planchette. Placed them on the floor and sat cross-legged before the board.

Then she smiled up at her friends. "Well? What are you waiting for?"

The girls giggled nervously and shuffled their feet.

Brittany said, "Really? Are you serious? A Ouija board?"

"Why not? It's almost Halloween, right? This is the perfect time for a little stroll down Supernatural Lane."

The girls seemed unconvinced and she persisted. "Come on, Chelsea, you just called the rest of us wusses, where's your sense of adventure?"

Julie's three friends looked at each other doubtfully.

She tried again, pushing a little harder. "Maybe we can learn something. Kara, you've been trying to decide what to major in when you go off to college, right?"

Kara shrugged. "Well, yeah, but I don't really think—"

"And Chelsea, you've been bugging your dad to buy you a car for graduation next year. Maybe we can find out if you'll actually get one!"

"Dude, I don't think this toy is going to—"

"And Brittany." Julie changed her tone, going to spooky to vampy. "Oh, Brittany. Maybe we can finally discover if you'll find true love and happiness with…God forbid…my brother…"

The girls dissolved in laughter.

"And don't forget babies," Kara said excitedly. "Let's find out if you're going to have lots and lots of babies with Jake!"

"Guys, I'm not—" Brittany's objections were drowned out in laughter and increasingly absurd suggestions as to how their love affair would unfold.

"But I'm not even dating Jake. I don't even want to—"

It was no use. Kara and Chelsea joined Julie on the floor, clustered around the Ouija board, and finally Brittany gave up as well. She shook her head and dropped to the floor, smiling and insisting she wasn't even interested in Jake Beebe.

*　*　*

They started out in high spirits, joking and laughing and nudging each other in the ribs as they took turns pairing up with their fingers on the planchette, two girls asking questions of the board while two sat to the side, observing.

And, of course, drinking wine.

It took a little time to rustle up any response from the spirit world. For a while, there was no action at all. They continued but with a little less enthusiasm each time a question went unanswered. Julie could see their exhaustion kicking in again.

Then the damned planchette moved.

It actually moved.

Kara and Chelsea were sitting at the board, with Julie and Brittany looking on. The question was a simple one: "Will Kara attend college?"

For a long moment nothing happened. Brittany stage-whispered, "Great idea, Jules, this is scary as hell. I don't know if I'll ever be able to sleep again."

Julie laughed in spite of herself but then the smile froze on her face as the planchette jerked into motion. She nodded at the board and Britt fell silent, her mouth hanging open comically.

The little board piece moved fitfully but steadily toward a word stamped on the corner of the board: YES. It arrived at its destination and stopped.

"You did that on purpose," Brittany whispered.

Kara shook her head wordlessly.

Chelsea looked over at Britt, saying nothing, before returning her gaze to the board. "What school will Kara attend?" she said, her voice a papery whisper as well.

Once again it took a moment before the planchette moved. This time there was no joking around. No wise-ass remarks. No laughter. The four girls sat silently before the board.

And then the game piece began to scratch its way across the surface again, moving from letter to letter: U to M to A to I to N to E.

"University of Maine," Chelsea said.

"That's your first choice, right?" Julie asked Kara.

Her friend lifted her fingers from the planchette. "I-I haven't made up my mind yet."

"I guess you have now," Brittany said with a chuckle.

Kara stood and moved away from the board. "Your turn," she said, nodding to Julie and Britt. "Let's find out about Jake and all those babies!"

Her tone was light but Julie could tell she was spooked.

Chelsea slid away from the board without a word, and Julie and Brittany took their places.

"Okay," Julie said softly. "Here's a question for you, All-Knowing-One: is Brittany going to marry—"

Before she could finish, the sound of heavy footfalls clambering up to the attic caused all four sets of eyes to swing away from the

Ouija board and toward the extendable stairway.

Jake's grinning face appeared, rising up from the hole in the floor like a conjured spirit. His shoulders and upper body followed as he took another step. He didn't seem to feel confident enough to step into the attic fully, but he waggled his eyebrows and said, "Mind if I join the party?"

"Ugh," Julie said. "I asked you to leave us alone and give us some privacy tonight."

He spread his hands innocently. "And I did. But I was walking down the hallway and I couldn't help but overhear you ladies playing with that old game—" he nodded at the Ouija board with a nose wrinkled in distaste—"and I thought I'd offer you the chance to ramp up the excitement."

He looked around and shrugged. "'Cause it sure looks like this party could use a nudge."

"Just go," Julie said in exasperation.

Before he could retreat down the stairs, though, Brittany interrupted. "Ramp up the excitement how?"

Her eyes were shining. Not for the first time, Julie wondered if the prospect of her brother and her best friend getting together might not be the completely laughable notion she'd thought.

"Ugh," she said again.

Jake had kept his hands behind his back since climbing into view, but now he brought them together in front of the girls with a flourish worthy of a Las Vegas showman. Or at least, Julie assumed it was worthy of a Vegas showman. She'd never been, so she really had no idea.

In his hands he held a book.

It was an old book. It looked ancient. It was thick and its pages were yellowed—Julie could see that much even with it held closed—and its cover wasn't made of pressed cardboard like a regular book. Instead, it was bound in leather that was no longer soft and supple. It was stiff with age, and cracked and dirty.

And it had a strange illustration on the front: an animal that looked to Julie like a goat. But it wasn't any ordinary goat. This one was standing up on its hind legs, and it was cavorting, dancing obscenely. Long horns sprouted from its head, one on each side behind its ears.

It was grotesque.

And that wasn't even the worst part.

The worst part was that the book radiated evil.

Julie could feel the evil from across the attic, waves of malevolence emanating from the damned thing. It might as well have been dripping black ooze. She didn't understand how Jake could even stomach holding it.

But he *was* holding it. He displayed the book proudly, reverently almost, like a religious artifact or something.

And then he said, "This is how we ramp up the excitement. Instead of playing some silly game, we use a genuine book of magic."

2

Julie scoffed. "Book of magic, my butt. Get out of here and leave us alone."

She kept her voice strong and dismissive, mostly to convince herself she wasn't disturbed by the book. It was freaking her right the hell out.

She glanced at her friends for support and could see immediately that Kara and Chelsea were in her corner. There was no way of knowing whether they were as bothered by the strange-looking old book as she was, but their faces were dark and uneasy, and Julie knew they would offer no argument to her kicking Jake downstairs.

Brittany was another story. Her eyes continued to shine and a dazzling smile lit up her face and she said, "No, don't go. It sounds like fun!"

Julie's best friend tore her eyes off the book—or was it Jake?—and turned her attention to her sleepover partners. She seemed surprised by their lack of enthusiasm and said, "What? That doesn't sound fun to you? Who doesn't like magic?"

Julie felt a rush of annoyance. "Oh, come on, give me a break. A book of magic? Really? There's no such thing, Britt, and even if there was, do you actually believe one would end up in the hands of *my brother,* of all people? In a tiny town in the middle of nowhere?"

She didn't know why she was so upset about the situation. Maybe it was Jake's arrogance at interrupting her sleepover after promising not to.

Or maybe it was Britt's unbridled enthusiasm about what Julie thought was a stupid and corny idea.

Or maybe it was her unease—*terror, let's be honest here, Julie, that book scares the living shit out of you*—regarding what he held in his hands.

Hell, maybe she was just tired. It was late and she was buzzed from wine. What was supposed to be a fun party had taken a sudden turn into the realm of the dark and sinister, and just because Brittany Carson couldn't feel the shift didn't make it any less true.

Britt ignored her. Still smiling at Jake, she said, "Let's do some magic."

Jake climbed the last couple of stairs and stepped into the attic.

"Where'd you get that thing, anyway?" Julie's annoyance hadn't faded but it seemed obvious she wasn't going to get rid of her brother until he'd showed off and done his little magic trick. She would deal with Brittany's vamp routine later.

Jake walked halfway across the attic floor and stopped. Shrugged at the question. "Too much free time on my hands, I guess."

"What's that supposed to mean?"

"It means I was digging around in the barn, looking through some of the stuff that's been piled up in the back since forever."

The Beebe home had long since stopped being a working farm. Julie's dad was a software engineer, and she doubted he'd ever dirtied his hands in his life. Supposedly, their property had at one time been a real homestead, with cattle and plowed fields and acres of crops, but that was like a hundred years ago or more. The few times she'd asked about her family's history, her dad had just shrugged, clueless.

As usual.

But a decaying old barn remained, located far behind the house at the rear of the property. It somehow remained stubbornly upright, defying gravity and all odds, almost as if to provide proof of a family history unacknowledged in generations. The building was a rotting mess, tilting on its foundation like a drunk at last call. It had at one time been painted red, but the paint had long since faded away or hung from the spongy wood in flaking, papery strips.

For as long as Julie could remember, the entire wobbly structure had been threatening to fall to the ground in a cloud of dust.

It was strictly off-limits, for obvious safety reasons.

Julie and Jake had been warned as long as Julie could remember not to go near the place, threatened with serious punishment if either were caught so much as loitering in its vicinity. The threats and warnings had been more than sufficient to keep Julie away, even when she'd been young and curious.

She shook her head, half in concern and half in sisterly scorn. "You went inside the barn? Are you really that stupid? The whole thing could have fallen down on top of you!"

He grinned mischievously. "But it didn't. And you wouldn't believe some of the cool stuff I found in there."

Julie had heard enough already. She didn't care what might be in the decrepit old barn. All she wanted was to get rid of her dumbass brother and get on with the party, although the negative vibes coursing through the attic since Jake's arrival seemed to guarantee *that* wasn't going to happen.

She'd been so angry with her brother and so shocked he'd actually ventured inside the barn that she had almost forgotten her friends were still gathered around the Ouija board.

But now Brittany said, "Cool stuff? Like what?" She was still grinning like a lovesick fool and Julie wondered why she'd never noticed the extent of her best friend's interest in her brother before.

Or maybe it was a brand-new development.

If so it was a stupid one.

"Well, this book is a perfect example." Jake held it up for Britt's inspection and as he did, Julie felt a fresh wave of revulsion wash over her.

Her brother continued. "It was buried inside an old steamer trunk that had been double-locked and then secured with a huge chain and the biggest padlock I've ever seen."

Julie shook her head. "Wasn't that a pretty good indication that, you know, you SHOULDN'T HAVE GOTTEN INTO IT?" The words came out in a hoarse, almost hysterical-sounding shout. She felt silly for screaming but couldn't help it.

Jake shook his head dismissively. "Just the opposite, dipshit. It was a pretty good indication that if I was going to find anything interesting, it would be inside that trunk."

"If it was locked up so tightly, how did you get in?" Brittany was hanging on Jake's every word. It was embarrassing.

"That barn's been rotting away back there since Christ was in diapers. The chains and locks were all rusted so badly there was no way I'd ever have been able to open them even if I had a key, which I didn't. But the top of the steamer trunk had mostly rotted away. All it took was a few taps with a sledgehammer to cave the whole thing in. Then I cleared away the debris and slid the chains over as far as I could. That gave me enough room to reach through the top and start digging through the stuff inside."

He waggled his eyebrows again. "And that was how I found this baby."

Julie sighed deeply. She said, "And you think that old book has magic tricks in it?"

"Oh, there's more inside this baby than you can possibly imagine," he answered. "But for tonight, I'll stick to something simple, because I've only had the book a couple of days and some of the spells are really complicated. I haven't had a chance to really decipher them yet."

"Simple is as simple does," Julie mumbled.

"I'll ignore that," Jake said. He continued to lock eyes with Brittany and a thought flashed through Julie's brain, fully formed and definitive: *something is not right here. Britt's never given Jake a second glance and now she's looking at him like she just won a rose on The Bachelor.*

"Everybody ready?" he asked.

"Just get on with it," Julie said, "so you can get out of here and we can finish our sleepover."

He flashed her a dark look and then lifted the book to his face. He glanced at it for a moment before placing it carefully on the floor and moving closer to the four girls, still seated around the Ouija board.

He reached into the back pocket of his jeans and removed a utility knife. Crouched behind Brittany and began carving a narrow trench in the plywood floor, dragging the tip in a surprisingly accurate circle, taking his time and eventually ending up back behind Britt. Nobody said a word while he worked, but all four girls followed his progress with sharp-eyed interest. Even

Julie had to admit to a certain amount of curiosity about what the hell her idiot brother was up to.

Once he'd encircled the girls with the knife—*you'd better hope Dad doesn't see what you just did you his flooring,* she thought, *or you'll be grounded for so long you'll need magic to ever leave the house again*—Jake knelt four times at the edge of the trench and etched the four cardinal compass points into the floor, one after the other: "N" behind Brittany, "E" behind Kara, "S" behind Julie, and "W" behind Chelsea.

Then he returned to the book and buried his nose in its pages.

He studied its contents carefully and then set it down again and once more approached the girls. Reached into his pocket. Withdrew a steak knife this time.

Britt giggled nervously. "How many things do you have in your pockets?"

"That's everything," Jake answered. "Hopefully it's all I'll need. I'm supposed to use a sword, but for obvious reasons I had to substitute something else. If this doesn't work, we'll know why."

Julie snorted derisively and Jake ignored her. Brittany, however, fixed her with an angry glare, the likes of which she'd never seen from her friend. The feeling that something was very wrong intensified.

Jake bent down behind Brittany and placed the steak knife on the floor. He positioned it so that the tip of its sharp end was directly above the "N" he'd scratched into the floor and pointed directly toward Britt.

She started to pivot on her butt to watch him but he shook his head and placed a hand on each of her shoulders.

"You have to stay still," he said.

She looked up at him with wide eyes. *She looks exactly like a love struck moron,* Julie thought. *What the hell?*

Britt allowed herself to be repositioned and then Jake returned to his magic book. He lifted it to his eyes once again and then began speaking. His voice was muffled and the words unclear because he was saying them so softly, but it sounded to Julie like he was reciting a list of names.

But they couldn't be names because none of them made sense and not a one was anything she'd ever heard before.

The nonsense went on for maybe ninety seconds and then Jake set the book on the floor one last time. He extended his right hand and pointed at Brittany.

He stood still for a moment. Then he began to lower his hand, moving slowly. His index finger was still aimed directly at Britt and at first Julie was so focused on her brother's bizarre actions that she didn't recognize what was happening.

Kara gasped and lifted her own hand. She pointed wordlessly at Britt and Julie shifted her attention to her best friend.

Brittany was dressed in footie pajamas, the onesie kind equipped with a zipper in front running from the top right shoulder to the right knee. The wearer was supposed to slip into the PJs and then zip them up, and that was exactly what Britt had done earlier in the evening.

The zipper on Brittany's PJs was lowering.

She wasn't touching it.

She wasn't moving.

Nobody was moving.

And yet the zipper continued to descend, revealing—so far—a black bra strap and nothing more. That would soon change, however.

Jake continued to lower his index finger ever so slowly, and Brittany Carson's pajamas continued to unzip.

Julie stared in shocked silence for one second.

And then two.

The zipper dropped further, revealing the swell of Britt's right breast. She continued to sit unmoving on the attic floor like a god-damned Macy's mannequin—a *lovestruck* Macy's mannequin, gazing at Jake with shining eyes like he was Harry Styles or something, instead of the disgusting small-town pervert he was only now revealing himself to be—and finally Julie found her voice.

"Stop it." The words came out weak and ineffectual, and nobody moved. Nobody reacted. Not Jake, not Kara or Chelsea, not even Brittany, who continued to be undressed—somehow—as if an invisible sicko was squatting right in front of her.

Julie glared at Jake, too furious even to form words besides the ones she'd already tried to no avail. She stared him down and then looked back at her friend and for the second time in a matter of seconds froze in disbelief.

The steak knife Jake had placed on the floor behind Brittany was glowing.

Its serrated steel cutting edge had lost the typical dull silver sheen one would expect to see in an eating utensil. Instead it blazed a bright, radiant red. It was as if the knife-blade had been held under a blowtorch long enough to become superheated.

Julie stared in shock, the blade pulsing and throbbing with energy.

Evil energy. The thought leapt into her head unbidden as the unearthly glow of the knife continued to darken, and brighten, and become even more terrifying.

And she found her voice.

Finally.

Julie climbed to her feet and screamed, "Stop it!" and as if a switch had been flipped, chaos erupted in the Beebe attic.

The blade stopped glowing. Instantly. Julie watched as its deep red—*evil*—color disappeared and once again it became nothing more than a steak knife, a prop in a teenager's cheesy trick.

Jake's shoulders drooped and his arm fell to his side, finger still extended. He wrinkled his forehead and stared down at his own hand as if seeing it for the first time, like perhaps it was a foreign object and he couldn't quite fathom what it was doing down there.

Brittany gasped and yanked at her pajamas, pulling the two sides of the onesie together to cover her chest, which was by now almost fully exposed.

Kara and Chelsea began babbling, talking over each other in a panic, asking what the hell had just happened.

And Julie advanced on her twin brother like an avenging angel, fury oozing out of every pore like a disease. She stomped across the attic and stopped inches from her brother, whose eyes were blinking in confusion and maybe even fear.

Julie saw it and didn't care if he was confused or afraid. He *should* be confused and afraid. He'd just assaulted her best friend—somehow; she had no idea what the hell had just happened here but that was a concern for another time—and she'd be goddamned if she was going to put up with it any longer.

"You get your sorry ass out of this attic right now," she said, her voice a low, angry growl.

"I-I don't—"

"Save it," she spat. "Get out of here. Turn around and go down those stairs before I push you down them, and take that…that… *disgusting* book with you."

He stood unmoving. Glanced across the attic at Brittany.

And she screamed, *"NOW!"*

Julie's mother shouted from her parent's second floor bedroom. "You kids keep it down up there, some of us are trying to sleep." Her voice was angry, but Julie knew her mother couldn't possibly be as angry—or as frightened—as she was at this moment.

The sound of their mother's voice seemed to break through Jake's confusion, or his reluctance to leave, or whatever the hell was keeping him here. He turned without another word and descended the attic stairs.

Julie stayed at the opening until the sound of his footsteps faded away as he entered his bedroom. She heard him slam the door and only then felt comfortable turning back toward her friends.

"What the hell?" Brittany muttered as she tossed her things into the backpack she'd brought to the sleepover.

"What the hell?"

"What the hell?"

She repeated the words over and over, like a mantra. She'd re-zipped her pajamas closed and her face was crimson with humiliation and shame, and she hurriedly filled her backpack and zipped it closed and then stood and faced Julie.

"Britt, I don't—"

"I have to go," she said, staring at the floor.

"No, don't go. Please. Stay a little longer." Julie tried to argue but she knew it was pointless. There was no way Brittany Carson would stay in this house tonight, or ever again, probably, after what had just happened.

And Julie couldn't blame her.

Brittany brushed past, still mumbling, her face flaming almost as brightly as the knife-blade had. She descended the stairs and broke into a sprint when she reached the second floor hallway. Her pounding footsteps raced past Jake's closed bedroom door and down the stairs to the first floor. Seconds later, Julie heard the front door slam closed. A car's engine started and then quickly faded away.

And Brittany was gone.

Julie turned toward her other two friends, only now realizing her eyes had filled with tears and were threatening to overflow. She struggled to keep from crying and tried to think of something to say and then realized it didn't matter what she said because it wasn't going to make a damned bit of difference.

Kara and Chelsea were packing their things as well.

Kara avoided Julie's gaze, exactly as Britt had done, but Chelsea's reaction was worse, if that was possible. She stared at Julie with a shocked look on her face, as if somehow *Julie* had perpetrated the twisted magic trick on them, and then she dropped her gaze and finished throwing her things together.

"Guys, please, I—" Julie still had no idea what to say, literally no clue. None. But she didn't need to worry about it, because Chelsea didn't let her finish, anyway.

"No," she snapped. "Just, no. I don't know what happened here, but it was totally fucked up and I want to go home right now."

Julie had no answer for that.

She couldn't argue because she agreed with her friends. Assuming they still *were* her friends. It was fucked up. From the moment Jake had climbed into the attic until the moment he left, it had been one sick, fucked-up misadventure.

She stood in desperate silence as they grabbed their things and crossed the attic.

Moved aside to let them pass.

Then she followed them down the stairs and through the house to the front door, still saying nothing because what the hell was there to say?

The girls had arrived together earlier in the evening in Chelsea's mother's car, and now Julie watched as the little Volkswagen sped down the driveway and turned toward Paskagankee.

The headlights had fully disappeared before she broke down in tears.

3

"What the hell happened last night? What did you do?" A few hours of restless sleep overnight hadn't done much to blunt Julie's anger, and she'd stomped into Jake's room without even the courtesy of a knock.

He was sitting at his desk when she entered, staring bleary-eyed at something on its surface with rapt interest. Based on his reaction at her entrance, she thought it might be the damned book from last night: he jumped in his seat like he'd been hit with an electric shock and then jerked his head around, his eyes wide and surprised.

It only pissed Julie off more.

He coughed into his fist. "I-I'm not exactly sure what happened, but I—"

"But nothing," she fumed. "What were you thinking? That shit you pulled last night is called sexual assault, dumbass."

He looked away. Julie couldn't tell whether it was in annoyance or guilt.

She shook her head. "How did you do it, anyway? I don't mean how could you be so stupid, although I'd like to know that, too, but specifically, *how did you do it?"*

The words came out in a jumble, fueled by anger and humiliation and, she knew, fear. How *had* he done what he did? Jake had always been impetuous and a little uncontrollable, like a wild puppy, prone to foolish actions. But this was a whole new level of stupid, even for him.

Still, *how the hell had he done it?* He'd been at least ten feet away from Britt the whole time her zipper was descending. He could no more have reached across that distance with his hand than Julie could sprout wings and fly to the moon.

Had he somehow attached fishing line, or wire, or something similar to Brittany's zipper while doing his strange prep work, carving stuff into the wooden floor and manipulating the steak knife?

But no, that was impossible. For one thing, Jake wasn't clever enough to misdirect four people's attention while fastening fishing line around something as tiny as a zipper, especially one located, as it was, just below a girl's jawline.

And for another thing, even if Jake had somehow been able to do all that, it wouldn't explain the knife blade Julie had seen glowing bright red with her own two eyes. The knife wasn't some prop purchased at a magic shop, it was part of a cutlery set the Beebe family had been using at the dinner table since Julie was a baby.

And that knife had been glowing, pulsing with—*evil*—dark red energy.

And it had been pointed at Brittany's back.

Julie shivered involuntarily.

"I'm waiting for an answer, Jake. You scared the crap out of me and my friends last night and I'm not leaving this room until you tell me how you did it."

"It's the book," Jake mumbled quietly.

"That's no answer. You can't read a bunch of mumbo-jumbo out of an old book and make magic happen. That's the stuff of fantasy and horror movies. I'll ask again. *How did you do it?*" Her voice was rising in intensity as her anger increased, becoming shrill and hysterical, and she hated it but couldn't control it.

One thing she knew, though: she would not stop pushing until he answered the question.

"How, Jake? Tell me, how did you—"

"I don't know, alright? I don't know how it happened. I did exactly what you claim is impossible. I followed the instructions in that book like following a fucking recipe, and what you saw up in the attic last night was the result."

"That doesn't make sense. You're telling me there's a magic trick published in a book that tells you how to sexually assault a girl? I'm not buying it, Jake."

"It's not like that, Julie. It wasn't a 'magic trick.' You keep using that expression and it's not accurate."

"Then what is accurate? Enlighten me."

He sighed heavily. "I found the book in the barn, exactly as I said last night. The second I picked it up out of that trunk I felt...I don't know...an energy of some kind, or an attraction."

"What is that supposed to mean?"

He shrugged. "I can't explain it, other than to say it felt like somehow I was meant to have this book."

He looked up at her and she could tell he was being sincere. The words were crazy but he believed them, and she bit back the sarcastic response that tried to leap out of her mouth. He was finally talking, even if the words were nonsense, and if she jumped down his throat now she knew he would clam up and probably never talk about the book again.

She glanced at the surface of Jake's desk and as soon as her eyes fell upon the book, the creeping revulsion she'd felt last night returned.

And something clicked in her brain.

What she was thinking didn't make sense, but last night's incident in the attic made no sense, either. Was it possible the book was causing a similar visceral reaction in Jake as it was in her, only instead of sensing evil and being repulsed, he felt something positive? Opposite ends of the same spectrum?

Was such a thing even possible? Or was that just nonsense?

She shook her head, unable to quite grasp the theory.

Jake saw her and said, "If you don't believe me, fine. You asked a question and I tried to answer it the best I could."

"I didn't shake my head out of disbelief. I just don't understand, but I want to. Tell me more. So you found this book inside an old trunk in the barn, and then what?"

He held her gaze for a moment in defiance and then made the decision to talk. "I started flipping through it, curious about the fact it's written half in some kind of weird English and half in another language entirely. It only took a few minutes to realize the book was special. The more time I spent reading, the more I began to realize just how special."

"I don't follow."

He shrugged. "You asked how I did what I did last night. I assume you're talking about the thing with the zipper."

"Of course I'm talking about the thing with the zipper! What the hell else would I be talking about?"

He ignored her outburst and kept talking. "This book is filled with spells, Julie. One of them is a telekinesis spell."

"Telekinesis? What?"

"It's the ability to move things with your mind."

"I know what telekinesis is, I'm just not following you."

"Haven't you noticed I've been spending a lot of time in my room recently? More than usual?"

"It might shock you to learn I don't monitor your every movement. I have a life of my own, you know."

Jake pursed his lips angrily. "I'm trying to explain what happened last night. Do you want to hear it or not?"

"I'm sorry. Yes, I want to hear it. And to be honest, I had noticed what you mentioned."

"Well, I wasn't just in here surfing the web. I was studying the contents of this book. One of the spells it contains is a telekinesis spell, although that's not what it's called in the book. I spent some time learning the spell and when I tried it, I was able to move a pen across my desk without ever touching it."

"Telekinesis."

"That's right. And it worked. It's exactly the same thing I did last night, only with a zipper on a pair of pajamas instead of a pen on a desk."

Julie stared, torn between disbelief at her brother's words and anger—and humiliation—as she recalled the events of last night.

"It was meant as a joke, Julie. I was trying to be funny and I guess I took it too far. I-I don't know what came over me."

The anger threatened to erupt again and she tamped it down. Screaming at her idiot brother would accomplish nothing, even though she doubted she'd ever wanted anything more in her life than she wanted to scream and yell and kick things right now.

"Say for the sake of argument I believe you," she said quietly.

"You can believe it or not, it's the truth. You wanted to know what happened and I told you."

"Okay, fine. You found this book and learned how to do tele-kinesis. So it *is* a book of magic tricks," she said quietly. "You said when I came in here that it wasn't, but you just admitted that's exactly what it is."

"No," he said simply. "Not a book of magic tricks. A book of magic spells."

"You're talking in circles," Julie said in exasperation. "What's the difference?"

"There's a world of difference between a trick some carnival magician might do and the conjurations contained inside this book." He touched the pages reverently and Julie had to suppress a shudder.

"I don't understand. And you're going to explain it to me."

"You don't want to know, Julie. Trust me on this."

"That's where you're wrong. I may have lost my best friend in the whole world last night because of you. I *have* to understand what's going on."

"I'm not even sure I understand, at least not so I can explain it."

"Try."

Another sigh, this one deep and, it seemed, tortured.

After a long silence he raised his eyes and met hers. "What do you know about necromancy?"

4

Julie took a step back. It was an involuntary movement born of shock. This conversation was getting stranger and stranger. Not to mention scarier.

"Necromancy? Isn't that when people get, I don't know, sexually aroused by dead people or something?"

Jake smiled despite the tension hanging in the air like a toxic cloud. "That's not necromancy, that's necrophilia. Now who's the dumbass?"

"Sorry I'm not up to speed on sex with corpses. And by the way: ewww."

"You were the one who brought it up, not me."

"Whatever. Keep talking."

"Okay. But remember, you asked. Necromancy is the art of divination through communication with the dead. It's considered a black art."

Julie wrinkled her nose. "You don't talk like that, so those aren't your words. They sound like something you might have memorized, like for a test."

"I did. That's the dictionary definition of necromancy."

"And you actually believe that crap? You think you can somehow communicate with the dead using this…book of the black arts?"

"You were in the attic last night. You tell me."

The temperature in Jake's room felt like it had dropped fifteen degrees since they'd started discussing necromancy and black arts and communication with the dead. Or maybe it was just Julie's blood freezing in her veins.

Jake had always been a bit of a troublemaker—Julie was the "good" twin and her brother seemed to revel in being known as the "bad" one—but his idea of "bad" had always been something less than necromancy: missing their two a.m. curfew on a Friday night, say, or drag racing along a remote section of Route 24.

Dabbling in black arts and communicating with the spirits of dead people seemed far beyond anything she'd ever thought him capable of.

She realized she was staring at him unblinkingly and holding her breath, so she exhaled deeply and tried to decide how to respond. Before she could, he surprised her by continuing the conversation.

"Some people call necromancy by a different name."

"What name would that be?" She wasn't sure she wanted to know but couldn't stop herself from asking.

"Demonology."

Julie felt her eyes widen and her bladder contract.

"Demonology. Like summoning the devil?"

He shrugged.

Nodded.

Refused to look at her.

"Jesus Christ, Jake," she whispered. "Whatever you've been doing, you've got to stop. Like, right now."

He raised his eyes to hers again. "Did you see how Brittany was looking at me last night?"

"Oh, God, Jake. I knew something wasn't right with Britt last night. Was that your stupid book, too?"

"There's an experiment in the book that allows the user to 'gain the love of another.' But there's no mention in the book about the spell being temporary, and when you stood up and screamed at me last night, it seemed to break the connection somehow."

"Break the connection? Jake, if you have to use some kind of demonic spell to 'gain the love of another,' as you put it—"

"It's not me putting it that way, it's the book. There are a lot of weird phrases and funky translations in there that I don't really understand."

"That's not the point. Try and keep up, will you?"

"Fine. Then tell me, since you seem to have all the answers. What's the point?"

"The point is that if you have to use a demonic incantation—I can't believe I'm even saying this—to make a girl fall in love with you, don't you think you might be doing it wrong?"

"But I've had a crush on Brittany like forever, and she's never paid a damned bit of attention to me before. Last night everything was different. She looked at me like I was Jake Gyllenhaal, not fucking Jake Beebe from fucking Paskagankeee, Maine."

Julie shook her head firmly. "That last statement might be the truest thing you've ever said. It certainly makes the most sense out of this whole conversation."

Jake wrinkled his forehead. "What are you talking about now?"

"You said Britt's never paid a damned bit of attention to you before last night. A 'damned' bit of attention is exactly what that was. I'm not saying I believe all that stuff about summoning dead spirits, and about using demons to do your bidding, and about... whatever else is in that book. But you're playing with fire, and you have to stop right now. Like, right this very minute."

"Don't be such a drama queen, Julie. It's not that big a deal. A lot of the stuff contained in the book is just silly, stuff that might have applied a thousand years ago when the thing was probably written, but is irrelevant now. Like, for example, there are spells in it to conjure a magical banquet, or to make a castle appear out of thin air. There's a spell designed to conjure a horse. There's even a spell someone can use to make himself invisible. Invisible, Julie! Can you imagine? You loved the Harry Potter books and movies, right?"

"Yeah, so?"

"Well, imagine having your own invisibility cloak. Think about how cool that would be!"

"That was fiction, dumbass. It wasn't real. And even in the fiction, Harry didn't have to summon a goddamned *demon* to become invisible." Julie felt her anger beginning to spike again, along with her fear. Talking to her brother about anything tended to be like talking to a brick wall, but he seemed even less interested than usual in listening to reason on this subject.

Jake continued as if she hadn't even spoken. "And speaking of cool stuff, there's even a spell in the book you can use to make someone appear dead. Holy shit, Julie, isn't that just about the most awesome thing you ever heard?"

"Goddammit, Jake, you'd better get rid of that book before somebody gets hurt. I mean, even more than you hurt me and Britt last night with that idiotic prank you pulled."

"I'm sorry about Brittany, all right? I got carried away. I admit it. And when I see her in school, I'll apologize to her, too. Will that make you happy?"

"Happy? No it won't make me happy. None of this makes me happy. It's too late for happy. The only way you can salvage anything out of this is to march your ass down to the barn and stick that book back in the trunk and forget you ever saw it."

Jake shook his head in disgust and mumbled something under his breath. He dismissed her with a wave of one hand and turned back toward his desk.

Toward the book.

Julie stomped out of his room and slammed the door so hard it shook the house.

Her mother yelled up the stairs, something about taking it easy and not destroying anything.

Julie ignored her. She was too busy stewing in her anger and trying to decipher what Jake had said under his breath after she told him to return the book to the barn.

It had sounded a lot like, *Not gonna happen.*

The temperature in the house seemed to have dropped even further. Julie stepped into her room and slammed her door as hard as she'd slammed Jake's.

Then she started to cry.

Again.

5

It was going to be hard to face Brittany.

It was going to be more than hard, it was going to be damned near impossible, but Julie knew she had to do it, and the sooner the better. Her best friend—all three of her friends, really, but especially Britt—had been freaked right the hell out last night when they left, and she couldn't blame them a bit.

She didn't know what she was going to say or how she could possibly explain the weirdness, but one thing she did know was that her explanation was *not* going to include anything about demonic conjurations or whatever the hell Jake was playing at.

Julie had tried texting Brittany last night. She waited thirty long minutes after the girls' sudden departure and then could wait no longer. She dashed off a tearful apology that offered no explanation for Jake's behavior or for the bizarre occurrences of the evening because she didn't have any more of a clue what had happened than did Britt herself.

The text went unanswered.

That in itself didn't mean much. Paskagankee was an isolated community, a stone's throw south of the Canadian border in the extreme northernmost portion of Maine. Cell towers had been constructed over the years, of course, and sometimes cell communication for the town's residents was even possible.

Sometimes not.

It was always iffy.

Whether due to the mountainous terrain or for some other

reason Julie couldn't comprehend, there were plenty of occasions she would try to send a text or make a cell call and nothing would happen. The text would remain unsent or the call would result in nothing but dead air. It was as though the nearest cell tower was a thousand miles away.

Other times she would try her text or call *from the exact same location* and it would work just fine. The unreliability was just another aggravating—and inexplicable—hassle, another reason living in Paskagankee felt most of the time like living in a remote, century-old wilderness outpost.

But Julie didn't think the lack of response from Brittany on this particular occasion had anything to do with a lack of cell coverage. Last night's message had been delivered. It had just been ignored.

Which made connecting with her friend all the more critical today.

Unfortunately, now that she had talked to Jake and gotten a little more information, she didn't feel any better about things than she had last night. What could she say? *Yeah, my brother's dabbling in the black arts. He tried to use a demonic spell to make you fall in love with him. Oh, and he used similar spells to partially undress you. You know, just the typical teen crush. Boys, right?*

Julie's aim was to repair a decade-plus-long friendship, and she doubted bringing any of what she'd learned into the conversation would do much to advance that cause.

She took a deep breath and picked up the phone. She tried to recall the last time she'd been this nervous about speaking to Brittany and could not. They'd hit it off on their very first meeting as little girls and had been practically inseparable ever since.

Of course, Britt had never been sexually assaulted by Julie's twin brother until last night, either. If anything was going to put a damper on a friendship that would probably be it.

Julie realized she was putting off the call, intentionally delaying because she was afraid of Britt's reaction.

She blew out a nervous breath and punched in her friend's number. What would she do if the call went unanswered? It was late Saturday morning and she couldn't imagine having to wait until school on Monday to talk, but if Britt refused to pick up, that might be the only option. She couldn't very well drive to Britt's house and demand to see her if her friend wouldn't even talk on the phone.

The line buzzed and her eyes started to tear up as it seemed to become clear Britt would continue to ignore her.

Julie was just about to disconnect the call when Britt picked up.

"Hello?" The voice was frosty, cold, the polar opposite of Britt's normal bubbly self. But at least she'd answered. It was a start.

"Hi, Britt, it's Julie."

"I know who it is."

"Well…um…how are you doing? Are you okay?"

"I didn't sleep much last night."

"That makes two of us," Julie said with a nervous laugh.

"What the hell happened, Jules? What was that all about last night?"

"My brother's a moron."

"You're going to have to do better than that, Julie. It was a normal sleepover until Jake came up into the attic. The Ouija board was weird, but it was a normal weird, you know? Once Jake came upstairs, it was like the world tilted sideways or something. Everything went off the rails."

"Jake's been messing around with a magic book. He's learned a couple of tricks and in typical Jake fashion he had to show off in front of you. He likes you, in case you've never noticed."

"I'm sot stupid, Julie."

"So you *have* noticed."

"That's not what I'm talking about. Yes, I know Jake has a crush on me, but something else was going on last night. Maybe I could accept the thing with the zipper being some kind of illusion a sixteen-year-old boy could pick up from a book of magic tricks—maybe, if I really push the limits of credulity—but…"

Britt's voice trailed off. They'd been friends a long time and Julie could sense her fear, right alongside her confusion and the anger. She was trying to hide it but it was definitely there.

"But what?" she said quietly.

"But you know as well as I do that last night was about a lot more than some pervert boy figuring out how to pull a zipper down from across a room. When Jake climbed into the attic, everything changed."

"Changed? What do you mean? Changed how?"

"It was as if I'd never seen him before. My head got fuzzy, like I'd had two bottles of wine instead of two glasses, and I got all warm and tingly and couldn't look at anyone or anything but him. A feeling of...I don't know how to describe it—affection? Love? Lust?—came over me and I couldn't control myself. It was embarrassing and humiliating."

"I..." Julie had no idea what to say. "I'm so sorry."

Britt continued as though Julie hadn't spoken. Her voice was thoughtful, hesitant. "When you jumped up and screamed at Jake, it was like you stuck a pin in an invisible balloon surrounding me. The balloon popped and the weird feeling evaporated and I was myself again. But if you hadn't done that...I don't know..."

Julie still had no idea what to say. Britt was barely managing to control her terror; Julie could feel it lurking around the periphery of the conversation like a dark cloud. *Like a demon.*

"I'm sorry," she said again.

"That's not good enough," Britt said quietly.

"I talked to my brother," Julie said. "I told him what an asshole he was last night and made it clear he needs to stop what he's been doing." She left out the part where she was certain he would ignore her.

"Tell him to stay away from me," Brittany said, the hesitancy still in her voice. "I mean in school, out of school, everywhere. I don't want to see him and I definitely don't want to feel...whatever that was last night...again."

"I'll tell him." Julie felt her face flush with humiliation just for being Jake Beebe's sister. She hesitated and then forced herself to continue with a question for which she wasn't sure she wanted to know the answer.

"Are we still friends, Britt?"

"I need time, Jules. Last night was weird and scary, and not in a fun, let's-go-through-the-haunted-house-at-Halloween kind of way. Even after talking with you, I don't have a clue what happened in your attic, and it's terrifying..."

Brittany's voice faded away and Julie desperately wanted to fill the silence, to reassure her friend, to offer promises she knew she couldn't deliver, but she couldn't bring herself to speak because the tears were about to break free and she knew there would be no way to hide her sobs if they did.

"I need time," Britt repeated. Then she hung up and was gone.

Julie pulled the phone away from her head and stared at it, all too aware her best friend—or was it her former best friend?—had never answered the question.

6

"Stay away from Brittany? How am I supposed to do that? Paska-gankee High School isn't exactly the size of a college campus, you know." Jake spread his hands and stared at his sister. She'd burst into his room without knocking for the second time in an hour, this time with tears running down her cheeks and fury in her eyes.

"That's not my problem," she spat. "You brought this on your-self with your juvenile actions and your stupid book, and you can figure out how to deal with the consequences. Just leave my friends alone!"

She turned and stomped out of the room, slamming Jake's door closed, also for the second time this morning.

He cursed and glared at the door, waiting for Julie to enter a third time, maybe to finish yelling at him just in case she hadn't done enough of that already. When thirty seconds went by and it hadn't happened, he relaxed and turned his attention back to his desk.

And the book.

He didn't know what its title was, specifically, because the cover was written in the strange foreign language he couldn't decipher. But he knew what the book was called, thanks to his Internet research.

It was called a grimoire, and it was fascinating. The more he delved into it, the more he realized it held nearly an infinite number of secrets. He didn't care about anything else anymore; all he wanted to do was study the book.

And that was odd, because the writing inside its pages was stilted and strange and hard to follow, and Jake Beebe had never been what anyone would consider a dedicated student.

This was different than trying to learn school stuff, though. This wasn't a book filled with math equations he would never use in the real world, or boring American History that held zero relevance to the life of a twenty-first century high school kid.

This was a grimoire, and it offered entry into a world of mysticism and power the likes of which no one in Paskagankee—hell, no one in Maine, or even in all of the United States, probably—had ever accessed, whether teenager or adult. Julie was whistling Dixie if she thought there was any chance in hell he was going to slam the book closed and return it to the rotting old steamer trunk and pretend he'd never seen it.

Maybe he'd gone overboard last night.

Okay, he'd *definitely* gone overboard last night. For all his struggles in school, Jake wasn't stupid. He also wasn't too proud to admit to himself he'd fucked up. Hell, he'd *tried* to admit it to Julie, but she didn't want to hear it.

No, the answer to last night's fuck-up was not to turn his back on the grimoire and all it offered. No, the answer was to study it *harder*, to immerse himself even *more* deeply in its pages, to learn more about spells and conjurations and, most importantly, how to control spirits.

Because while the parlor trick with the zipper had been cool— Jake felt his breath quickening as he replayed the sight of those PJ's opening up and that sexy black bra coming into view—that hadn't been the best part of his initial foray into black magic.

Far from it.

The best part had been seeing the look in Brittany Carson's eyes as she stared at him in adulation, hanging on his every word, clearly wanting nothing more than to be with him, and just as clearly willing to do anything—and everything—he desired.

Close the book and return it to the steamer trunk?

Fat fucking chance.

He shook his head at his sister's denseness. For all her booksmarts, she was one stupid girl when it came to issues outside the halls of learning. He almost felt sorry for her, to the extent he ever considered the issue at all, when he thought about what the future might hold for someone so ill-prepared for life in the real world.

He flipped idly through the grimoire's pages, smiling at some of the more fanciful spells contained inside. The possibility of conjuring a medieval castle was amusing, if a little unrealistic, as was the spell for conjuring an entire feast, and the one for imparting on your horse the ability to fly.

But those were peripheral conjurations, light-hearted amusements that had undoubtedly provided hours of entertainment back in the Middle Ages, when the book was written.

The more important spells, the more frightening—and thus useful—conjurations, were buried much deeper in the text, and it was to those pages Jake turned next.

Invisibility spells. Spells designed to bring the dead to life and to make a live person mimic the characteristics of death. Even spells that, if the text was to be believed—and Jake had no reason *not* to believe—would summon demons and force them to do the bidding of the person performing the conjuration.

The prospect was terrifying but exhilarating.

The possibilities limitless.

He read steadily, struggling through the complicated wording and odd phrasings, absorbing everything like a sponge and studying the text without a break. Before he knew it, the afternoon had passed and it was dinnertime.

Stopping to eat was a pain in the ass and the last thing he wanted to do, but he knew blowing off dinner would result in a flurry of questions from Mom that he had no desire—or even ability—to answer.

So he reluctantly pushed the chair back from his desk and trudged downstairs to the kitchen. He ate quickly and in silence, thinking of nothing but returning to his room to study his book further. He ignored Julie and her grim-faced, festering anger.

When he finished eating, he left the table without a word. He felt off somehow, edgy and upset, the entire few minutes he was away from the grimoire, and the sensation stayed with him until he was back in his room, lamp turned on, once again examining the pages of the thick book.

The next thing he knew, midnight was approaching. His eyes

itched and burned, he found himself yawning constantly, and he knew it was time to crawl under the covers and get a good night's sleep.

He ignored his exhaustion and kept reading.

It was almost like he physically *could not stop.*

The Sunday morning sky was starting to lighten before he finally slept. His head drooped over the book until it settled onto his crossed arms and he dozed fitfully, dreaming of Brittany's undying love, and of flying horses and medieval castles and other, darker things he could not recall upon wakening.

When he did reopen his eyes after a few short hours, he kept reading.

Kept studying.

Kept absorbing.

7

Jake Beebe was cold. The nighttime breeze worked its way through his heavy down coat and his boots with grim relentlessness, chilling him. He stopped several times as he walked through the forest to retie the bootlaces, pulling them tightly with fingers turning numb.

It didn't help. Midnight was approaching rapidly and the autumn temperature had dropped rapidly after sunset.

Jake had given more than a little thought over the last several days to his sister's insistence that he dispose of the grimoire and put it out of his mind.

Even as he studied the book and marveled at its potential, he had tried to convince himself he was only playing around, that after the way his conjuration had gone so wrong with Brittany Carson he would never try another, that his interest in black magic was theoretical and nothing more.

Somewhere in the back of his mind, though, he had known he was bullshitting himself. Somewhere in the back of his mind he'd known he would try another spell, and why not?

Would a poor man be expected to ignore a treasure trove of riches he'd discovered? Of course not.

So how could Julie expect him to pretend he hadn't stumbled upon what might turn out to be the most significant source of knowledge in the last thousand years?

The only real question, he now knew as he trudged through the primeval forest surrounding Paskagankee, had been *which* spell he would attempt. And the more he read, the more he studied the mystical book that seemed to so frighten Julie but so fascinate him, the more he came to the conclusion it would be a big one.

The big one.

Never mind lighthearted flights of fancy like summoning a banquet or a medieval castle. Those kinds of things would be cool and all, but Jake had decided that if he was going to tromp through the woods and freeze his ass off at midnight with November just around the corner—and to complete any of the really interesting spells, that was exactly what he would have to do—he was going to go for all the marbles. Swing for the fences.

He would summon a demon.

His very own demon.

A demon who, according to the conjuration spelled out in the grimoire, would materialize in front of him in a form he could see and understand—presumably a human form—and who, if the spell was performed properly, would be prohibited from harming Jake and would be compelled to follow Jake's instructions precisely.

No matter the contents of those instructions.

The way Jake saw it, if he were to pull off this conjuration, he would have his own slave, a supernatural one with the ability to complete all the other spells contained in the grimoire's pages, plus so many more.

The possibilities were literally endless.

If he wanted to compel Brittany Carson to love him, Jake's personal demon would make that happen. It would be like last weekend's disaster in the attic had never occurred.

If he wanted to stay home from school every day without getting in trouble, and still receive his diploma following senior year, Jake's personal demon would make that happen.

The world would be at Jake's fingertips. The only limit to what he could have would be his own imagination.

And Jake liked to think he had a pretty goddamned active imagination.

Was it risky summoning a demon from Hell? Of course it was, but specific text contained in the conjuration was said to prevent the demon from harming the person who summoned it.

Provided the spell was performed correctly.

Jake was simultaneously excited and frightened.

At last he burst through a tangle of tree branches and underbrush and stepped into the clearing he'd prepared over the last couple of days after school. He felt a rush of determination as he placed the grimoire gently onto the cold ground and turned his flashlight beam onto its pages.

He wasted no time getting to work. The night was cold and windy and it wouldn't be getting any warmer out here.

He stepped away from the grimoire to find a couple of rocks with which to hold the pages open and then stopped, eyeing the book suspiciously. The wind ruffled his long hair against his scalp and yet the pages remained flat.

They didn't riffle.

They didn't flap.

They didn't move at all. They remained utterly still, as if someone had taken the time to glue the book's pages together, one by one, on either side of the chapter Jake had selected.

But of course that was silly, not to mention impossible. The only other person in the world aware of the grimoire's existence was Julie, and she wasn't about to waste her time on a stupid prank, especially not where the grimoire was concerned. She was terrified of it. Her fear was obvious every time she so much as looked at the special book.

And besides, Jake clearly recalled riffling the pages just moments ago when he had opened the grimoire to the demonic conjuration spell. Its pages had been as loose and free as the pages of any book he'd ever read.

The breeze continued to blow, stronger now if anything, and still the pages lay perfectly flat and unmoving, as though made of stone themselves.

Jake swallowed heavily.

His stomach felt heavy, like he might need to take a crap.

He ignored the chill that suddenly seemed to have worsened and got to work.

8

The basics of the spell were simple. To perform the demonic conjuration, one must refrain from sexual relations for five days—no problem there, since despite his best efforts Jake was still a virgin—and must fast for twenty-four hours.

The fasting part was a little more problematic than the no-sex part. One thing Jake loved more than practically anything else in the world to eat. But he'd dutifully avoided doing so all day, even begging off dinner with claims of an upset stomach. He drank plenty of water and chewed through four packs of gum but was proud he'd maintained the willpower to avoid food for a whole goddamned day.

It was a first for him.

Aside from those two strictures, the only requirement was to follow the spell exactly as laid out on the grimoire's pages, and Jake set about doing so, alone and fearful in the dark, desolate forest.

The specifics of the spell were similar to the one he'd performed in the attic last weekend, albeit more complex. They involved carving a circular trench into the clearing with a sword, along with symbols and letters, and then filling the trench with gasoline and lighting it on fire while chanting a bunch of bizarre names and some other stuff Jake didn't understand.

He didn't have a real sword and also didn't have the slightest clue where to *get* a real sword, so he made do with what he did have. In this case, that meant digging through crap in the attic until finding an old plastic ninja sword from one of the Halloween costumes he'd worn years ago as a kid.

He'd felt silly lugging the sword down to his room and hiding it until tonight, but what the hell. Nobody had seen him do it, not even his busybody sister, and why should the spirit world give a shit whether the sword was real or fake? A sword was a sword, right?

Jake worked carefully, taking his time and trying to do things right, even as the breeze blew and the temperature dropped. He carved his circle into the dirt, and then filled it with a more or less faithful representation of a pentagram.

Then he marked the four compass direction points just outside the circle, exactly as he had done last weekend in the attic with his Brittany spell.

Then came the only real hard part: drawing four horned goats capering on their hind legs, one adjacent to each of the four compass direction points. That took some time and concentration.

At last he stepped back and examined his work. The drawings were surprisingly good; especially considering he'd rendered them with a plastic sword in the dirt, with nothing more than a flashlight beam for illumination. Hopefully they would do the trick.

He stepped next to the grimoire and retrieved a two-gallon plastic gasoline can and then began pouring its contents into the trenches he'd carved so painstakingly. It was a slow process, but again he forced himself to move slowly and carefully.

Jake lost himself in his work, and when he finally stretched and glanced at the time on his iPhone, he was surprised to see that well over an hour had passed since his arrival in the clearing. His back was aching and it cracked loudly as he straightened.

He barely noticed. His excitement had begun to build as he poured the gas into the grooves, until now it overshadowed even the dread he'd been feeling almost from the moment he snuck out of the house.

He flicked his lighter with shaking hands and held it to the southernmost portion of the circle. The gasoline flared and flames raced away in both directions and through the pentagram in the middle. By the time Jake had dropped his lighter back into his pocket, the entire circle was ablaze, fire pulsing in the breeze and licking toward the sky.

Jake had no idea how long it would take for the gasoline to burn out, so he grabbed the grimoire and wasted no time, beginning to read, chanting in a voice that surprised him by its steadiness. He announced the weird names, and then requested the presence of the demon, repeating the entire passage three consecutive times. Then he sat back on his haunches and waited.

The wind moaned in the trees and the flames danced inside the pentagram and for some time nothing happened. Jake felt his confidence—and his terror—begin to ebb. He'd failed somehow and all his efforts had been for nothing. He would have to—

The flames began to change color.

They had initially been almost exclusively yellow, but now they began to turn red, rapidly and noticeably, within sixty seconds becoming the bright crimson of arterial flow, every bit as thick and lush as the blood of a slaughtered victim in the most realistic video game Jake had ever played.

He was shaking and he realized he had no idea how to stop this unnatural occurrence if he decided he'd gone too far.

And then it was too late anyway.

In his peripheral vision Jake detected movement, subtle and somehow threatening.

He shifted his attention to where he thought he'd seen the movement and gasped at the sight of a black mass undulating on the far side of the burning circle. The mass was amorphous and swirling, so utterly dark it stood out against the murky background of the forest trees.

Swirling and churning, the mass at first appeared stationary, but as Jake watched he realized it was, in fact, moving. It approached slowly, almost imperceptibly, but then it picked up speed, racing through the flames directly toward him.

The flames, now so bright crimson he could barely stand to look at them, disappeared as the undulating black mass advanced. Then the mass burst through the circle and enveloped Jake, choking out the light from the flaming pentagram, and the light from the flashlight, and the ambient light cast by the moon and the stars.

A faraway buzzing sound began to fill Jake's consciousness. It became loud and insistent and it was nowhere but it was everywhere and it was relentless and loud and eating away at Jake's brain until he could no longer stand it and he knew he was about to die, and he wished he *would* die, anything to end the torment of the void and the buzzing, and in his tortured mind he apologized to God and to Julie for the abomination his carelessness and stupidity had called forth into the world, and he apologized and he begged to die, to be released from this terror and misery, and then the blackness granted his request, it granted it by strangling him and choking him and he could feel his life leaching away, and at last Jake was released from his pain, and as consciousness left him he was thankful it was all finally over.

9

Julie had been pissed off at Jake all week, and rightfully so. The best thing she could say about his actions in the attic and in the time since was that they were stupid and mean and immature.

The worst thing she could say was that he'd committed sexual assault and proven himself to be a thuggish brute.

Britt hadn't mentioned anything about pressing charges, and maybe to take her anger that far would have been a bit of a stretch, but she was clearly still confused and upset. She'd barely acknowledged Julie's presence in school this week, even though they had practically all their classes together.

The cold shoulder came as no surprise, but it still hurt like hell.

And as if it wasn't bad enough that Jake had driven a wedge between Julie and Britt, he'd taken things even a step further, basically telling Julie he was going to continue to play around with that awful book, and to hell with what she wanted.

Jake doing stupid things wasn't exactly a novel situation. He tended to be impetuous and rash, two personality traits Julie had never understood. Her default state was almost always care and caution. Thinking things through before acting. The exact opposite of her brother.

Their wildly divergent personalities meant Julie had long-since become used to being annoyed with Jake. That scenario was nothing new.

But something else was going on here, something over and above a sibling spat caused by idiotic behavior.

Something seemed different about Jake.

Something was…off.

It was more than just the fact they weren't getting along. Their current simmering hostility was to be expected, given the events of the past week.

This was something else.

And it wasn't constant. At times, Jake seemed like the same goofy, trouble-prone brother he'd always been, if currently aloof and dismissive to her personally.

But at other times, he seemed to…transform. Something would come over him, his eyes darkening and his posture changing and his entire aura becoming…intimidating.

Menacing.

Sinister.

It had happened two or three times so far, and while Mom and Dad hadn't seemed to notice, that didn't mean anything. They hadn't paid much attention to their only two children in years. With them it was all about work and their business on the town council.

The Beebe clan had resided in Paskagankee for centuries, longer than almost any other family in town, and they'd been one of the driving forces in local politics for decades. Julie couldn't imagine why they could possibly care about running a tiny little shithole like Paskagankee, but it seemed to matter a hell of a lot to her parents.

But with the two of them so preoccupied, it was probably too much to expect either one to notice a little thing like Jake's personality changing in the middle of dinner, and his manner becoming dark and threatening toward their only other child.

Julie noticed, though. She couldn't help noticing.

And when the change came over Jake it was terrifying.

The situation last night at the dinner table was a perfect example. Mom and Dad were chattering away, discussing nothing remotely of interest to two sixteen-year-olds, while Julie and Jake were preoccupied with trying to ignore each other. The time dragged, Julie feeling awkward and unhappy, but that wasn't the scary part. That was just the new normal since last Saturday.

The scary part came when the meal finally ended. Mom and

Dad left the table to have their coffee in the living room, leaving Julie and Jake to clean up the dinner dishes as they always did.

No sooner had their parents turned the corner and disappeared from sight than Jake's eyes narrowed to slits. Julie would have sworn they transformed from their usual mud-brown to something glittering and almost obsidian.

A chill seemed to radiate out of him—not the anger and resentment he'd been displaying toward Julie all week, but rather an *actual chill*, a drop in temperature that made goosebumps rise on her arms and caused her to shiver like she'd gone out in the middle of winter without her coat.

He sat slumped in his chair like a petulant child while he ate, but the minute Mom and Dad left he rose up, straightening and almost seeming to elongate, although Julie decided that must have been her overactive imagination.

What wasn't her imagination, however, was how he leaned forward, aggressively invading her personal space until he towered over her, his face inches from hers, his eyes hard and cold. Then he reached out, quick as lightning, and wrapped one hand around her wrist.

Then he began to squeeze. His hand felt frigid, like Julie imagined a dead person's hand would feel, and he steadily increased the force of his grip until she feared the bones in her wrist would snap.

And he never said a word. He stared into her eyes with a horrible shark-eyed gaze and said nothing while crushing her wrist.

She gasped, first in surprise and then in pain, and the pain grew immense, and she couldn't yell at him to stop, and she couldn't scream for Mom and Dad, because the pain was so bad she couldn't even *breathe*, and he never said a word, he just kept squeezing and crushing and staring at her with those cold, dead eyes.

Just when she thought she would end up in a cast for the next two months, he finally eased his grip. He glared at her and then he pulled his hand away and leaned back in his chair.

Then the dead-eyed Jake vanished.

He blinked rapidly and shook his head and his eyes were once again their normal color. He shot her a look of what she took to be confusion.

"What the hell?" Julie whispered. She massaged her right wrist with her left hand in an effort to get some blood flowing back into the joint, which ached and throbbed. She eyed him fearfully while easing her chair away from the table.

Jake remained silent, but Julie got the distinct impression he had no idea what had just happened. It was as if he'd blacked out or something for the last couple of minutes and then suddenly come back.

And that in itself was scary, as if she needed something *more* to be terrified of following the bizarre scene that had just played out in virtual silence. She was angry; of course she was. Who wouldn't be?

But more than anything else she was afraid.

The scraping of her chair legs across the worn linoleum sounded like screams of pain from invisible victims, and Julie shuddered involuntarily. She stood, still moving with the utmost caution, like a rabid dog were sitting in the chair next to her, rather than her twin brother and—with the possible exception of Brittany Carson—the person she knew better than anyone else in the world.

He continued to gaze at her curiously as she reached forward and lifted her dishes off the table. She carried them to the sink without turning her back on him and dropped them into the basin. They clattered and she jumped nervously.

"Ill take care of the dishes," she said, trying to make her voice cold and hard but succeeding in sounding only small and frightened.

Jake's eyebrows knitted together, his suspicion clear. Julie didn't think she'd ever offered to do the dishes by herself before, and her statement had obviously added to his confusion.

Typically it was an epic struggle to get Jake to help with anything around the house, and until tonight Julie would sooner have chewed off her own arm than offered to do anything for her lazy twin. But at this point all she wanted was for him to skulk off to his room—where he'd been spending virtually all of his free time anyway—and right now she thought offering to do his dishes for the next year might be a decent trade-off if he would just go the hell away.

He sat motionless and stared at her appraisingly. For one brief, horrible moment she thought he was going to refuse her offer, and the prospect of sharing the kitchen with him for even another minute felt like more than she could bear.

Then he said, "Fine, whatever," and he shoved his own chair across the floor with the backs of his legs, exactly as Julie had done but at roughly ten times the speed. The screams of the invisible victims were shortened but every bit as intense.

She tried to remain impassive but winced despite herself.

Jake held her gaze for a few seconds longer before stalking out of the kitchen.

His heavy footsteps pounded all the way up the stairs and his bedroom door slammed shut before she allowed herself to cry.

Then she couldn't stop.

10

Something was very wrong. Jake had the strong suspicion he'd fucked up badly last weekend out in the forest north of Paskagankee.

Maybe he'd messed up the conjuration somehow.

Maybe he'd done and said everything exactly the way he was supposed to but the grimoire's author had fucked up the spell's translation from the weird language into English.

Maybe his current problem had nothing whatsoever to do with the grimoire. Hell, maybe he was blacking out several times a day because he'd suffered a brain aneurism or something. That possibility seemed laughably unlikely, but who the hell knew?

Whatever the cause, Jake's problem was getting worse. Quickly. He was losing time more and more often, blacking out at random times and for no discernable reason. He would feel normal, and then out of nowhere and with little warning, would just slip away.

It was what he imagined falling into a coma would feel like.

Then, after a period of time, sometimes as little as a few minutes and sometimes as long as a few hours, he would reappear, sliding back into his own head and reawakening.

But Jake knew he hadn't been slipping into and out of comas for the last five days. For one thing, he had to believe that even his uninterested parents or his angry sister would notice if he suddenly lost consciousness and became unresponsive for a period of time. It didn't seem like the sort of occurrence that could be easily missed.

And for another thing—and this was the truly scary part about what was happening to him; even scarier than the fact that he was blacking out in the first place—every single time the coma-like state had overtaken him, Jake had regained consciousness *in a different place* than he'd lost it.

Which meant of course that he'd been moving around and doing things, sometimes even interacting with people, while remaining completely unaware of his actions.

The first time it happened was right after he'd finished chanting the strange names and the prayer-like words of the demonic summoning spell out in the forest last weekend. He clearly remembered reading the lines from the grimoire, taking his time and being careful not to mispronounce anything.

He remembered repeating the spell three times, exactly as specified.

He remembered the flames of the burning pentagram transitioning from a normal yellowish color to a vivid red, becoming simultaneously darker and brighter until they damned near burned his retinas to look at.

He remembered the dark mass that had appeared on the far side of the fire, coming together like nothing he'd ever seen before and then undulating and swirling as if somehow gathering strength before darting through the fire and coming straight at him.

He remembered the dark mass overwhelming him, enveloping him while being accompanied by a buzzing noise originating inside Jake's own head, the sound intensifying until all he wanted was to die if that was what it would take to make the buzzing noise stop.

And that was the last thing he remembered until waking up just before sunrise Monday morning.

He couldn't remember walking out of the forest.

He couldn't remember entering his own house.

He had no recollection of how he'd spent nearly four hours of time in the middle of a freezing-cold night.

And then there was the weird situation with Julie at the dinner table last night. He'd felt himself slipping away, being pulled out of his body in the now-disturbingly-familiar way. He tried to stop it from happening, just as he'd tried to stop it from happening every time he felt the sensation coming on.

He was unsuccessful.

This time when he regained consciousness, Julie was staring at him like he'd grown a third eye.

It was a look of horror, of confusion and of fear. She was regarding him in a way he'd never seen *anyone* look at another human being. No matter how much they'd fought in the past or how angry they were with each other—including last weekend in the attic and then in his room the next morning—his sister had never come close to matching the look she'd had on her face last night at the dinner table.

It was as if she wasn't looking at her brother at all. It was as if she was looking at something subhuman. Something...monstrous. Tears shimmered in her eyes and her lower lip trembled and she was rubbing her wrist like it had just been run over by a train.

And the way she'd backed away from him. She got up from the table like she thought he was going to leap out of his chair and beat the shit out of her.

What the *hell* had he done while he was...out of his body? Or maybe the better way to put it would be: out of his mind. His body didn't seem to have gone anywhere.

Whatever it was had obviously been pretty bad. Julie offered to wash his dishes because she wanted to get rid of him; her intentions couldn't have been any clearer.

Jake had taken her up on the offer, not so much because he wanted to get out of doing the damned chore as because he wanted—needed, really—to get out of the kitchen every bit as badly as Julie wanted him to. He was confused and scared and beginning to very much regret ever opening the goddamned grimoire.

Of course, the minute he closed and locked his bedroom door, he sat down at his desk and begun studying the book. Again. He hadn't wanted to, but he also hadn't been able to stop himself from doing so. It was as if the accursed thing had sunk hooks into his mind and could reel him in anytime it wanted.

Nothing had happened since the dinner table incident. He'd been conscious and aware of his surroundings—and in control of himself—the rest of last night and so far today.

Eighteen hours and counting.

Enough time to ignite a glimmer of hope in Jake's mind that whatever was happening to him had run out of steam and things would now return to normal. Maybe the effects of the grimoire were like a virus attacking his body and eventually running its course.

It was now Friday afternoon. He sat slouched in the back of Miss Dunn's classroom at Paskagankee High, puzzling over everything that had gone down in the past week and trying to determine whether he'd actually managed to escape the clutches of the book of spells. Algebra wasn't close to being his favorite subject—not that he actually *had* a favorite subject—at the best of times.

This was far from the best of times.

So when Miss Dunn called on him out of nowhere, asking about the hypotenuse of a fucking triangle or some such shit, to say he was unprepared to respond would have been an understatement.

He straightened in his chair and cleared his throat, playing for time while he searched desperately in his memory for some kind of answer that wouldn't make him look like a total dipshit in front of the entire class.

He couldn't come up with one.

He cleared his throat a second time, wondering how in the hell this situation could get any worse.

Then he found out.

The darkness came and he fought it for as long as he could—maybe a second or two—and then it overwhelmed him.

And he was gone.

Again.

11

Lucie Dunn had been an educator for a long time, all of it spent right here in Paskagankee. She'd received her teaching degree from the University of Maine almost ten years ago and immediately returned to her hometown, painfully aware from her own experience as a student of the desperate need for teachers in such a tiny and isolated community.

The first few years were difficult because she was not much older than the kids she was teaching. Some of the students to come through her classroom were younger brothers and sisters of girls she'd been friends with during her own time at PHS. There had even been one or two siblings of boys she'd dated.

As those initial years passed and fewer students were kids she knew personally, the job became a little easier. But even during the roughest periods, she'd never once regretted her decision to come home.

Meeting the right man and starting a family would be a challenge, and as she passed her thirtieth birthday and began to watch it shrink into the distance in the rear view mirror it was something she found herself considering more and more often. Lucie still believed the family situation would work itself out, though.

Exactly how that was going to happen was anybody's guess.

In the meantime, there was plenty to keep her busy. At the moment, that meant trying to get and keep the attention of one of her most frustrating students. Jake Beebe was bright; he was every bit as intelligent as his twin sister Julie, who, even as a sophomore everyone on the staff at PHS could see would probably wind up valedictorian of her graduating class.

But one thing Jake lacked was Julie's inquisitive nature and enthusiasm for learning. Jake was all too happy to put forth just enough effort to scrape by with barely passing grades. It was a common problem in a town offering much more in the form of alcoholism and drug abuse than any kind of real opportunity, especially for its youngest citizens.

Today, though, Jake seemed even less focused than usual. He sat in the last row of the class—*nothing unusual there,* she thought wryly—slumped behind his desk, his gaze wandering restlessly around the room, not even pretending to pay attention.

Lucie put up with it for a while. Even though she'd been teaching for almost ten years now, she wasn't so far removed from the travails of high school life she couldn't remember what it was like to be sixteen and feel the weight of adolescence on one's shoulders.

She continued to engage the class as much as possible. She knew math was considered dry and boring by most, so her preferred method of combatting that boredom was a spirited back-and-forth teaching style that forced kids to stay on their toes, participating by choice ideally and by coercion when necessary.

Eventually she made the determination it was time for coercion. Time to remind Jake gently why he was here. Otherwise his fifty minutes spent inside her classroom today would end as a total waste of time, both hers and his.

So she called on him. She asked him a relatively easy question, something from yesterday's material, from when she was pretty sure he'd been paying at least marginally more attention than he was today.

He hemmed and hawed and delayed and she knew there would be no answer forthcoming, at least none that bore any relationship to the material she'd taught. His reaction wasn't terribly unusual; she'd seen it hundreds of times over the years from kids who'd been caught daydreaming.

What *was* unusual was what happened next.

Jake's eyes seemed to glaze over. His head drooped for a split-second and her immediate thought was that she was seeing a sixteen-year-old suffer a stroke right in the middle of her classroom.

Then the moment was gone and Jake straightened up once again in his chair.

Lucie met his gaze and did a doubletake as his glittering eyes looked almost…black. Empty. Like a window into a barren soul.

She took an inadvertent step backward and banged into the blackboard. Stuttered once before regaining some semblance of control over her emotions. And her voice.

"You were saying, Mr. Beebe?" she managed.

"I hadn't said anything yet," he growled. His voice sounded different. It was definitely Jake's, but seemed somehow deeper, more guttural, like he was speaking through one end of a long tube. The words were clipped, their cadence radically different from his typical speech pattern.

For a moment Lucie said nothing, stunned into silence by the sheer Bizarro World weirdness of the situation. She felt the eyes of the other students on her and cleared her own throat, aware she was doing exactly what Jake had just done but unable to stop herself.

"I'm waiting for an answer, Jake," she finally managed.

"You can keep waiting," the guttural voice said. "In fact, why don't you just ask someone else your little question and leave me the *hell* alone."

Then he snickered, like he was sharing a private joke.

If he was, nobody else got it. The kids cast puzzled glances around the room, looking from Lucie to Jake and then back again. The classroom had grown deathly silent as everyone waited to see what would happen next.

She had to regain the upper hand, and immediately. It wasn't just about Jake Beebe anymore, or even about the current strange situation. It was about maintaining a reputation for discipline with the kids. Once lost, that reputation was exceedingly difficult to regain.

Lucie spoke quietly. "I'd like to speak with you for a moment after class, Jake."

No response. He didn't argue, didn't take the semi-mocking tone he'd used before. He simply didn't answer.

But at the moment, she decided not to push the issue. If he got up and tried to leave without coming to the front of the classroom when the bell rang, she would deal with it then.

In the meantime, she turned and walked to the blackboard and tried to continue. Her pulse was racing and her heart hammering in her chest. She was about as rattled as she could ever remember being inside a classroom. Jake had never been the best student, but this open rebellion had come out of left field.

She began diagramming an equation, speaking loudly so the students could hear, when out of her peripheral vision she saw something that looked like a tiny missile strike the blackboard and bounce to the floor.

A glance down confirmed what she already knew: someone had thrown a spitball.

Something landed in her hair and a couple of students chuckled.

Lucie whirled and focused on Jake. His right arm was just following through on the launch of a third mini-projectile. It whipped through the air with surprising accuracy and she had to dodge left to avoid taking it square in the face.

"That's it!" she shouted. Her voice screeched shrilly and with difficulty she swallowed back a bit of her fury before continuing. "Detention for you, Mr. Beebe. My classroom immediately after dismissal." It took every last bit of her crumbling self-control not to curse at him.

Jake smirked and looked away and the clanging of the bell saved Lucie from further humiliation. The wayward student shoved his chair back and stalked out the rear classroom door without any sign of acknowledgement or even a look back.

Lucie was shaking, angry and upset, nearly hyperventilating. What in God's name had come over a kid who'd never been a major disciplinary problem for her, or for any other teacher as far as she knew?

She reached back and felt around in her hair for the spitball that had lodged back there. Once located, it took three tries to grasp it firmly enough to pull it out. Her hands were trembling badly and the spitball was slimy and disgusting and she felt her hair tangling as she pulled.

Finally she yanked hard, tugging the nasty piece of junk free of her hair and tossing it into the trash basket next to her desk. Several strands of hair came along with it, and she barely noticed and didn't care. She stifled a sob and tried to compose herself as a new group of kids filed in for the next class.

She was initially unsure why this incident bothered her so deeply. Her revulsion was visceral, much more than just the natural reaction to being on the receiving end of spitball target practice. She'd dealt with unruly students before, if never quite in the manner of Jake Beebe.

Then it occurred to her. It wasn't Jake's actions that bothered her at all, not really. It was how he'd literally transformed from a typical, if reticent, student into something…unnatural.

Something predatory.

Something offensive at the most basic level.

Something almost inhuman.

And she'd demanded it return after school for detention.

What the hell had she been thinking?

12

This time when Jake returned to his body he was still in school but no longer slouched in the back of Miss Dunn's classroom, no longer desperately trying to come up with the answer to her question or at least recall what the question had been.

He blinked his eyes and took in his surroundings and tried to reorient himself as quickly as possible. It wasn't easy because he was surrounded by a gaggle of chattering kids, but after a moment he realized he was walking down the hallway just *outside* Miss Dunn's classroom.

Jake's heart fell as his pulse began to race. This nightmare he'd brought on himself was getting worse. Much worse. Whatever he'd summoned, or awakened, or invited into himself out in the forest last weekend—*the spirit. It's a spirit. A demon,* he thought, and his pulse kicked into an even higher gear—was becoming bolder.

This was far worse even than last night. At least last night's shit show had been witnessed by just one person, and his sister at that. Today he'd left his body in front of a classroom full of kids plus a teacher, and while he had no idea what had happened during his blackout, he guessed it wouldn't take long to piece everything together.

Because the swarm of kids in the hallway were all chattering at *him.*

Mike Crowley jabbed him in the ribs and said, "Dude, that was awesome!" and Jake's heart fell a little more. If a degenerate like Crowley was calling something Jake had done "awesome," it couldn't be good.

Monica Bouchard said, "That was not awesome, that was totally disgusting. A spitball? In her hair? Nobody deserves that, not even a teacher. What is wrong with you?" and the bottom dropped out of Jake's heart. Even worse than Monica's comment was the look she was giving him. It was something she might have reserved for a bloody carcass squashed on a Paskagankee back road.

Jake knew he had to respond but had no clue what to say. "I—"

"You should blow off detention!" Crowley said. "You're in trouble already, what's the worst that could happen?"

Christ. Detention. As if this day couldn't gave gotten any worse.

Crowley continued excitedly, thinking out loud. "Yeah, picture Miss Dunn waiting in her classroom after school. She's tapping her foot, staring at the clock, waiting for you to show, *and you never do!*"

The last four words were spoken with the unbridled glee of a nine-year-old on Christmas morning, and finally Jake found his voice. "You're an idiot, Crowley, you know that?"

The grinning student snapped his head back as if he'd been punched in the face. He flushed bright red and Jake flashed on the flames of the pentagram last weekend.

"What are you talking about?" Crowley said. "You're already in trouble. Send a message. Or are you just that big a pussy?"

Jake stepped forward and shoved the bigger kid back on his heels. "I'll say it again. You're an idiot. If I blow off detention, what do you think's gonna happen next?"

Crowley's immediate instinct had been to shove Jake back, but now he stopped and considered the question. After a moment he shrugged as if to say, *Who cares?*

"I'll tell you what'll happen next," Jake said. "Calls to my parents. Possible suspension. Grounding by my folks until I'm eighteen. Yeah, Mike, sounds great."

Crowley stepped forward and shoved Jake, but most of the instinctual anger in the act seemed to have dissipated. Jake got the feeling he did it only to show he hadn't been intimidated, as a way to get in the last word, testosterone-wise. Jake let him do it and then walked away.

He had bigger problems to worry about than Mike Crowley and some stupid teenage dick-measuring contest.

Much bigger problems.

13

Lucie managed to get through the last class of the day. She wasn't quite sure how. Her heart pounded in her chest like a jackhammer for basically the whole period, and she could hear her voice trying to shake and crack as she spoke.

Hopefully the class didn't notice.

Jake Beebe's bizarre…transformation…had occurred during E period, which meant she'd only needed to keep herself together for less than an hour before the end of the day.

Unfortunately, the end of the day meant detention.

For Jake.

In her classroom.

It wasn't official PHS policy for a teacher to hold detention in her own classroom; in fact, Lucie was the only teacher at Paskagankee High who regularly did so. Official school policy was that detention would take place in the classroom directly opposite the principal's office. Teachers rotated through detention duty, meaning each teacher was responsible for staying after school and presiding over official detention roughly once every three weeks.

But Lucie had always done things a little differently. She didn't like the idea of "official" detention for a couple of reasons. First, she believed it detrimental to the very students who needed guidance the most to saddle them with a label of "troublemaker" or "problem." The straight-A students rarely found themselves sitting across from Mr. Weems's office from 2:10 to 3:10 p.m., and Lucie believed the kids who regularly found themselves in detention would benefit much more from guidance than from the negative labeling that accompanied "detention."

The second reason she objected to "official" detention was that in her experience it was usually nothing more than a waste of time: one bored teacher mostly ignoring a classroom filled with anywhere from one or two to more than a dozen kids for an hour, while those kids snapped gum, cracked jokes and passed notes.

By holding unofficial detention in her own classroom, Lucie believed it helped students avoid the tag of troublemaker while also allowing her to give some personal attention to kids who needed it most.

For ten years, PHS administrators had been telling her she couldn't hold unofficial detention. For ten years she'd been ignoring them and doing it anyway, and for ten years they'd looked the other way.

Lucie Dunn was an excellent teacher in an area of the country where it was next to impossible to get and keep even mediocre ones. PHS administrators weren't about to risk losing her over something as unimportant as a disagreement over how to best run the after-school detention program.

Her unofficial detention policy had made her extremely popular with the kids during her decade of teaching, if not necessarily with the other teachers and administrators. Lucie liked to believe she'd made a real difference in more than one young life through communication and personal attention, and she'd never regretted her decision to stick to her guns in the face of the school's opposition to her unofficial detention policy.

Until now.

Now, with the school's final bell having rung, and with Jake Beebe due in her classroom any minute now for his very own Lucie Dunn Detention, she wished fervently that she'd never developed her own unofficial policy, that she was one of the teachers who just packed up their materials and left the building as soon as possible after last bell.

She thought back to Jake's lack of response at the end of E Period when she'd demanded he report to her classroom at the end of the day. Maybe he hadn't heard her and wouldn't show up. Maybe he *had* heard her but would ignore her demand.

She could pretend he hadn't heard her and just let the whole thing go. She could—

What are you thinking? Jake's behavior is clear indication of a problem, and it's up to you to get to the bottom of whatever's troubling him. You're supposed to be the adult, remember? Why don't you start acting like one.

The mental pep talk calmed Lucie's nerves slightly, but she still couldn't ignore the nagging thought in the back of her mind that things would be much better for all concerned if Jake simply walked out of the building and went home this afternoon.

But he didn't go home. Lucie busied herself correcting quiz papers, and when she looked up from her desk five minutes after last bell, there he was.

He walked through the rear classroom door, the one he'd sauntered out of barely more than an hour ago after peppering Lucie with spitballs and generally acting not like a high school student but like a particularly unrepentant prison inmate.

He seemed hesitant. Shy almost. Embarrassed.

He looked nothing like the dangerous, somehow inhuman entity that had disrupted her classroom, and she offered him a warm smile. Obviously her concerns had been unwarranted. Jake was nothing more than a kid with a problem, acting out for some as-yet unknown reason.

He wasn't dangerous or in any way frightening; he was a teenager who needed help.

Lucie would provide that help, or at least would try to. She followed up her smile by speaking softly. "Come in, Jake, please."

Her trudged into the classroom and dropped a mostly-full backpack onto the desk at which he'd been sitting earlier in the day.

He started to take a seat but Lucie said, "Why don't you come up to the front of the room? I've got some work to do at my desk and we can chat while I go through it. How does that sound?"

He didn't answer but he picked up his backpack and moved to a desk in the front row. This time she didn't stop him from sitting.

She stood up from behind her own desk and walked around it to the front. Then she shoved her papers to the side and perched atop the desk's surface with her legs dangling off the side. Her goal was to make Jake comfortable, to chat with him not as a teacher lecturing a wayward student, but on a more equal basis, or at least as mentor and mentee.

"What happened during E Period, Jake?" Again she spoke softly, unthreateningly.

"I-I don't know, Miss Dunn." Lucie's teaching experience had brought her in contact with hundreds of students in after-school scenarios like this one, and she had started out by asking exactly that question almost every time.

Their answers had run the gamut from denials of wrongdoing, to outlandish excuses justifying their wrongdoing, to tearful confessions of problems at home, or alcoholism or drug abuse or bullying issues or any number of other problems faced by twenty-first century teens.

But she didn't think she'd ever seen such a genuine expression of bewilderment on a student's face. It was almost as if Jake not only didn't understand why he'd thrown the spitballs and disrupted class, he wasn't even aware he'd done it.

His reaction was so unusual she followed her question up with one she'd never before asked. It popped into her head based entirely on his look of confusion.

She said, "Tell me what was going through your mind when you were throwing those spitballs. I'd like to know what you were thinking."

He looked up at her and she noticed his eyes had filled with tears. *This* was not a novel occurrence. This was a reaction she'd seen before. He was about to confess some deeply personal problem, and while she had no idea yet what that problem might be, she felt finally like she had returned to familiar ground.

She would let him pour his heart out.

She would listen without interruption.

And she would help him begin to deal with whatever was affecting him so deeply. This, more than anything, was why she'd become a teacher. She lived to help adolescents navigate the minefield that was their teen years.

"That's just it," he said. He blinked and one tear dripped out of his right eye and rolled slowly down his cheek. He didn't seem to notice. "I don't know what I was thinking, because I—"

He stopped speaking mid-sentence and his eyes blanked. It was like someone had pulled the plug on his brain and it was powering down.

And then he began...to...change.

14

Jake's facial expression slackened, morphing from agonized confusion to...nothing. It was like he was conscious but unaware. And then, after maybe a half-second of that disturbing nothingness, the change continued and a look of cunning—*of evil; he looks exactly like evil personified*—crept over his face.

And his eyes.

Oh God, his eyes.

Lucie watched, stunned, as Jake's brown eyes transformed. They had never been what anyone would consider striking. They weren't the piercing blue a Hollywood leading man might exhibit. They weren't wide and impressive or focused and earnest. They weren't particularly noteworthy in any way.

But now they were not even human.

The pupils enlarged as Lucie watched, horrified. They darkened and within seconds had turned black as coal.

And they began to glow, pulsing with malevolence.

The thing began to rise from the desk.

Lucie felt herself edging backward on the desk in an effort to add distance between herself and...whatever this was. She was operating without conscious thought, terror causing her brain to seize up.

The thing with the glowing eyes smiled, a facial expression lacking in warmth or humor or good nature. The gesture was evil to the core. It made this obscenity before her no more reassuring than it would have been had the monster drawn a knife and plunged it into Lucie's chest.

And then the thing spoke. Its voice was low, gravelly and discordant. It sounded like a razor blade sawing through an out-of-tune guitar string.

"What was the question again?" the black-eyed horror said. It continued to creep closer to Lucie and she continued to push herself backward.

Her laptop tumbled off the desk and crashed to the floor, and in her panic and fear she barely noticed.

The coffee mug filled with pens and pencils she kept on the corner of her desk followed a half-second later. It dropped onto the computer and scattered its contents across the floor, and she barely noticed.

Her Paskagankee High School desk blotter was next, covering the mess like a burial shroud, and she barely noticed and certainly didn't care.

Because she'd reached the edge of her desk and had nowhere else to go. Any further and she would tumble onto the floor, exactly as her computer and pens and pencils and blotter had done.

Even worse, the Jake-thing had closed the gap between them and now stood before her, its face a leering rictus of amused animal hostility. Somewhere in the dim recesses of the tiny portion of her brain that hadn't turned to mush Lucie realized she hadn't used the bathroom since before lunch and that suddenly she needed to pee worse than she could recall ever having to go in her life.

The thing reached one hand out and placed it on her knee. Lucie had worn a long, flowing skirt today, but the hem had ridden up her leg to her thighs and through her nylons she could feel fingers every bit as ice-cold as those of a corpse. They slid up and caressed the thigh like the clumsy advances of an uncertain lover, and she thought she might be sick.

"Oh, yes," the razor-blade voice rasped when it became clear Lucie Dunn would not be responding any time soon. "I remember now. You wanted to know what I—excuse me, what *Jake*—was thinking pelting you with those disgusting, unsanitary little balls of paper and saliva."

Lucie felt herself shaking, her body vibrating under her clothing. Otherwise she remained perfectly still, as if perhaps by offering no response to this abomination it might grow tired of provoking her and shamble away.

"Allow me to share a little secret with you, although you've probably guessed most of it by now, anyway. It's not Jake in here. At least not right now. Jake was kind enough to invite me into his body and now is forced to share."

Lucie swallowed heavily, trying to decipher the monster's words but mostly grateful its hand had stopped sliding up her leg. Maybe someone would come along and save her while the thing with the razor blade voice that used to be Jake Beebe explained itself.

Maybe another teacher would open her classroom door to ask her a question.

Maybe—

"You see," the thing continued after a long moment when no one opened the door to ask her a question. "While I've been forced to remain, shall we say, *dormant* for a very long time, I've always known eventually another young man with more curiosity than brains—and can't we include virtually *all* young men in that statement?—would come along and summon me again, and over the long centuries in exile I've comforted myself with the knowledge that when I finally *did* get the opportunity to…visit your world, shall we say…I would make absolutely the most of it."

Despite Lucie's best efforts to follow what passed for the monster's logic, or reasoning, or whatever the hell it was, his words had devolved into nothing more than senseless babble to her.

Still it continued speaking, hand absently tracing circles with its thumb on her thigh. It felt like an ice cube was being pressed into her nylons.

"As you can imagine," the thing said, "I felt as giddy as a child, finally being invited into this world after so much time away. The spitballs were just my way of having a little fun. Of blowing off steam, so to speak. You can't blame me for having a little fun, can you, Lucie?"

She realized she'd started to whimper, small, pathetic sounds escaping her lips for which she was dimly ashamed but which she stood no chance of stopping. The whimpers were like lava escaping an active volcano: they were going to come out no matter what.

The Jake-thing lifted one hand to its mouth in a mocking parody of modesty, or perhaps shame. It fluttered its eyelids coquettishly. "Please forgive me for being so forward, Lucie. I know as one of your students I'm supposed to call you *Miss Dunn*, but now that I've revealed myself to you as something other than awkward teen Jake Beebe, such formality seems pointless, don't you agree? Especially when you consider how…intimate…we're about to become."

The monster squeezed her thigh hard, its frozen fingers feeling much longer and bonier through the thin material of her nylons than they should. Then the hand resumed its journey up her inner thigh and Lucie was suddenly roused out of her near-stupor of fear.

She kicked out with her right foot, catching the Jake-thing in the gut and shoving hard. It stumbled backward and windmilled its corpse-hands in an attempt to maintain balance as the force of the kick sent Lucie tumbling backward off the desk.

She landed heavily on her back, the pencil-holder coffee mug shattering under her weight and driving a shard of porcelain through her skirt and into her hip. The back of her skull bounced off the floor with a *crack*, and a bright flash of lightning inside her head was followed immediately by a curtain of darkness trying to drag her into oblivion.

Lucie fought to stay awake.

If she passed out she would die.

She shook her head in a desperate attempt to reboot her internal hard drive and a piercing jolt of pain caused her to gasp in agony. It took her breath away. It felt like an icepick being driven into her skull.

And still she moved. She rolled onto her side and wobbled to her feet and then sprinted for the door.

At least, her intention was to sprint. But she was injured, maybe badly, and the best she could manage was a side-to-side stumble, like a Ridge Runner drunk at closing time, aiming for the door more through blind animal instinct than any real conscious design.

The darkness continued to close in, threatening to overwhelm her. The pain in her head screamed a warning that she'd fractured her skull, that she was about to pass out, that she'd better get her ass in gear. But her legs felt heavy and foreign and she seemed to be moving in slow motion.

She never saw the Jake-thing until she ran straight into it.

15

It was like crashing into a brick wall. A frozen, unyielding brick wall.

Lucie bounced off the monster and stumbled backward, faintly aware of a sibilant giggle coming from its the razor-blade throat. One corpse-hand flashed out and grabbed her before she could fall to the floor a second time, and she knew she should be grateful for not hitting her already-damaged head on the floor again but she couldn't manage gratitude when gut-clenching terror was taking up so much of the afternoon's agenda.

The thing that used to be Jake Beebe—*demon, it's a demon, with those glowing black eyes and that ice-cold skin it can't possibly be anything else*—clamped a hand over her throat and began walking forward, forcing Lucie toward her desk and the mess she'd made on the floor. She no longer felt like she needed to pee worse than she ever had, because in her intense fear and pain she'd pissed all over herself.

It was the least of her worries.

The thing was propelling her backward toward her desk and she knew exactly what was going to happen. The monster would force her down on her desk and it would rape her and then kill her and everyone's last memory of her would be that she was found flat on her back with her legs spread and her skirt up around her waist and—

The thing—*demon, it's a demon, it has to be a demon*—made a sudden, ninety degree right turn just before reaching the desk.

Instead of forcing her onto it he shoved her up against the blackboard, his hand still firmly clamped around her throat. He'd started off pushing her slowly but then had picked up speed, and now her feet skittered, barely keeping contact with the floor, as they tried to keep pace with the monster.

Her spine cracked painfully against the chalk/eraser holder and sharp pain flared where she'd been gashed by the shard of smashed coffee cup. The back of her head bounced off the blackboard and for the second time in less than a minute, lightning flashed inside her skull and consciousness threatened to desert her.

This time she almost wished it would.

The monster—*the demon, oh Lord in heaven it's a demon*—held her by the neck against the blackboard, its stony hand allowing just enough slack for her to force oxygen into her lungs. For now.

It leaned forward until its face was just inches from hers, those horrible black eyes glowing with demonic intensity. Even in her fear and pain and panic, Lucie could feel the chill emanating from the monster's skin, like super-cooled air floating out the open door of a freezer.

It opened its mouth to speak and Lucie nearly gagged from the stench. It wasn't bad breath; it was a hundred times worse than bad breath. A thousand times worse. It was a combination of raw sewage and rotted flesh and things that were even worse, things Lucie did not want to consider.

"Where were you going in such a hurry?" the demon said with a hideous, taunting smile. "I open myself up to you and this is the thanks I get? The first time in centuries I spill my own guts instead of someone else's, and you rush off at the first opportunity? I hope you can appreciate the delicious irony. I certainly can."

As the thing talked it gradually tightened its grip around her neck until her airway was completely cut off. She flailed her arms and kicked her feet, aiming a weak punch at its face and missing entirely, aiming a weak kick at its groin and connecting but eliciting no reaction.

In her mushroom cloud of panic it took Lucie a moment to realize the demon had begun lifting her off the floor, pushing her body up the blackboard by her neck until she hung suspended, kicking and punching and feeling the darkness closing in for good.

"You wanted to know why I threw spitballs at my sweet, goodhearted teacher, correct?" The thing loosened its grip for a half-second, allowing Lucie to drag one deep, shuddering breath into her burning lungs before resuming its death grip on her throat and cutting off her airway again.

"ANSWER ME," it hissed, its eyes flashing a deep crimson before settling back into their awful coal black.

She nodded desperately, focused mostly on trying not to lose consciousness but somehow aware that refusing to respond to the demon would not in any way help her accomplish that goal.

"So, if that's the case," the demon continued serenely, "you must be *extra*-curious about why I'm doing...all this."

Another nod. The breath of air Lucie had been able to grab moments ago had felt like the sweetest thing she'd ever experienced, but the relief was fleeting and now she could feel her lungs starting to burn again and the darkness, which had reluctantly retreated, crept back and continued to advance.

"I did it, and I do it, for one reason, and it's a much simpler reason than you might think. I do it BECAUSE I CAN."

The demon's vice-grip fingers closed around Lucie Dunn's throat for the final time, and as she continued to hang suspended over the floor the demon pulled her away from the blackboard and then slammed her head against it, over and over, and the lightning inside her skull flashed again and again and just before she lost consciousness she heard/felt bones breaking in her neck.

And she welcomed the darkness.

PART THREE
CHAOS

1

The autumn air on Mount Katahdin was crisp, but the sun was warm and the sky cloudless, a picture-perfect day for a fall wedding in New England.

Mike McMahon had never considered getting married on a mountain. Hell, until a few months ago he would never have considered getting married again *anywhere*.

So to say he was skeptical when Sharon Dupont broached the subject of a mountain wedding would have been a laughably inadequate description of his concerns, particularly since the wedding was to take place in October. He pictured high winds and freezing temperatures, probably rain and possibly snow.

She'd scoffed at his concern. "Have a little faith, will ya?"

He wasn't sure how many times he'd heard that particular phrase in the six months between her acceptance of his proposal and the morning of her first—and his second—marriage.

But since all he really cared about was making one beautiful woman happy, he'd pushed his concerns aside and cheerfully agreed to the venue, not to mention everything else she wanted regarding the wedding. He was determined to do anything he could to make it the best, most memorable day of her life.

It turned out his meteorological concerns had been groundless. The conditions couldn't possibly have been better.

Mike had discovered to his surprise that mountainside weddings were popular in the area, and to accommodate them, a large post and beam platform had been constructed upon which the ceremony would take place. The platform was big enough to hold even a large wedding party—which theirs most certainly was not—and had been carved right into the side of the mountain.

Guests were seated on a series of benches constructed behind the platform. The benches were tiered up the mountainside, allowing every guest an unobstructed view of the ceremony as well as of the scenery.

And the view was spectacular.

From the perspective of the guest benches, the platform upon which Mike and Sharon would be married appeared suspended in space, hanging off the side of Katahdin. In the distance, dozens of mountains and rolling hills provided a stunning backdrop, the reds and yellows and purples of changing leaves a dazzling celebration of autumn in northern Maine.

Mike's eyes began to water and he wiped the back of his hand across his face, embarrassed. He hoped no one noticed because if anyone from the department saw him tearing up he knew he'd never hear the end of it.

But it was hard not to be overcome with emotion in this place and circumstance. He was standing on the platform, gazing at the scenery in the distance when the wedding march began to play, far above the platform at the DJ's station.

He turned away from the scenery and gazed up the side of Mount Katahdin to see his bride. She'd been awaiting the start of the ceremony around a corner on a paved walking path. As the music started up, she materialized through the trees, walking slowly, smiling widely.

And she was stunning.

Literally breathtaking. He had to remind himself to draw in oxygen as she started the long walk that would lead her between the rows of guest seating and to his side where she belonged.

Her parents were both gone, her mother having died years ago when Sharon was a young girl, her father passing shortly before Mike's arrival in Paskagankee. Her father's illness had brought Sharon back to the town she'd thought she had escaped for good after being accepted into the FBI academy.

Without a living father, and with her mentor—and former Paskagankee Police Chief—Wally Court having died last fall,

Sharon had shyly asked Paskagankee PD dispatcher Gordie Rheaume to walk her down the aisle.

Gordie, who'd been a dispatcher for decades, had known Sharon both in her previous life as an alcoholic, drug-abusing young woman with no mother, an absent father, and no direction, and her current incarnation as a dogged, focused and dedicated police officer. He was so touched by her request that he had actually broken down in tears inside the station.

"It would be my honor," he said when he could finally speak, a time lapse of maybe five minutes. The wedding was all Gordie had been able to talk about from that moment on, and more than once Mike caught himself thinking the old dispatcher might be more excited than the bride herself.

Now Gordie walked proudly with Sharon, arm in arm, looking more dapper in his three-piece suit with yellow rose pinned to the lapel than Mike had ever seen. They approached slowly along the path, moving not just with the measured cadence appropriate to the occasion, but also because the damned mountainside was extremely steep.

Sharon wasn't exactly what most would consider a "girlie-girl," and between her long, lacy, crisp white wedding gown and the heels she'd chosen, Mike thought there was every possibility she might lose her footing and roll right off the side of the mountain if she tried to hurry.

They reached the top of the platform's stairway and paused. Katahdin's wedding coordinator had suggested they stop at that point and delay at least five seconds before proceeding, enough time to allow the guests and the wedding photographer ample opportunity for photos.

After what felt to Mike like forever, they continued their wedding march.

And then she was next to him.

Mike's Best Man was Officer Harley Tanguay. Mike wished his friend Pete Kendall could have been standing with him on this special day, but Pete was another Paskagankee resident who had died too soon. Harley was a good man and a solid cop, and one of the few Paskagankee officers who had refused to indulge in the whispered sniping about the chief sleeping with the most junior officer on the force right after his arrival in town.

The wedding would be officiated by Rose Pellerin, another life-long resident of Paskagankee who had known Sharon since she was a little girl. In addition to being the longtime owner of *Needful Things,* the antique shop on Main Street, Rose was an ordained minister and had welcomed the chance to marry the couple.

Mike had come to know Rose as a generous and good-hearted woman, but she could seem severe and forbidding when she wanted to, and she used that ability to her advantage now. She quieted the buzzing crowd with nothing more than a glance, a raised eyebrow, and a cleared throat.

Then she started speaking, welcoming the guests and wedding participants to what she termed "a very special, love-filled day."

Mike glanced sideways at Sharon and winked. Her face was shining, the product partly of beautifully applied makeup but mostly of excitement and happiness.

Out of the side of his mouth he whispered, only half-kiddingly, "It's not too late to get the hell out of here and elope to Vegas, you know."

He thought he'd been discreet, but realized too late that the microphone Rose was using to amplify their voices to the back of the viewing area had caught his comment.

The guests chuckled and Rose said, "You shush! I worked hard getting ready for this ceremony and spent three hundred bucks on my dress. You're damned well going to stand there and listen like a good boy."

"Yes, Ma'am."

This time the crowd laughed and Sharon giggled and Mike decided his life could not possibly get any better.

* * *

They'd written their own vows, and Sharon was in the process of reading hers off, of all things, her cell phone. She produced it from somewhere in the folds of a gown that had no pockets, like a magician pulling a coin from behind an observer's ear.

"I memorized my vows," she swore to the onlookers before

starting, an embarrassed smile on her face. "But I knew that once I got up here I'd be so nervous my brain would shut down and I'd end up looking like a fool. So please excuse me."

Then she started reading.

Her words were simple and touching, an acknowledgment before the world—or at least the small crowd that had gathered to honor the couple with their attendance—of her love and dedication to her new husband and to their life together.

"You saved me," she said simply, looking from her phone up into Mike's face. "From myself, from the voices inside my head that whispered for years that I wasn't good enough, or pretty enough, or smart enough, or ambitious enough."

You're all of those things and more, Mike thought as he stood before her, awe-struck by her beauty and intelligence, still amazed someone like her had chosen a broken-down wreck of an older man with whom to spend her life when she could have had so much more.

"As you've always been there for me," she continued, "I will be there for you. No strings attached, no caveats, no questions asked. Always and forever."

Mike reached up and ran the back of his hand across his face, but he was too late. The tears had begun, and nothing he could do now was going to stop them.

* * *

Time had been set aside immediately following the ceremony for photographs of the bride and groom to be taken amid the mountain backdrop of fiery foliage and stunning scenery.

As uncomfortable as Mike had been showing his emotions during the wedding, he was equally so posing for pictures afterward. This was not the photographer's first rodeo, however, and although she remained friendly and smiling throughout the process, she was all business. She issued instructions with a staccato delivery that would be the envy of any drill sergeant:

"Turn to the side."

"Lift your chin."

"Hand in the pocket of your suit."

"Turn to the other side."

"Drop your chin."

Within ten minutes, Mike had had enough. He whispered to his new bride, "Remember how I swore in my vows that I would put you first for the rest of my life and that any sacrifice for you, great or small, would be a privilege?"

"Well, it was only twenty minutes ago, so yes, I remember. Only one of us is old and suffering from a failing memory."

"Very funny. But if this torture continues much longer I might have to request a ceremony do-over, just so I can scrub that statement from my vows."

"Suck it up, old man. There are no do-overs in the wedding game."

"Oh. Now you tell me."

"Hey!" the drill-sergeant photographer barked. "Have your first fight as a married couple on your own time. Right now, you belong to me. Mike, lift your chin. Oh, and put your hand in your pocket."

* * *

Eventually the photographer decided she had enough material and the small group drifted toward the gondolas. The reception was being held inside the lodge at the base of Katahdin, and all the guests had ridden down the mountain and gathered there to begin celebrating while the newly married couple was being photographed.

As they walked, Mike and Sharon made small talk with Harley and Gordie, joking and laughing, teasing each other about being out of uniform. Initially Mike worried the conversation might be stilted or awkward—four cops thrown together in an outside-work scenario unlikely ever to be repeated—but after the pomp and circumstance of the wedding ceremony, all four appreciated the opportunity to relax.

The group had just settled into a gondola car for the fifteen-minute ride to the reception when Mike's phone rang. The muffled buzzing from his suit coat pocket caught him by surprise and he glanced at Sharon with raised eyebrows. Anyone likely to call him—and it was a small group of candidates to begin with—was probably already here at Mount Katahdin for the wedding.

"What the hell?" Sharon said.

Mike shrugged. "Maybe it's someone down at the lodge wondering what's taking us so long. They're probably wondering when they can start drinking."

"Get real," she answered with a laugh. "They didn't wait for us. It's more likely they're already drunk and somebody butt-dialed you by accident."

Mike fished the phone out of his pocket. He looked at the screen and felt the first stirring of concern. The number for the Paskagankee Police Department flashed on the Caller ID screen.

He held the phone up so Sharon could see.

Whatever the reason for the call, this could not possibly be good news.

Most of the small police force was here on Katahdin for the wedding. They'd left a skeleton crew back in Paskagankee for the day, and night dispatcher Rob Cornell—working a double shift so Gordie could attend—would be too busy to call with congratulations.

Mike sighed and answered.

His suspicions of a problem were immediately confirmed.

2

"Hello?"

"Chief, we have a problem. I mean, a really big problem."

"Slow down, Rob. Take a breath and tell me what's going on."

Gordie Rheume had been day shift dispatcher at the Paskagankee Police Department for as long as anyone currently on the force could remember. A widower, Gordie's entire life revolved around his position at the department, and while he had a tendency to gossip, Mike had found him to be reliable and solid.

But Gordie was seated across the small gondola car, watching Mike take the call from his temporary replacement with rapt interest.

Rob Cornell had been in his position less than six months, and Mike hadn't yet made a final determination as to the quality of Cornell's job performance. But the duties of a night dispatcher in a town as small as Paskagankee didn't typically put the dispatcher in a position where outstanding judgment was required. Drunk driving arrests, drug possession and the occasional domestic disturbance formed the bulk of the law enforcement duties on a busy night in Paskagankee.

Rob took Mike's words to heart. He paused, breathed deeply and then continued. "We need you back here right away, Chief."

"Rob, I got married less than an hour ago. Sharon and I are on our way down the mountain right now, where a reception hall full of people are waiting to celebrate with us. I can't leave now."

"Chief, there's been a murder."

"What are you talking about? Who's been murdered?"The other three passengers inside the gondola could hear only Mike's end of the conversation, and at his words they snapped to attention as one. They'd been watching and listening with interest before, but now a tense electric buzz filled the car's interior.

"One of the teachers at the high school was found dead in her classroom shortly after school ended."

"What was the teacher's name, Rob?"

"Uh…let's see." Even over the rumble of the gondola car and through a scratchy cell connection, Mike could hear papers shuffling, and he shook his head as he tried to tamp down his irritation. The dispatcher should not have to search for a murder victim's name immediately after the crime has occurred.

"Ah. Here it is. Dunn. Lucie Dunn."

"Age of the victim?" Mike was having a hard time believing someone would be bold enough to murder a teacher inside a school building with other adults and students presumably still inside. Maybe the death was nothing more than an elderly teacher falling victim to natural causes.

"Uh…" More paper shuffling. Then, "Thirty-three, Chief. The victim was thirty-three."

Oh boy. So much for natural causes.

"Who was the responding officer?" Only two cops had been left to patrol the town on the chief's wedding day. One was someone Mike trusted implicitly and the other…not so much.

It had already become clear Mike would not be attending his wedding reception, but the name about to be relayed by Rob Cornell would go a long way toward determining how much trust he could place in that officer's handling of the situation.

"Boykin."

Ugh. Miles Boykin was relatively new to the department and someone Mike had begun to suspect did not possess the temperament or the judgment necessary to be a good cop. Mike had received a number of citizen complaints regarding Boykin, and feared Miles might be one of the small minority of officers who entered police work not to give back to their community or to protect its citizenry, but for the opportunity to carry a deadly weapon on their hip and push people around.

He suspected Miles was little more than a small-town bully.
The fact Boykin had been the one to draw the call at the high
school meant that in all likelihood, Mike would already be starting
his investigation on the wrong foot. Hopefully Boykin would at
the very least not contaminate the scene.

"Okay." He met Sharon's eyes and shook his head.

Into the phone he said, "Tell Miles to secure the scene if he
hasn't already done so. You said the teacher was found inside a
classroom?"

"Yes, sir."

"I want the classroom sealed. Nobody comes or goes until I get
there. Once Miles has secured the scene I want him to canvass the
school for witnesses. Someone must have seen or heard something,
and I want to speak to that person or persons as soon as possible."

"Yes, sir."

"You got all that, Rob?"

"Yes, sir."

"Okay. Tell Miles I'll be at the high school by..." he glanced
at his watch and did a little quick math in his head. Mount
Katahdin was located forty miles of winding, hilly back roads east
of Paskagankee, and even utilizing his siren and flashers, Mike
guessed it would take close to an hour to get back to town.

"Four o'clock," he said. "I should be there by four."

"Yes, sir."

Through the gondola's Plexiglas window Mike could see the
lodge growing larger in the distance. They would be at the base of
the mountain soon.

Before disconnecting the call, he said, "Tell me everything I
want you to do, Rob."

The dispatcher responded immediately. "Tell Miles to secure
the scene. Nobody goes in or out. Instruct him to canvass for
witnesses and if he finds any, detain them until you arrive."

Mike felt a flash of optimism in Rob Cornell's response, which
actually sounded professional.

The flash disappeared in an instant, though. One thing he'd
learned in Paskagankee was that events were rarely as bad as they
seemed: they were almost always worse. And this particular event
felt bad already.

He disconnected the call and before he could say a word, Sharon said, "I'm going with you."

He shook his head. "Sharon, we have a banquet hall filled with people who drove all this way to celebrate our wedding. I might have to leave, but you don't. We can't both ditch them."

"We won't be *ditching* them, we'll be doing our jobs. And besides, most of the people inside that lodge are law enforcement anyway, or at the very least friends or family of law enforcement. They recognize the nature of the job, and they'll understand if we have to leave."

Mike shook his head and ran a hand through his thick black hair. He knew he should try to convince Sharon to stay, but he also knew arguing with her once she made up her mind would be like tying to prevent the sun from rising in the east.

He shook his head and chuckled. Smiled at his bride as they prepared to climb out of the gondola car at the base of Mount Katahdin. "Do you want to explain to our guests that they'll be celebrating without the bride and groom or should I?"

She tilted her head and winked. God, but she was beautiful.

"Let's do it together," she said. "We're officially a team now, right?"

"Right on, babe. Plus, they'll be less likely to kill both of us."

3

It took five minutes to explain to the guests that a law enforcement emergency had arisen in Paskagankee and that Mike and Sharon had to leave immediately.

It took five more for the couple to hurry to their hotel room and change out of their wedding clothes.

Five minutes after that they were inside the cruiser, driving as fast as Mike dared on the narrow, winding roads, siren blaring and blue lights flashing. Extreme speed wasn't strictly necessary—the dead teacher would remain dead whether Mike and Sharon arrived in forty-five minutes or ninety—but every crime's trail tended to grow colder as time passed, and that was truer of murder investigations than most others. Hours mattered, as did minutes.

Traffic was light and the weather good, and in just over half an hour the Explorer had crossed the Paskagankee town line. Ten minutes after that, they pulled into a parking space just outside the high school's main entrance.

An ambulance had parked one space over. Its engine idled as red lights flashed atop the cab, inside which two EMTs sat drinking coffee. They offered identical halfhearted waves to Mike and Sharon as the cops exited the Explorer but otherwise remained motionless. Obviously they'd been the first to arrive after a panicked call from whoever found Lucie Dunn's body. The EMTs had discovered her dead and shortly afterward been banished from the scene by Miles Boykin. They'd probably been cooling their heels in their vehicle for close to an hour.

A middle-aged man with thinning hair and a rumpled demeanor rushed to the school's entrance the moment Mike and Sharon entered. His tie was loosened and his sleeves rolled up to his elbows. It was PHS Principal Sheldon Weems, and he'd clearly been waiting for the arrival of someone besides Officer Boykin to tell him what to do.

In his capacity as chief of police, Mike had dealt with Weems many times. The man had always struck him as earnest and dedicated, if perhaps overly officious and fussy.

"Thank God you're here," Weems said as he shook Mike's hand and then Sharon's. "What took you so long?"

"I was busy getting married," Mike answered drily. He didn't bother to explain he'd been getting married to the officer standing next to him. He figured if Weems didn't already know, he'd find out soon enough.

Weems ignored Mike's response anyway. It was as though he hadn't even heard it. He was flustered and upset.

And understandably so, Mike thought. *A thirty-three year old teacher dies under suspicious circumstances inside your school. In addition to the horror of the situation, it can't do much for your job security to have teachers being snuffed out right under your nose.*

"Why don't you tell us everything you know about what happened," Mike said gently.

"Don't you want to see for yourself?"

"Of course. But first I want to hear it from you."

Weems breathed a deep, shuddering sigh. He picked at his tie in what seemed an unconscious habit and said, "There isn't much to tell. One of our students was walking past Miss Dunn's classroom and noticed her door ajar. She thought it odd and poked her head inside. That was when she saw…the…the body. She ran to the office and told my secretary something had happened to Miss Dunn, that she was passed out on the floor. My secretary told me and I went to investigate. I rushed to the classroom, saw that Miss Dunn wasn't breathing and called 911."

Mike nodded. "Did you start CPR?"

"Of course, but it was pointless. She wasn't breathing, had no pulse. The medics arrived within minutes and took over but…"

"I understand. We'll need the name of the student who found Miss Dunn, as well as any other potential witnesses you can think of: kids who stayed after school for whatever reason, student's with disciplinary problems, other teachers."

"But you don't think…"

"What?"

"Surely you don't think…one of our students, or, oh good Lord, one of our *teachers*…could have done this?"

"I don't think anything yet. But I'll still need that information."

Weems nodded distractedly. "Of…of course. I'll compile a list. The student who stumbled on Miss Dunn's body is still in my office, by the way. She's very upset, as you might imagine, and is waiting for one of her parents to pick her up."

"Thank you," Mike said. "If you could show us to the classroom now?"

Sharon hadn't spoken but was taking everything in, her eyes narrowed, her focus sharp. It was hard to imagine she'd been standing on the side of a mountain barely an hour earlier, reciting her wedding vows.

Weems nodded. He seemed about to say something but then picked at his tie again and turned without another word. He hurried down a long hallway to the right of the school's administrative offices as Mike and Sharon followed behind.

Halfway down the long corridor Mike spotted the open door with yellow police crime scene tape strung across it. The victim's classroom was at the end of the hallway on the right side, located as far from the offices and the main wing of the school as it was possible to be.

Sheldon Weems stopped in front of the door and indicated Lucie Dunn's classroom with one outstretched hand. Mike thought he resembled a TV game show host, minus the good looks and personality.

"This is it," Weems said, somewhat unnecessarily. "If there's nothing else you need at the moment…"

"Not at the moment," Mike said. "I'd appreciate that list of potential witnesses as soon as you're able to provide it."

"Yes. Of course," Weems said. He nodded, almost to himself, then tugged at his tie and then began walking in the direction of the offices. His footsteps echoed down the corridor and eventually faded away.

4

Sharon ducked under the crime scene tape and then Mike followed her into Lucie Dunn's classroom. A grim-faced Miles Boykin stood just inside, hand on the butt of his holstered weapon as if perhaps expecting the school to be overrun by a gang of armed perps at any moment.

Mike glanced around the room and then addressed Boykin. "No one's disturbed the scene?"

"Not since I got here. I can't speak for what might have happened before that. The medical guys were working on the vic when I arrived, and I have no idea how many people tramped through here before that, but nobody's come or gone since."

"Okay. Good work, Miles, thank you. I'll take it from here and you can resume patrol."

Boykin looked from Mike to Sharon and then back again, his eyes hard and cold, his thoughts as clear as if he'd spoken them aloud: *What's she doing here? I'm the responding officer and I have almost as much time on the force as Sharon. How come she gets to stay and be part of the investigation, and I'm dismissed like a nosy little kid being sent to his room?*

In a way Mike couldn't blame him. He would probably have felt the same way himself, were he in Boykin's shoes.

But he wasn't in Boykin's shoes. He was in charge, and his responsibility was to the victim. He trusted Sharon Dupont— *McMahon,* he reminded himself. *It's Sharon McMahon now*—in a way he doubted he would ever trust Miles Boykin, and not just because she was his wife.

Sharon was intelligent and intuitive, sharper in some ways than Mike himself, despite the fact he had nearly fifteen years more law enforcement experience than she. And they'd been through the wringer together more than once since his arrival in Paskagankee, sharing experiences most observers would probably not believe.

Sometimes *he* had trouble believing them, and he'd lived through them.

Mike met Boykin's indignant gaze and held it until the other man looked away. Then he said, "Is there something you'd like to say, Officer Boykin?"

The younger man cleared his throat, his hand still on the butt of his gun. Then he shook his head and stalked to the door. He ducked under the tape and disappeared.

Mike sighed and then turned his attention to the victim. Sharon had already begun examining the scene during the little mini-showdown between employee and supervisor, doing her best to pretend she didn't notice.

The young teacher was crumpled at the base of the chalkboard, her head twisted to the side at an unnatural angle, feet and legs tangled beneath her as if she'd fallen straight to the floor. A small amount of blood was splattered around her skull, and bruising was evident on both sides of her neck.

On the floor to the side of Lucie Dunn's desk was everything one would expect to see on *top* of it. Pens. Pencils. A ruler. A smashed ceramic coffee mug. A desk blotter partially covering the other items, as if it had been the last thing to fall.

Mike walked forward from the door, where he'd been standing when he had his moment with Boykin. He glanced from the desk to the victim to the chalkboard and then back to the desk.

Sharon followed his gaze and nodded. "I'm thinking the same thing," she said. "The teacher was assaulted first on the desk, and then again against the board. The assailant enjoyed the first attack so much he decided to go back for seconds."

"Or maybe she tried to get away *as* she was being attacked on the desk, but couldn't make it to the door. This pissed off the bad guy and he assaulted her the second time."

Mike squatted by the desk, careful to remain clear of the blood spatter. "Judging from the distance of this blood from the clutter on the floor, I would say she was shoved off the desk, or maybe scrambled off it on her own in an attempt to escape. She fell, struck the back of her head and began bleeding."

"So she's assaulted on the desk. She falls or is pushed off and maybe tries to run for the door, but she doesn't make it. Then the assailant really gets down to business. He pushes her up against the blackboard and strangles her. Then he drops her dead or dying body to the floor and takes off."

Mike nodded. "He didn't *just* strangle her, though. Look closely at the blackboard."

Sharon followed Mike's gaze. Her eyes widened when she spotted what he had already seen. A significant amount of blood was smeared on the board, with blood spatter shooting off in all directions from the impact point.

"So he strangled her, *and* he smashed her head against the board," she said.

He nodded. "The level of violence is staggering. This wasn't an attempted rape gone bad, or at least not *just* an attempted rape gone bad. There's rage here, a simmering anger that flashed and then burned out of control, a potential for deadly violence that goes way beyond a simple assault that got out of hand."

He climbed to his feet, trying to get a better perspective of the crime scene.

Took three steps back.

Something was bothering him.

Something was wrong, above and beyond the disturbing sight of the young teacher lying dead on the floor. He couldn't quite put his finger on what it was, but it was there and it was real and it wouldn't leave him alone.

Sharon watched him without a word. Her curiosity was evident, even to Mike, even as distracted as he was.

But the time wasn't right to share his concern, because he still didn't know what it was specifically about the scene that bothered him so much.

He walked to the rear of the classroom, turning his back on the fallen victim until reaching the rear wall. Then he pivoted and faced front again.

Narrowed his eyes.

Looked at the teacher crumpled on the floor and then up to the blackboard and then back to the body of the victim.

And then he saw it.

He couldn't quite believe he'd missed it.

"What would you estimate as Lucie Dunn's height?" he said.

Sharon stepped back from the body and gazed down at it for a moment. "It's hard to say, given the way she fell. She's probably average height for a woman, or maybe a little less. I'd say a fair guess would be five feet, four inches, give or take."

"So she doesn't look unusually tall to you."

Sharon shook her head. "No. Definitely not tall. Like I said, if anything, she might be slightly shorter than average for a woman."

Mike walked forward again, joining Sharon at the front of the classroom. "Look at the blood smeared on the blackboard," he said.

She turned and lifted her eyes, then continued lifting them until they came to rest on the reddish-brown smear. Understanding came into her expression.

"Holy shit," she whispered.

Mike nodded. "Yes. That blood smear clearly came from the attacker smashing the victim's head against the board, any number of times. But the height of the stain doesn't fit. It's way off."

He walked to the board and lifted his hand until it was positioned at a height roughly in the middle of the now-mostly-dried bloodstain.

His hand was above his head.

Way above his head.

He was six feet tall and he was holding his hand close to a foot *above* the top of his head.

"I don't understand," Sharon said. "The killer forced her to climb onto a chair, and *then* he beat her to death?"

Mike shook his head. "That doesn't feel right. He would have had to stand on a chair as well, otherwise how could he get the leverage to smash her head against the board hard enough to kill her?"

"Maybe she died from strangling, and the injury to her skull was incidental."

"Maybe," Mike agreed. "But even if that's true, he still had to have struck her head against the board multiple times, and hard enough to leave a lot of blood."

"But why move chairs over to the board and then stand on one, while forcing the victim to do the same?"

"More importantly, why would he leave the rest of the mess all over the floor, but replace the chairs behind the desks before making his escape? None of the chairs are out of place."

Sharon squinted, thinking hard. "Okay, so say he didn't use chairs at all. What else could he have forced the teacher to stand on, and why? What are we missing?"

"It doesn't feel right," Mike repeated. "I don't think he forced the victim to stand on anything."

"Well, how is that possible? How could anyone not the size of an NBA center have the strength and agility required to lift the victim above his head while standing on the floor, and *then* generate the force required to strike her skull against the board hard enough to leave that much of a mess?" She pointed at the bloodstain, and Mike noticed her hand shaking just a bit.

He shook his head. "I don't know. We're obviously missing something."

They stood in silence. Mike tried to ignore the sick feeling in the pit of his stomach, the feeling he'd experienced more than once over his time in Paskagankee.

It was a feeling that said he was dealing with something that was not quite…natural.

5

Mike cleared his throat. One look into Sharon's face told him her feelings were exactly the same as his on the subject of supernatural occurrences in their little town.

"Where do we go from here?" she asked.

Mike considered the question. He'd been burned in the past by out-of-town investigators trying to cut him out of his own investigation, and the last thing he wanted was to repeat that distasteful scenario.

"I'm going to call the crime scene techs up here from Portland. Before they get here, though, I'm going to get Boykin back here with a camera and have him start taking our own crime scene photos, so we won't have to risk being cut out by CSI. Maybe Miles will feel a little more like part of the team that way, and I'll have some evidence I can use for my investigation.

"In the meantime," he continued, "I'd like you to go to the principal's office and interview our only witness."

"The student who found the body."

"That's right. Maybe she saw or heard something that can point us in the right direction."

Sharon nodded and turned toward the door.

"Wait," Mike said, and she turned back to look at him expectantly.

"It looks like our honeymoon might have to wait a while. I'm sorry, babe." They'd planned to spend a few days in Portland following the wedding, browsing the shops and walking the beach, their first real getaway since coming together as a couple. It wouldn't be anything extravagant, but Sharon had been nearly as excited about their trip as she was about the wedding, and Mike knew the prospect of postponing it would be painful for her.

"Don't give it a second thought," she said, smiling weakly. Normally her smile lit up his world, but this one was tight and forced. "I wouldn't be able to enjoy myself knowing the monster that did this—" she waved in the direction of the murder victim—"was loose and running around Paskagankee while we were off enjoying ourselves."

"Same here. But the minute we finish this investigation, we'll resume our honeymoon, I promise."

She nodded. "I know."

Once more she started for the door. Mike reached for his radio to call dispatch but before he could, Sharon turned around again.

He raised his eyebrows expectantly. "What is it?"

She nodded in the direction of the body. "She's not going to be the last victim, is she?"

Mike looked at the mess on the floor next to the desk. Looked at Lucie Dunn, still crumpled in an undignified pile on the floor. Looked up at the thick swatch of sticky, partially dried blood positioned so high up on the blackboard.

And then he shook his head.

"I don't think so," he said quietly. "Not unless we work fast and get extremely lucky."

6

Sharon double-timed down the long hallway, not quite sprinting toward the administrative wing of Paskagankee High School, but not dawdling, either.

As she moved, she wondered at the irony of such a horrific crime occurring on what should have been among the happiest days of her life. She'd fallen for Mike McMahon almost from the first time she laid eyes on him.

She remembered sharing a patrol car right after his arrival in Paskagankee as the new police chief. He decided to accompany an officer on patrol for several days as a way of learning the ins and outs of policing in his new jurisdiction. Since she was the officer with the lowest seniority on the force, she'd inherited the job.

She'd wanted to dislike her new boss. The man he was replacing, retiring chief Wally Court, had been her idol and mentor, almost single-handedly saving her from a life of alcohol and drug abuse. Chief Court had instilled in the young woman a sense of discipline and direction that had been lacking since the death of her mother nearly ten years earlier.

But as much as she *wanted* to dislike Mike McMahon, she hadn't been able to manage it. He was older, mid-thirties to her early twenties, a man she should never have been interested in. His easy smile and boyish charm had broken down her resistance immediately, though, and she'd been drawn to him in a way she'd never been drawn to anyone.

Despite his easygoing manner and quick wit, she'd sensed in

her new boss a sadness, a heaviness of spirit that said his road had been as difficult as hers—maybe even more so—if in different ways.

A killing spree that erupted just after McMahon's arrival in town—one in which her mentor Wally Court was unfortunately involved—threw the new police chief and the rookie cop together intimately, and they'd remained a couple ever since.

The principal's office came into view and Sharon picked up her pace. She shook her head at her hometown's dark history. Statistically, a village the size of Paskagankee should suffer one murder or unexplained death perhaps every thirty to fifty years.

Paskagankee's rate was higher.

Much higher.

And now it seemed the darkness lurking beneath the town's rocky soil had resurfaced again.

*   *   *

Through the glass of the closed office door Sharon could see Principal Sheldon Weems involved in an earnest discussion with a woman and a distraught young girl. It was obviously the student who had found the body of the deceased teacher. Just as obvious was the fact that the girl's mother had arrived and was insisting on taking her daughter home.

Sharon knocked on the door and then entered the office without waiting for an invitation.

"Ah," Weems said, clearly relieved. "Here's the officer now."

Sharon smiled at the principal and introduced herself, first to the student and then to her mother.

"I'm Mary Kuzinski," the older woman said crisply. "And this is my daughter Marta, and we're leaving now."

"It's nice to meet both of you," Sharon said, focusing her attention on the witness. "I'm sorry it has to be under these circumstances."

The girl looked pale and had clearly been crying.

"Marta's been through a trauma," the mother said, "as you can plainly see. She's upset and I'm taking her home now."

"I completely understand," Sharon said. "But it's critical we talk to Marta immediately. Details that are fresh in her mind now may fade quickly, and it's the smallest of those details that may allow us to apprehend whoever did this terrible thing before they hurt someone else."

Mary Kuzinski shook her head firmly. "Look at her. She needs to—"

"It's okay," Marta said. "I can talk now. If there's anything I can do to help, I want to."

"This won't take long," Sharon said. "I promise. We'll get preliminary information now and then follow up with Marta at home if we have any additional questions, does that sound fair?"

The mother huffed unhappily as Principal Weems busied himself setting up four chairs in an intimate circle. His relief at being spared the hassle of dealing with Marta Kuzinski's mother was palpable. He placed the chairs in front of his desk and then sat and folded his hands expectantly.

"I'm sorry," Sharon said to Weems. "I'll have to ask you to wait outside. An officer will want to speak with you as well about the incident, and it's important we get the information from all witnesses separately."

He looked like he was about to complain, but Sharon turned away and opened the office door. She held it and locked eyes with Weems until he frowned and stalked past.

She closed the door and smiled again at Marta Kuzinski. "Have a seat," she said kindly.

She waited until the girl chose one before sliding one of the chairs next to her and sitting. "I couldn't help but notice how far from the main building Miss Dunn's classroom is," she said. "What brought you to that part of the school at the end of the day?"

"Well," Marta said with a long, shuddering sigh. "I had gone to see my guidance counselor after classes ended. She's helping me with the college application process, and we had an appointment to work on some apps today."

"And that teacher's classroom is near Miss Dunn's?" Sharon's felt a surge of optimism. If a teacher had been in a nearby classroom it could mean a second witness.

That optimism faded quickly, however, when Marta shook her head. "No, Mrs. Chadwick's room is all the way at the other end of the school."

"Then what brought you past Miss Dunn's classroom?"

"The student parking lot I use is on that side of the building, so instead of going out the main entrance and walking along the front of the school, I usually go down the corridor and exit the door just past Miss Dunn's room."

Sharon nodded. It made sense. She'd done exactly the same thing hundreds of times during her own years as a student at PHS.

"I see," she said. "And what made you take notice of Miss Dunn's classroom on your way by?"

"The door was half open."

"And that was unusual?"

"Well, yes, but it wasn't the sort of thing that I would normally have noticed. Miss Dunn is…was…one of my teachers this semester, and she's very sweet. She'd had kind of a hard time today during Algebra class, and when I saw her door ajar like that I assumed she was still there. I just wanted to step in and make sure she was okay. That was when I saw…I saw…"

She started shaking and Mary Kuzinski drew in a breath to speak. She was going to insist—again—on taking her daughter home, and this time Sharon doubted she could say anything to stop it.

She spoke quickly, before the protective mother could get a word out. "It's okay, Marta. Slow down and let's take it one step at a time. Miss Dunn had a problem during Algebra class?"

Marta nodded.

"What kind of a problem?"

"Spitballs."

"I'm sorry?"

"Miss Dunn and a boy in the back of the class during E Period had a little confrontation, nothing major, no big deal, but when she turned around and faced the blackboard, he started making spitballs and throwing them at her. "

"A confrontation." *And later one of the two people involved in the confrontation ends up dead.*

Marta's eyes widened as the significance of what she was

saying occurred to her. "Oh, no," she said, shaking her head. "It was nothing like that. It wasn't anything where someone would get killed. It was just a high school discipline thing. It was only unusual because the boy involved never causes trouble. He doesn't pay much attention in school, but he's not usually a troublemaker. I only mentioned it because Miss Dunn finally got mad and told him to report to her classroom after last period for detention."

According to Marta the in-school confrontation had been "minor," but Sharon had been a cop long enough to know that what seemed like no big deal to an onlooker didn't always feel like no big deal to the participants. Could the angry student have returned to the classroom after school looking to settle a score, and things got out of hand?

Then she pictured the swatch of blood so high up on the blackboard and tried to imagine a high school student, no matter how tall or how strong, lifting a grown woman that high and then smashing her head multiple times, hard enough to kill her.

It just didn't fit. Still…"What's the name of the boy who was throwing the spitballs, Marta?"

"I'm sure he didn't have anything to do with…you know…"

"I'm sure he didn't," she agreed. "I'll still need his name, though. We'll need to talk with him, just like we're talking with you."

Marta looked up at her mother, who nodded without speaking. "It was Jake Beebe."

Great. The Beebes had lived in Paskagankee for generations. The family was extremely active in the local political scene, and Jake's father was currently serving as chairman of the Paskagankee Town Council. The Beebe family was as close to political royalty as it was possible to get in such a small town, and Sharon could easily picture their status getting in the way of questioning the boy.

Sharon considered her next question carefully before continuing. "You said Jake isn't typically one to cause trouble in school?"

"Not at all. But anybody can have a bad day, you know?"

"Of course. Miss Dunn certainly had a bad day. Now, let's talk about when you walked into Miss Dunn's classroom to check on her after school. Tell me exactly what you saw and heard."

Through a voice shaking and hitching with sobs, the young girl outlined the traumatic experience of finding one of her favorite teachers dead on the floor. Sharon felt for the girl but quickly realized she would be no help as far as offering any new information. The teacher's attacker had already exited the building—likely through the exterior door next to Lucie Dunn's classroom—and Marta's words only corroborated what Sharon and Mike had already observed.

After several minutes spent leading the girl through her experience and trying to keep her from breaking down in tears, Sharon decided there was nothing to gain by continuing to question her.

The only potential lead she'd developed was the disciplinary issue with Jake Beebe, and while it was certainly worth following up on, it didn't feel right. Sharon had seen the Beebe kid around town, and while she couldn't claim to know him, she had interacted with him a few times. He'd always struck her as aimless, a small-town kid paralyzed by a lack of direction, but nothing she'd seen gave any indication he was capable of the kind of unrestrained violence that had been perpetrated on Luce Dunn.

"Okay," she said. "Thanks very much for taking the time to talk with me. I know it was hard, but you did a great job. If we have any more questions, we'll get in touch with you through your mom, okay?"

Marta nodded and sniffled and dabbed at her eyes. Sharon stood, and next to her Mary Kuzinski rose as well and turned toward the door.

"Um, there's one more thing," Marta said in a small voice. She still hadn't risen from her chair. Her eyes were focused steadfastly on the floor.

Sharon took her seat and waited quietly for Marta to continue. Her cop instincts screamed that whatever was to come out of Marta Kuzinski's mouth next would be important, and anything she said now would just serve to screw it up.

So she said nothing.

"I sit right in front of Jake," Marta said.

"Okay."

"And when I saw the spitballs come flying by, I knew right away they had been thrown from the desk behind mine."

"Jake's desk."

"Yes. It was obvious."

"Okay."

"And I was surprised, because like I said, Jake doesn't always pay attention in class but he never causes trouble, certainly not that kind of trouble."

"And?"

"Well, I was so surprised, I turned around, you know, just to see for myself that it was still Jake sitting there, that he hadn't maybe changed seats and someone else was launching spitballs at Miss Dunn."

Marta stopped talking. Sharon noticed she'd begun shaking again, even worse than she had been when they first met. She felt the looming presence of Mrs. Kuzinski behind her and feared the woman would shut Marta down just as the girl was preparing to relay something important.

So she reached out and took Marta's hands in her own. They felt hot and sweaty.

"It's okay," she whispered. "You're safe here. You turned around and…"

"When I turned around," Marta continued, "his eyes were… they were…"

"Go on."

"I'm sure it must have been a trick of the light or something, because his eyes…they looked…black."

"Black? You mean he had a black eye, like he'd gotten into a fight?"

She shook her head. "No, no nothing like that. I'm not talking about the skin around his eyes. I mean the *actual eyes*. The pupils. They were huge and black and…and…you're going to think I'm crazy, but they were…"

"They were what, Marta?"

"They were *glowing*. They were black and glowing."

A chill enveloped Sharon like a blast of Arctic air. It started in her belly and mushroomed out to her extremities.

Because she didn't think Marta Kuzinski was crazy at all. She'd lived in Paskagankee far too long and had seen far too much to dismiss the girl's words. She thought about the bloodstain located almost seven feet off the ground on the teacher's blackboard and swallowed heavily.

She released Marta's hands and tried to smile at her reassuringly. She failed.

7

Jake stumbled through the woods, confused and afraid. Branches swiped across his face, scratching the skin and occasionally drawing blood. He barely noticed. He tripped over fallen logs and raised tree roots, dropping to the ground on his hands and knees, only to push to his feet and stumble on.

He'd spent virtually his entire life tromping through the thick forest surrounding Paskagankee, on fire roads and trails, on pathways that were known to most of the citizenry and on others he doubted had been used by another human being in decades, maybe centuries.

At the moment, though, he had no idea where he was. Didn't much care, either. He knew he was making his way slowly in the direction of home, and that was good enough.

He'd taken this route because after what had happened at school he didn't trust himself to be around other people. And while in his opinion Paskagankee was nothing more than a lightly-inhabited, dying flyspeck of a shithole, Jake knew there was still almost no way he could expect to walk Mountain Home Road all the way from the high school to the Beebe home and not cross paths with a single soul.

And he was terrified of what might happen if he *did* cross paths with anyone. Because he'd seen the horror that had been inflicted on Miss Dunn—that *he'd* inflicted on Miss Dunn—after school, and he was terrified it might happen again.

To another innocent person.

He replayed the events of the afternoon as he picked his way through the forest, wanting nothing more than to banish them from his memory but knowing that would never happen; not even if he lived to be a hundred fucking years old.

He'd felt himself slipping away again almost immediately upon returning to Miss Dunn's classroom to serve detention. He fought against it as he'd fought against it every single time, knowing it would do no good but trying anyway.

And of course it *had* done no good. But this time was a little different than the others. This time he never lost consciousness, was never pushed completely out of his body as had been the case in the past.

And that was infinitely worse.

Jake was forced to watch through horrified eyes, helpless and unable to control his body as it carried out its horrific attack on Miss Dunn. The whole ugly scene played out before him, a passenger inside his own skin, until the teacher's lifeless or dying body dropped unceremoniously to the floor.

And now Jake knew his worst fears had been realized. He could no longer ignore the blackouts he'd been suffering with increasing frequency, could no longer assume they were simply the result of a rapidly growing brain tumor, or some obscure blood disease, or some weird psychological disorder that caused him to become unconscious while still somehow remaining a functioning human being, living and breathing and interacting with—and terrorizing—the rest of the world.

He could no longer assume any of the above, because he now knew with one hundred percent certainty what he'd suspected from the beginning: the blackouts were directly related to that damned book.

Damned book is right, he thought, chuckling sickly to himself, choking back the nausea that threatened to expel his partially digested lunch to the forest floor.

He had become possessed.

By a demon.

As insane as that sounded, even to Jake, he knew it was the only thing that made a lick of sense, assuming *any* of this nightmare made any sense, assuming he hadn't gone mad and was even now strapped to a gurney in some fucking hospital mental ward, living the entire scenario out inside his own mind.

A demon is living inside me. Jake shuddered as the thought flashed through his head. He felt his skin crawl, the faraway whisper of a demonic cackle echoing inside his skull as if to provide confirmation of his disturbing theory.

As if he *needed* confirmation.

Somehow he'd done the summoning spell improperly. That had to be it. He'd screwed up the spell in such a way that allowed the demon—who was supposed to appear in a form *visible* to Jake but also *harmless* to him, and then be bound to Jake's every wish—to enter his body.

Once inside, the demon had demonstrated quite convincingly it could take over and orchestrate Jake's every action whenever it wished, like a remote pilot flying a drone. A deadly, sadistic, remorseless drone.

Oh God oh God oh God.

It was an emotion more than a conscious thought. Jake suspected very strongly that he was now beyond help. He was well and truly fucked.

He could feel the evil infecting his body, pulsing and black and menacing, a wildfire of darkness that was beginning to burn out of control. The demon's willingness to allow Jake to observe the damage he was causing—taking part in it, however unwillingly—was a sign that its power was growing, that it was utterly confident in its ability to regulate Jake's every move whenever it wished.

As frightened and confused as Jake was, he nevertheless recognized the irony of his situation. He had summoned a demon because he wanted an entity that would be forced to do his bidding, to execute his every desire.

What he'd gotten was exactly the opposite: a demon capable of fulfilling *its own* every wish through the use of Jake's body.

And that demon was getting stronger and bolder.

And more violent.

Jake continued to thrash through the woods almost blindly. He almost wished he would get lost in the forest and starve to death, but doubted very much the demon would allow that to happen.

And once he arrived home nothing about his situation would

change, he would still be a menace to anyone and everyone.

But for now all he could handle was the most basic of plans: get home. Hole up inside his room. Try to figure out what to do next.

That was a tough one. He didn't even dare go to the police and turn himself in. If he were to try such a thing, what would stop the demon from taking control of his body, as it had done with Miss Dunn, and attacking them? It could very quickly turn into a bloodbath, because even though they would be the ones with the guns, the cops would think they were dealing with a scared sixteen-year-old kid.

The reality would be so much different. How many could the demon wipe out before the police even had a chance to react?

Jake paused to catch his breath. Even for a healthy sixteen-year-old, hiking the rough terrain surrounding Paskagankee was an arduous task, and he was breathing hard and sweating heavily.

He looked around, surprised to see he was almost home. He'd been so distracted with the horror-movie scene of Miss Dunn's murder running through his head on a nonstop loop that he hadn't been paying much attention to his progress. Soon he would break through the screen of thick underbrush behind the Beebe barn.

Another quarter-mile beyond the barn he would enter his home and face the next obstacle: getting up to his room without running into his sister and potentially beating her to death.

Mom and Dad wouldn't be out of work yet, and Jake thought he remembered one of them saying something about a Town Planning Commission meeting right after work today, so they likely wouldn't arrive home until nine or ten tonight. That should keep them safe, at least for a while.

But what if the demon decided it might be fun to play more of its sick games with Julie? What if it decided to amuse itself by torturing and killing the day's second victim?

Jake shuddered and ran a hand over his face. It felt haggard and old. *Keep it together, asshole.*

Their home was old and rambling, a centuries-old farmhouse that had been built with a large family in mind, not the four people who currently occupied it. The odds of him running into Julie were slim, especially since they weren't currently on speaking terms.

Jake would sneak in quietly and make his way to his room.

Julie would never even know he'd arrived home.
He hoped.
Because she might not survive any other scenario.

8

Mike checked his watch. He sighed and ran a hand through his hair.

More than four hours had passed since he became a married man for the second time, and the majority of those four hours had been spent examining the scene of a particularly disturbing murder. The copper/iron scent of spilled blood lingered in the classroom, heavy and cloying, a noxious cloud of violence and death.

He had been present at dozens of murder scenes in his career, from his early patrolman days in Revere spent securing them, to his time taking part in investigations in that city, to the most recent couple of years leading the department in Paskagankee.

Every murder scene was different, obviously, in terms of the methodology used to kill and the evidence left behind, but Mike had discovered long ago that they all shared one characteristic: the overwhelming sense of despair that filled the crime scene. It was like the remnants of a scream, a cry for justice echoing across time and through the murky grey area between life and violent death.

He'd felt it at every murder scene he'd ever attended, and no matter how many times he experienced the sensation, it never got any easier. It was uncomfortable and sad, and spurred in him the desire—the *need*—to find the perpetrator and provide the victim some measure of justice, however small, however insignificant.

It was what drove him as a law-enforcement professional. It was also what threatened to overwhelm him when faced with the shattered remnants of the victim's dignity that were inevitably left behind at the scene of a violent crime.

He pursed his lips and sighed again. Then he got back to work.

*   *   *

Miles Boykin was back at the high school within twenty minutes of Mike's call. He returned with the department's digital camera and a vastly improved attitude.

And he did what Mike considered a pretty good job photographing the scene, too. Mike hadn't been sure what to expect, so he kept a close eye on the officer, concerned mostly with ensuring Boykin stayed on the periphery of the scene and avoided contaminating it in any way before the arrival of the CSI techs from Portland.

Boykin had been careful but thorough, particularly for a young officer working his first murder scene. Maybe there was hope for the kid.

Shortly afterward, the techs showed up and began the tedious process of tagging and photographing evidence. By now the blood had mostly congealed, the nausea-inducing mass on the blackboard appearing greenish-black and vaguely alien.

Sharon returned after maybe forty-five minutes, and they conferred in the rear of the classroom while Mike kept a close eye on the proceedings up front. Her face looked grim, a greyish tint to the skin that was about as far removed from a bride's happy glow as Mike thought it was possible to get.

"Are you okay?" he asked.

She'd told him earlier that she hadn't slept much last night. "I was too excited to be marrying my dream man!"

Mike had answered, "Jesus, and I thought you were marrying me." The comment earned him a punch on the upper arm and a wicked grin from his bride-to-be.

He smiled wanly recalling the exchange, thinking it felt much longer ago than roughly eighteen hours.

She ignored his current question, clearly preoccupied.

He looked her up and down. It seemed exhaustion plus the events of the day might be catching up to her. "You should head home."

She shook her head firmly and said, "I'm fine."

He wasn't sure he agreed with her diagnosis but held his tongue. For now.

"How did it go with our witness?"

"You won't believe me when I tell you."

"Try me. You might be surprised."

"Well, she didn't see anything of value when she found the victim. The perp was long gone by the time our student walked past the classroom. It was just a lucky break she decided to stick her head in the door in the first place."

"You spent an awfully long time with a witness who had nothing to add to the investigation."

"I didn't say she had nothing to add, I said she didn't see anything when she discovered the body."

Mike cleared his throat. He glanced up toward the front of the classroom, where a crime scene tech was busy photographing the bloody smear on the chalkboard. The tech had affixed a length of measuring tape to the board next to the smear and trailing downward. It indicated the height of the bloody evidence as six feet, ten inches from floor level.

"Okay," he said. His stomach felt sour. "Something's thrown you off since you went down to the principal's office. Hit me with it. What did our witness tell you that's gotten you so off-stride?"

Sharon followed Mike's gaze to the blackboard. She stared at the evidence for a moment before dropping her eyes to the floor.

He waited patiently.

A moment later she lifted her head and locked eyes with him. "She didn't see anything when she discovered the body, but she was in this classroom for the second-to-last period of the day, and she may have given us a potential lead on a suspect."

"Explain."

"There was a confrontation during the class between the victim and one of the students. Not much of a thing, really, the kind of minor disciplinary issue that happens all the time in high school. It involved a smart-mouthed kid, a teacher who tried to refocus the student, and spitballs."

"Spitballs."

"Yes."

"Doesn't sound like much to me, Sharon. It's a hell of a reach from some teenager throwing spitballs at a teacher to the violent murder scene we have here. I just don't see it."

"I agree, and that's not what got my attention."

"Okay. What got your attention?"

"The girl I talked to, the one who found Lucie Dunn, happens to sit right in front of the spitball-throwing outlaw. She said the kid is not the greatest student in the world, but doesn't typically cause trouble in class, either."

"All the more reason to consider him a pretty unlikely suspect."

"Maybe. But…"

Mike felt himself getting annoyed. It had been a long day, and Sharon's reticence about spilling what she'd learned from their only witness was starting to get under his skin. It wasn't like her to beat around the bush; she was normally direct to the point of occasional perceived rudeness.

He spread his hands. "But what?"

Now it was her turn to clear her throat. She took in a deep breath and blew it out harshly.

Then she said, "But she said she was so surprised when the spitballs started flying, she thought the kid who normally sits behind her might have moved seats."

"But he hadn't."

"No, he hadn't. And when she turned around and looked at the kid, she said, uh…"

"Jesus Christ, Sharon, just spill it."

"She said his eyes were black. And they were glowing like charcoal briquettes."

9

Mike stared hard at his bride, unsure how to respond.

He'd fully expected to hear something bizarre—it was obvious just from the way Sharon was acting that something had thrown her for a loop—but this truly came out of left field. Hell, this came from beyond the left field fence. Way beyond.

"Glowing black eyes," he finally said, his tone revealing his skepticism.

She nodded and offered him a tired smile. "That was pretty much my reaction, too."

"The witness is obviously mistaken." He shrugged, searching for some explanation that would make sense. "She was still upset from finding the victim, or the classroom lighting reflected off his eyes, or maybe her story is some bizarre cry for attention…" Mike's voice trailed off as he struggled to continue.

"She was definitely upset about from finding the victim, there's no question about that. But I don't think you can attribute her story to any trick of the light, or hysterics, or anything else."

"Why not?"

"Because she was terrified, Mike. Not just upset about finding one of her teachers dead on the floor, which she was, as anyone would be. She was afraid. She was almost paralyzed by fear."

He stood, hands on his hips, unconvinced.

"And it was absolutely not a cry for attention."

"How can you be so sure?"

"She didn't want to tell me about the thing with the kid's eyes.

149

I practically had to flog her with a rubber hose to get it out of her, and even then she almost wouldn't spit it out."

He shook his head. There was a time, before moving to Paskagankee and experiencing a series of inexplicable events over the past two years, when he would have dismissed the young girl's observation outright. He might have chuckled wryly or made the scenario into a joke, but one thing he would definitely *not* have done was offer the observation any serious consideration.

Those days were long gone.

He eyed the crime scene techs, now nearly finished with their painstaking work. Soon they would pack up their materials and exit the scene. Once that happened, the ambulance crew, which had left the high school upon the arrival of the police, would return to transport the victim's remains to the medical examiner's office for autopsy.

He returned his attention to Sharon. She'd waited patiently by his side while he worked through the peculiar information.

"Did you tell Weems to compile a list of potential witnesses?"

She nodded. "I said I wanted a roster of every student and faculty member who might have had occasion to interact with Lucie Dunn today."

"Good job. We've got a lot of work ahead of us."

"I know."

"I'm sorry about how your wedding day turned out."

"I know. And it's *our* wedding day, ya big lug."

He smiled and checked his watch. "It's barely past dinnertime. I suppose it wouldn't hurt to drive out to the black-eyed kid's house and ask him a few questions, maybe lean on him a little."

"I knew you were going to say that. You're nothing if not predictable."

He huffed. "I prefer to think you just know me really well."

"Whatever gets you through the night, Chief."

"Don't you mean *who*ever?"

She grinned and he said, "What's the name of our spit-ball-throwing desperado, anyway?"

"Jake Beebe."

He'd started walking toward the front of the classroom and now he stopped in his tracks.

Turned back toward Sharon.

"Did you say Beebe?"

"That's what I said."

"As in Paskagankee Town Council Chairman Beebe?"

"Also the only Beebe family in town, yes."

Mike groaned. "Jesus. As if this situation wasn't bad enough."

"Still want to head out there tonight?"

He considered the question. "What have I always said about any investigation?"

"Follow the evidence."

"Damn right. Let's go."

* * *

The ride out to the Beebe property was a mostly quiet one. Mike felt badly about Sharon getting cheated out of her perfect wedding day, but he knew what she would say if he brought up the subject: "Lucie Dunn got cheated out of a hell of a lot more than I did."

And she would be right.

But that didn't change his disappointment for her. Nor did it change the sick feeling in the pit of his stomach or the disembodied voice in his head chanting, *Here we go again.* His two years as a Paskagankee resident had been marked with supernatural encounters, mostly of the deadly kind, and the talk of glowing black eyes had brought every one of those encounters to the forefront of his mind with the force of a wrecking ball.

The prospect of once again having to deal with Medical Examiner Jan Affeldt niggled at the back of Mike's mind, just one more disagreeable aspect in a day that had gone rapidly downhill following the one p.m. wedding ceremony. Mike had butted heads with the sour-tempered ME on several occasions, and the violent manner of Lucie Dunn's death made it virtually certain he would soon do so again.

They were halfway to the old Beebe farmhouse when Sharon spoke up. "What are we going to do if Van and Lyn refuse to allow us to question Jake?"

"Why wouldn't they allow it? Their son's not suspected of anything at the moment. He's nothing more than a potential witness to a crime that occurred at the high school."

"Maybe," Sharon said. "But you know as well as I do if we try to pressure or intimidate Van to get access to Jake, the first thing he'll do is lawyer up and then we'll never speak with the kid. Not without filing charges, at least."

Mike turned and waggled his eyebrows at Sharon. "Then I guess it's a good thing there's a Town Planning Committee meeting tonight, isn't it?"

"Planning committee?'

"Yep. The planning committee meets once a month, and would you care to guess how their meetings are structured?"

"Not particularly."

"Then let me enlighten you. The committee gathers at the Katahdin Diner for dinner and drinks right after all the members get out of work, and then afterward they move to the town hall basement, where they convene the official meeting at seven. That meeting typically takes two to three hours."

"I see," Sharon said. Mike could here the smile in her voice. "I've never paid much attention to the makeup of Paskagankee's planning committee. Am I to assume Van Beebe is a member?"

"You are to assume exactly that," Mike said. "Just as with everything else in this little slice of heaven, Van *runs* the planning committee."

"But…"

"Hold on now. Before you voice your next concern, let me put your mind at ease. Lyn Beebe is also a member of the planning committee, which of course means—"

"Neither of the Beebe parents will be home to deny access to Jake."

"Exactly."

"That's why you were in such a hurry to run out to the Beebe farm tonight."

"I prefer to think of it as an example of my dedication to duty, but if you insist on attributing crass ulterior motives to me, I suppose there's nothing I can do about that."

Sharon chuckled.

"Besides," he added. "You already screwed up and married me. Now you're stuck with me. There's no longer any reason to hide my true personality."

This time Sharon laughed out loud. She sounded exhausted, but Mike doubted he would ever tire of hearing her laughter. Even in the midst of a horrific murder investigation he thanked God, or fate, or karma, or whatever other force had delivered this beautiful woman to him.

"You know," she said. "You may have forgotten to consider one factor in your diabolical plan."

"Really? That sounds unlike me."

"Maybe so, but Jake Beebe still has the right to refuse to talk to us if he so chooses. And if he's somehow involved in Lucie Dunn's death, glowing black eyes or no glowing black eyes, he may well invoke that right."

"We'll see," Mike answered. "But at the very least, I want the opportunity to see this kid face-to-face, to get a look at those eyes for myself, and to gauge his reaction in person when we show up at his door."

The farmhouse rose out of the gathering darkness, set back from the narrow road by several hundred feet. Mike turned the Explorer into the long gravel driveway and eased to a stop next to the front walkway. Lights on inside the home indicated the presence of at least one of the Beebe children.

"Looks like it's show time," he said.

They climbed out of the truck and crunched up the gravel walkway to the front door.

10

The bell sounded inside the house and a moment later the front door swung open. Standing inside was a teenage girl. Mike knew there were only two Beebe children. Twins. A boy and a girl. This was obviously the female half of that equation.

The girl blinked in surprise at seeing two uniformed police officers at her door.

"Yes?" she said. "What's going on? Can I help you?"

"Hello," Sharon said. Mike was happy to let her take the lead, at least for the time being. "My name is Officer...uh...Dupont, and this is Chief McMahon of the Paskagankee Police Department."

"Um, hi. I'm Julie Beebe. Why are you here? I mean, what can I do for you? If you're looking for my dad, he's not here. He won't be home until later."

Sharon smiled. "We're not looking for your dad. May we come in for a moment? We won't take up too much of your time, I promise."

"Yeah, sure, I guess. But I don't understand, if you're not here to speak with my dad, why *are* you here?"

"You probably haven't heard yet," Mike said, "but there was a... serious issue at the high school this afternoon."

"Oh, yes, I've heard," Julie Beebe said. "Miss Dunn died. Everyone from school is talking about it on social media. They're saying she was murdered."

Mike almost grimaced. When he'd begun his law enforcement career, social media was in its infancy. Specifics regarding a crime like the one that had been committed this afternoon at PHS could be protected back then to a degree that was now no longer possible.

And even when specifics were available, rumor and speculation inevitably ran rampant. He could only imagine what was being shared online about the death of Lucie Dunn.

"That's actually why we're here," Sharon said.

"Miss Dunn's death is why you're here? I'm sorry but I don't understand."

"We'd like to speak with your brother, Jake."

"Why do you need to talk to Jake?"

"It's routine," Sharon said. "We're hoping he might be able to fill in some details surrounding the events of the afternoon for us."

"You don't think Jake—"

"We're not here to talk to him about the crime, specifically," Mike interrupted. "We actually just have a few questions about an incident that occurred earlier in the day. We're hoping he can clear those up for us."

"The spitballs," she said.

"You know about that?"

"That's the other thing everyone's talking about on social media." Julie Beebe's eyes flashed, not supernaturally but angrily. "Jake can be a moron sometimes," she said, "but it's hard to believe the stories about him whipping spitballs at Miss Dunn. That's just so unlike him."

"That's why we were hoping to speak with him, to eliminate the speculation so we can focus on the truly important issues surrounding this afternoon."

"I guess that makes sense," Julie said. "But I'm not even sure Jake's here. I've been studying in the living room since right after I got home from school and I don't remember hearing him come in."

"Would you mind checking for us?"

"No problem." The girl padded to the bottom of a flight of stairs. She turned her head and cupped her hands around her mouth and shouted, "Jake, are you here? Come on down, you have company!"

The shout was met with silence, and Julie turned back toward them "Like I said, I don't think he's—"

"Tell them to go away," came the response. "I don't want any damned company." The words floated down the stairs, muffled and fuzzy, like they'd been shouted from behind closed doors.

"Oh." Julie started in surprise. "Oh, I guess he is here. Should I tell him his visitors are the police?"

"That won't be necessary," Mike said. "We'll go upstairs and introduce ourselves."

He started moving toward the stairway and Julie trailed behind hesitantly. "Um…okay…shouldn't I call my parents, you know, make sure it's alright?"

"You can if it would make you more comfortable," Mike said. "It's definitely your right. But all we want to do here is ask Jake a few questions. He's not a suspect in anything at this time and it should only take a couple of minutes."

"Oh. I guess that should be fine, then."

Mike started up the stairs. Sharon followed, matching him step for step. Julie trailed along behind, clearly unsure whether she should accompany them or remain downstairs.

"I don't know about this," Sharon whispered. "When Van hears what we did he'll have your ass."

"No he won't," Mike answered, keeping his voice low. "Jake Beebe's not officially a suspect in any crime yet, and I asked for and received permission to enter the house, as well as to go upstairs and question Jake. Van might be pissed but there's not a damned thing he can do about it."

"But—"

"And if the kid refuses to talk, we'll leave, but at least I'll have the chance to observe his body language and see how he reacts to our presence."

They reached the top of the stairway and Mike stood aside to allow Julie to take the lead. A hallway ran the length of the second floor, with several doors on each side. All the doors stood open with the exception of the first one on the left, which Mike took to be Jake's bedroom.

"Is this it?" he asked Julie, pointing to the closed door.

She nodded and he said, "Would you go in please and let Jake know we'd like to speak with him?"

Mike feared that if he knocked on the door and identified

himself as law enforcement, Jake would simply refuse to open up.

Then they would have to leave.

Without seeing him or speaking to him.

And as Jake Beebe so far represented the only potential link to the dead teacher, Mike wanted very much to avoid that possibility.

Julie moved to the door, uncomfortable.

She rapped three times with her knuckles and said, "Jake, open up or I'm coming in anyway."

From inside the room came a flurry of activity. A loud *bang* indicated a door or desk drawer being slammed shut. Heavy footfalls followed as Jake crossed his bedroom floor.

He was cursing angrily, and as the door swung open he spat, "I told you I don't want to see anybody, dammit!"

Mike stepped forward, shouldering Julie aside. "Hello, Jake. My name is Chief Mike McMahon of the Paskagankee Police Department and I'd like a minute or two of your time."

Things went downhill in a hurry.

11

Mike's first thought was that Sharon's witness back at the high school had been full of shit.

When Jake opened his bedroom door Mike immediately took a good hard look into the boy's eyes. They were the very first thing he wanted to see.

They looked perfectly normal. Brown pupils, typical size, surrounded by bloodshot irises that indicated either a serious lack of sleep, or perhaps illness or severe stress.

But they weren't black and they certainly weren't glowing.

The kid looked unhappy or upset—*or scared; he actually looks terrified*—but otherwise he had the appearance of an ordinary male teen.

Jake stepped back from the door and blinked, obviously surprised at finding the police outside his bedroom door.

And then everything changed in an instant.

Mike opened his mouth to explain that they had a few questions about the spitball incident at school when Jake's eyes… morphed. It happened while Mike was still looking at them. The pupils darkened and enlarged, turning coal-black and eliminating the bloodshot irises.

And they…

They…

They…

Holy shit, they're beginning to glow.

Julie screamed and stumbled back in terror, smashing into the hallway wall hard enough to shake the house.

Jake—or whatever the hell this was inside the kid's room, because it certainly wasn't human—reached out to slam the door closed, but Mike had taken one step forward and the door struck his foot and rebounded. Then the kid retreated, backpedaling across the room until striking his desk.

Mike took another step into the room and placed a hand on the butt of his weapon. He was conscious of Sharon's presence, one step behind him and to the right as she crowded through the door. Jake's sister continued to scream in the hallway but he blocked it out, a distraction he didn't need at the moment.

Jake dropped onto his desktop butt-first. He stared hard at Mike, those glowing black eyes intensifying, filling with hatred and rage and unrestrained malevolence. Then he shifted his gaze to Sharon, and Mike moved a half step to the right in an unconscious effort to protect his partner and wife.

The Jake-thing sneered, its eyes pulsing as it pushed off the desk. Then it stepped to the side and backed into the bedroom wall between two windows.

It reached down and yanked open the window on the right. The ancient wood screeched a protest and the window banged hard into the top of the runner and somewhere in the back of his mind Mike marveled that none of the panes of glass shattered from the violence of the impact.

"Take it easy," Mike heard himself saying, his voice loud and authoritative, the product of nearly twenty years of police experience. "We just want to talk."

The Jake-thing ignored his words as its glowing black eyes shifted between Mike and Sharon.

Mike thought, *It's sizing us up, trying to decide whether to take us on.*

Then it crouched down and eased halfway out the window, the movement cat-quick and fluid. It sat like that for a half-second, its awful eyes still fixed on Mike and Sharon.

Julie Beebe had calmed slightly but now renewed her screaming as she saw her brother hanging half out the second story window.

Mike rushed forward, saying something about not jumping, that it was okay, that all they wanted to do was talk, and as he got close enough to touch Jake he reached out and grabbed a fistful of the kid's shirt and—

And the thing fastened one freezing-cold hand around Mike's fist and yanked it away, pulling his shirt clear. Then it slipped out the window and disappeared.

Mike shouted an instinctive, "NO!" He leapt forward and leaned out the open window, looking down, prepared to see a teenage boy crumpled on the front steps with a broken leg or a fractured skull or maybe even something worse.

But Jake wasn't injured.

He wasn't crumpled anywhere.

He clung to the exterior wall on the front of the Beebe house like a giant spider, defying gravity, glaring up at Mike with those malevolent black glowing eyes.

Mike had seen a lot in his time in Paskagankee. Unlikely things. Inexplicable things. Impossible things. But this was an event for which he was entirely unprepared and he froze, the hand with which he'd made a desperate grab for Jake still hanging out the window.

The Jake-thing glared up at Mike, its eyes still glowing black but now with a tinge of red. Then it hissed, and then it was speaking, saying something that was almost but not quite gibberish, something that might have been Latin or perhaps some weird offshoot of the dead language.

And then it hissed again.

And then, impossibly, it was moving, climbing down the wall.

Mike watched, astonished, as the thing defied gravity, its hands and feet clinging to siding where there were simply no hand-or-footholds. It moved steadily downward.

At last Mike overcame his paralysis. He turned and sprinted out of the bedroom. Past Sharon, who was asking what the hell had just happened. Past Julie, who was still screaming but now crying as well.

He clambered down the stairs, taking them three at a time, hitting the foyer floor with a crash. He charged through the front door and looked up and to the left, in the approximate spot he'd last seen Jake clinging to the front wall.

The wall was empty.

Mike leapt down the granite steps, dimly aware that Julie Beebe had finally stopped screaming. He looked left and then right, alert for any sign of a fleeing teenager, but there was nothing.

Jake Beebe—or whatever had been inside that house—was gone.

12

Mike trudged back into the house and up the stairs. Julie's screams had been replaced by deep, wrenching sobs and she had sunk to her knees in the hallway outside her brother's bedroom.

She looked up when he approached and said, "He fell out his window."

"Jake's okay," he told her. He placed a hand on her shoulder and gave a light squeeze. It occurred to him that neither Julie nor Sharon had been in a position where they could have seen the boy crawling down the exterior of the house.

"I was just outside," he continued, "and there's no sign of Jake, which means he's uninjured or at least not badly injured, since he was able to run off." At this point, he saw no benefit to adding to the distraught girl's hysteria by telling her that her brother had recently learned to defy gravity.

Julie nodded and breathed a shuddering sigh. Then she lowered her head and resumed staring at the hallway floor.

Sharon stood just inside the boy's bedroom door. She stared into the room with a single-minded intensity.

Mike stepped closer and she said, "Holy shit."

He couldn't really disagree with the sentiment. But he didn't understand why Sharon's attention continued to be focused on the now-empty bedroom when Jake was no longer inside it and the boy's sister was suffering a meltdown just a few feet away.

He stepped into the room and moved next to her. Put a hand on her shoulder, much the same as he'd done with Julie, and said, "Sharon, snap out of i—"

And then he stopped in his tracks, the words evaporating in his mouth. He turned to the left and then pivoted slowly, his gaze moving across the room, covering all four walls until reaching a full three hundred sixty degrees at the point where he'd begun.

He heard himself muttering "Holy shit," exactly as Sharon had done.

In the chaos that erupted after Jake opened his bedroom door, Mike hadn't noticed the walls. His attention had been absorbed fully by the boy's almost instantaneous transition from frightened, nervous teenager to terrifying supernatural entity.

But he noticed them now.

The walls were covered in bizarre drawings and symbols. Some looked like they might be letters to an alien alphabet, foreign to Mike and completely indecipherable.

Others were crude drawings of animals, most recognizable to a certain degree, but all of them weird, unnatural hybrids, combinations that made no sense and gave off an aura of blackness, of evil, of threatened harm.

Here was a goat's horned head atop a bovine body. There was a horse rearing up on its hind legs, a crow's head atop its long neck, with a curved beak and black, beady eyes.

There were symbols that seemed neither to be letters of the weird alphabet nor unnatural representations of animals. Something that looked a bit like a dollar sign, but adorned with spiky offshoots emanating from the S and a wiggly cap atop the vertical lines through the S. A sun that had been painted black, complete with murky beams shooting off it.

And there were pentagrams.

Dozens of pentagrams of differing sizes, some painted on the walls in what appeared to be blood, others carved directly into the drywall itself. Some of the symbols had been designed to appear as though they were burning, and in those the flames had been painted an intense red, unnaturally bright, striking and disturbing.

To Mike's astonished eyes it appeared at first glance like there was not more than a two or three inch section of wall anywhere inside the room that did not have some grotesque symbol or other design painted or scratched or carved into it.

The room was one of the most unsettling things Mike had ever seen, and that was saying something. Just standing inside it evoked a sensation of fear, of discomfort, of violence.

Of darkness.

He shook himself. The awful drawings and symbols seemed to have an almost hypnotic effect. Mike realized he wasn't exactly sure how long he'd been standing and staring, a torpor having fallen upon him that was similar to the grogginess of awakening the morning after taking a double-dose of Nyquil when suffering from the flu.

Only worse.

He turned and placed both hands on Sharon's shoulders. She continued to stare at the walls of Jake Beebe's bedroom, eyes wide, mouth agape. He eased her into the hallway, pulling the bedroom door closed behind them.

Then he dropped to his knees beside the still-sobbing teenage girl. He circled her shoulders with one arm and gently lifted her to her feet. Guided her to the stairway and said, "Can you get down the stairs by yourself?"

She nodded once but he held her by the elbow anyway.

They descended to the first floor and moved into the Beebe kitchen. Mike eased Julie into a chair at the kitchen table and then stepped back and regarded the girl. She stared steadfastly at a red-and-white checkered place setting.

When he spoke, he did so softly and, he hoped, non-threateningly. "How long has your brother's room been…like that?" he asked.

She took a moment to respond but then she shook her head. "Not long."

"Specifically," Mike said. "A day, a month, a year?"

She raised her eyes to meet Mike's. They were teary, red-rimmed and bloodshot. "I was in his room last weekend, on Sunday, and it wasn't like that then. It was normal."

"And you haven't been in it since Sunday?"

"Not until tonight. We haven't been getting along so we've mostly ignored each other. And it's not like we spend a lot of time hanging out together even when we're not fighting."

She dropped her gaze back to the kitchen table and muttered something Mike couldn't make out from his position halfway across the room. Sharon was standing right next to her, though, and she met Mike's eyes with a confused expression.

Mike shrugged: *I didn't hear her.* He nodded toward the distraught girl without speaking. His sense was that Sharon, being female and closer in age to the teen, might have better luck getting her to open up than he would.

Sharon nodded and addressed Julie. "Could you repeat what you just said? Chief McMahon didn't hear you."

"I said it's that damned book." Her raised voice was both angry and frightened, and Mike raised his eyebrows in surprise. A reference to a book was the last thing he'd expected to hear.

"What book are you talking about?" Sharon said, her voice soft and friendly.

Julie shook her slumped head, and when she spoke, her voice was shaking. "A couple of weeks ago Jake found a book in the barn. It's old and dusty and gross, and the cover is filled with weird drawings like…like…"

"Like the ones in Jake's room?"

She nodded.

Took a deep breath.

Continued. "Yes, exactly like those. I assume the inside of the book has the symbols, too, but I don't know. I wouldn't look at it. The stupid thing scared me right from the get-go, but Jake loved it. He almost seemed…drawn to it somehow, like once he started reading he couldn't stop."

"And you said he found the book a couple of weeks ago?"

"Something like that. I first found out about it last weekend, when Jake pulled a stupid prank on me and my friends."

Sharon met Mike's eyes again and said, "A prank? What kind of a prank? What did he do?"

"It was some stupid magic trick he said he'd gotten from the book. He stood across the room and somehow was able to lower the zipper on Brittany's pajamas during a sleepover. He also did some kind of weird mind-control thing for a couple of minutes before the spell, or whatever, was broken."

"Mind control?"

"Yeah. Jake has had a crush on Britt for a long time, and for a couple of minutes last Saturday night, while he was doing the zipper thing, he got her to look at him like he was Harry Styles or something."

Mike almost blurted out, "Who?" He'd never heard the name but it didn't really matter, the inference was clear. Harry Styles was someone desirable to teenage girls.

He held his tongue and Julie continued. "It was gross and weird and creepy as hell, and I told him so the next day. The thing Saturday night was when we started fighting. We haven't gotten along since."

"And you say you were inside Jake's room Sunday?"

Julie nodded.

"And it looked normal at that time?"

"Yes."

"And Jake has been absorbed in the book he found during most of that time?"

"Not during most of the time. *All* of the time. He goes to school and comes straight home, and the minute he gets home he shuts himself in his room and barely comes out until it's time to leave for school the next day. I guess that's what he was doing in there. He was busy putting all those...*things*...on his walls."

Mike thought about the strange book. He recalled the flurry of activity he'd heard coming from inside the room when Julie first knocked on the door.

He spoke for the first time since silently asking Sharon to take over the questioning. "Where is this book now, Julie, do you know?"

She shrugged. "I assume it's in his room, or maybe his backpack, but I really don't know. I've tried not to think too much about it because it creeps me out so badly. But I'll tell you this: since he started reading the damned thing he doesn't seem to like be too far away from it."

"I'd like to take a quick look for that book. Would it be all right if I go back upstairs and see if I can find it? Officer—" there was the slightest hesitation as he tried to decide what to call his new wife. She'd introduced herself upon their arrival using her maiden name so he decided, for the time being at least, to go with that—"Dupont will stay down here with you."

"That would be fine. Just keep it away from me if you find it."

Mike started for the stairway before stopping and walking to

Sharon's side. "Call her parents and get them back here," he said quietly.

"Will do."

"And then call the station and ask Cornell to have the patrol units keep an eye out for Jake Beebe. If they see him, I want him picked up. But be sure they're advised to use extreme caution."

He thought back to Jake's glowing black eyes and inhuman hissing noises and the sight of him crawling down a vertical wall with no sign of support. "He might be…disoriented. He might be dangerous."

Sharon nodded and he headed for the stairs.

13

Mike paused outside Jake's bedroom door. As much as he wanted to get a look at the mysterious book Julie said had begun to consume her brother's life, he needed a moment by himself to think.

To process what he'd seen.

The symbols carved and painted—some apparently in blood—on the walls of Jake's bedroom were unnatural. The fact that Jake's eyes had morphed from run-of-the-mill brown to pulsing, glowing black *while Mike watched* was clearly unnatural, as was the fact that he'd managed to escape the house by crawling down a vertical exterior wall.

It was more than unnatural.

It was inhuman.

It's demonic.

The thought leapt into Mike's head unbidden. He tried to push it aside, to label it ridiculous, but could not. Not after all he'd seen and been a part of in Paskagankee since his arrival here two years ago.

For whatever reason, this little village was a hub of supernatural activity. Almost none of the townspeople acknowledged it, not in so many words, but everybody knew it. Native American curses, dead people returning to life, men showing up in town straight from the 1800s, it had all happened.

There was no logical explanation for why any of it had happened, but Mike *knew* it had all happened because he'd seen it with his own two eyes.

Maybe Paskagankee had been built on sacred Native American ground.

Maybe the town had grown over a site that represented a confluence of supernatural forces incomprehensible to human beings.

Maybe…Mike didn't know what other possibilities might have caused the supernatural activity.

What he did know was that he'd been a lifelong skeptic when it came to the supernatural. He'd never believed in ghosts or revenants or paranormal activity. As a cop, he'd dealt with plenty of evil wrought by living, breathing people. Considering the possibility of other sources of darkness hadn't crossed his mind.

The things he'd seen and been a part of in Paskagankee had changed all that, and now he found himself unable to dismiss the notion that the events of the day—from Lucie Dunn's murder right through to the disappearance of Jake Beebe—might be of demonic origin.

And that possibility was terrifying.

*   *   *

Jake's bedroom was similar to the typical teen's in at least one respect—it was a mess. The bed was unmade, comic books and dirty clothes were scattered on the floor, and the room's one constant was a general sense of clutter.

Of course, the average teen didn't have bizarre demonic symbology jammed into every last square inch of his room, but then most teenagers didn't scale sheer walls or feature glowing black eyes, either.

Mike tried to remain focused as he scanned Jake's bedroom. He guessed the torpor Sharon had exhibited and that he'd started to feel when he was in here before was some strange effect of the symbology, and he steadfastly ignored the drawings.

The obvious first place to look was Jake's desk. It was located in one corner of the room, opposite his bed, and its surface was covered with papers, pens and pencils, and assorted other junk that included a couple of books. They were plainly identifiable as high school textbooks, though, nothing remotely resembling the kind of ancient text Julie had described.

Jake had placed his backpack on the floor beside the desk, and Mike shifted his attention to it next. It was scuffed and stained, a couple of its seams beginning to fray, clearly approaching the end of its useable life.

Mike unzipped its main compartment and picked through it. Like the desktop, the backpack contained a couple of books, but a quick examination revealed them as nothing more interesting than two more schoolbooks. Aside from the books, the storage compartment was filled with loose papers—school assignments and tests and quizzes—as well as more pens and pencils, a battery-powered calculator and one dirty sock.

He wrinkled his nose and checked the remainder of the backpack's storage compartments, certain he would find nothing of interest and finding his suspicions quickly confirmed.

He sat back on his haunches and glanced around the room. Maybe the book wasn't here after all. But if Jake had become as engrossed in it as his sister claimed, it seemed impossible to believe he wouldn't have kept it in here somewhere.

He leaned against the side of Jake's desk as he scanned the room, determined to avoid looking at the damned symbols covering the walls.

He ran a hand through his hair and pursed his lips in concentration. *Where would a teenage boy keep a book that was important to him?*

Then he smiled.

And you call yourself an investigator.

He pivoted and turned once again toward Jake's desk. There were three drawers to the right of the chair well and he opened the top drawer first.

And there it was.

The fist thing Mike noticed was that the book was very old. It was bound in leather, and over time the dirt-brown cover had become cracked and brittle looking. The volume was thick and heavy, and as Mike looked at it he felt a chill, a sense of dread that he could not deny was related directly to the book.

And he had to touch the thing.

He lifted it out and then slid the desk drawer closed. The book was heavy, and felt somehow unclean.

He blew out a breath forcefully and returned to the kitchen.

*   *   *

"Is this it?" Mike had no doubt he was holding the correct book but he needed confirmation. He held it in both hands with the cover facing Julie, who was still seated at the kitchen table. Sharon had made the girl a cup of tea, and steam curled lazily from the mug.

"Yes, that's it." She shuddered. "It's…doing something to Jake, isn't it?"

"I don't know," Mike answered, although he'd been thinking exactly the same thing.

"I don't want it here when Jake comes back," she said. "Get it out of here. It's making me feel sick, like it's emitting some kind of blackness, an aura of evil. Can't you feel it?"

Mike opened his mouth to answer, unsure of what to say. He most definitely *could* feel it, but the cop in him didn't want to admit to something like that, especially in front of a teenage witness.

He never got a chance to find out what he would have said, because at that moment the front door crashed open and into the house came Van and Lyn Beebe.

14

"What in the hell is going on here?" Van Beebe's face was flushed and furious as he skidded to a stop in front of Mike. He'd charged down the hallway so fast he nearly overshot and tumbled into the kitchen table.

Behind him, his wife Lyn looked pale and upset and she blurted, "We got a call from the police that something has happened to Jake. Is he all right? Where is he? What's happening?"

"And why are you inside this house without the owners being present?" Van interrupted. "You can't enter without permission, and you can't question a minor child without permission!"

Mike held up a hand. He spoke calmly and quietly. "Are you folks going to give me a chance to explain what's going on, or would you prefer to keep shouting questions and accusations?"

Lyn's mouth snapped closed and Van stopped talking as well, although only with obvious extreme reluctance. "Why are you inside my house?" he repeated slowly through gritted teeth.

"There was an incident at the high school today," Mike said.

"We heard about the teacher's death," Lyn answered. "That's just horrible. But what does it have to do with Jake and Julie?"

Mike cut a brief glance at Sharon. He prayed they'd shared enough time on cases and investigations that she would interpret his message correctly: *Don't share too much until we have a better handle on what the hell happened here tonight.*

He hoped for the best and turned to face the angry couple. "It may well have nothing to do with either of your children. But a teacher is dead and there was an…incident between the victim and your son barely more than an hour before the murder. We came here tonight simply to ask Jake a few questions."

"You can't do that," Van said forcefully. "You can NOT question minors without their parents ' permission and without them being present."

Mike stiffened. "You've made that statement more than once now and it's not accurate. You can continue to repeat it point over and over until you're blue in the face and it still won't be accurate."

"Is that so?"

"Yes, it's so. Here are the facts: if you're present when we question your children, you *can* deny permission if you wish. However, if you're *not* present, as was the case tonight, and your children agree to speak with us we have every legal right to question them. We were invited into your home and followed standard procedure throughout."

"That's ridiculous," Van said. His anger didn't seem to be abating but he'd at least dropped some of his belligerent self-assuredness.

"It may be ridiculous, but it's how the law is written."

"How interesting that you happened to decide to question my children during a Town Planning Committee meeting."

"Murders do seem to occur at the most inconvenient times, don't they?" Mike knew he should be treading carefully around the man who could terminate his employment at any time, but he'd had enough of Van Beebe's aggression. He realized he'd curled his right hand into a fist and he eased it open, hoping neither of the parents had noticed.

Van blinked in surprise. He seemed taken aback at the vehemence of Mike's response, temporarily stunned into silence.

As if to fill the void, Lyn spoke up. "If you came to question Jake, where is he? Why is he not here? And why did we get a call saying something had happened to him? Is he all right?"

"I'm sure he's fine," Mike said. "He became extremely…distraught…while we were talking, and—"

"He jumped out the window," Julie interrupted.

Van looked around the kitchen and glanced into the home's living room. "What window? Why would he leave via a window and not just walk out the door? That makes no sense."

"We were upstairs," Julie said. "He jumped out his bedroom window."

"On the second floor?" Lyn looked stricken. "He must have broken his legs!"

"I was outside within seconds," Mike said. "And he had already disappeared. He's perfectly fine." He wasn't about to mention the sight that would be seared into his memory forever: a teenage boy descending the sheer side of a house.

"What kinds of questions were you asking my son that would make him so desperate to escape the interrogation he'd jump out a second story window?"

"It wasn't an interrogation. In fact, we didn't even get the chance to ask him a single question. He took off before we could. But he was on foot when he left, and my officers are keeping an eye out for him. I have every confidence he'll be back home soon."

"I don't know what the hell's going on here," Van said. He seemed to have regained some of his equilibrium. He'd raised his voice again and gotten back in Mike's face. "But let me make this perfectly clear. You are to get my son home immediately. And when you do, you are not to speak with either of my children again without my express permission, or without me or my designated representative being present."

"I understand," Mike shot back. "But you need to understand something as well. If that's the case, the next time we speak with Jake it may well be in an interrogation room at the station."

"Get out of my house. Leave. Right now."

"Dad," Julie said. "It's okay, they were just—"

Van Beebe wheeled to face his daughter. "That's enough, Julie. I'll handle this."

She looked away and shook her head slightly. Her father didn't seem to notice.

While the little father-daughter skirmish took place Mike caught Sharon's eye and nodded in the direction of the hallway. They stepped silently past the Beebe parents and moved toward the front door.

Nothing would be gained by continuing to snipe with Van, and Mike's goal now was to get out of the house with the ancient, leather-bound book in his possession. He'd already received permission from Julie to remove it, but he suspected strongly that if the girl's father were to catch sight of it, that particular situation would change, and quickly.

And whatever the hell was happening here seemed centered on that book.

They reached the door and Mike pulled it open. Heavy footfalls behind them told him Van had followed.

"Remember what I told you," the angry man said. "You do *not* have permission to speak with Jake."

Mike turned and looked past Van Beebe to his wife, still standing at the far end of the hallway.

"We'll notify you the minute we locate your son," he said calmly. Then he closed the door and they walked silently to the Police Explorer.

He continued to clutch the book firmly in his left hand.

15

Even while he was doing it, Jake couldn't believe what was happening as he *crawled down the side of the house*.

When Julie had shouted up the stairs that he had visitors, he'd had no clue it was the fucking cops. In retrospect he realized it shouldn't have come as any great surprise, given what he'd watched the demon do to poor Miss Dunn using his body.

But they'd been alone in the classroom at the time and he was almost certain there hadn't been any witnesses to the attack. It had been swift and brutal. He was sure no one had entered the classroom from the moment he stepped through the door to complete his detention until the moment the demon stalked out of the school building after leaving its victim crumpled dead on the floor.

But once he'd opened his bedroom door to see the pair of officers standing grim-faced in the hallway he'd felt one brief initial rush of terror before the now-familiar sensation of…slipping away…overcame him.

And now, as he stumbled more or less blindly through the pitch-dark woods, he tried desperately to think of some way out of this mess he'd created.

But there could be no way, because he knew that every single thought flashing through his mind was being monitored by the unwelcome guest that had taken up residence inside his body. Any move he made, anything he decided to try, would be anticipated and countered almost before he could twitch a muscle.

And the situation was worsening.

As the demonic spirit more fully integrated its takeover of his body, Jake could feel additional changes occurring.

Initially he had blacked out when the demon took control of his body, but now was cursed to see the damage being wrought in real time. And he was beginning to suspect—although he could not yet be sure—that he could *sense the demon's intentions.*

It didn't happen all the time, and "sensing its intentions" wasn't entirely accurate, but that was the way Jake envisioned it in his mind: that every so often he could intuit the demon's next moves.

And that might just be the most frightening part of this whole God-awful situation. Because to label the entity's intentions dark or foul or malevolent would be absurdly inaccurate; in fact, all of those descriptors jammed into a blender wouldn't come close to capturing the blackness Jake could sense inhabiting his human form like a fast-moving and virulent cancer.

The rage he'd felt pounding through his body after the demon's takeover—when he opened his bedroom door to see the two cops and his sister standing in the hallway—had been all encompassing, chilling in its intensity.

His initial fear had been that the demon would go on the attack, wreaking the kind of havoc Jake had been forced to observe in Miss Dunn's classroom, except that this time the victims would be a pair of law enforcement officers and, even worse, his only sister. He'd never felt anything similar to the terror that gripped him at that moment, but even then he'd been unable to lift a finger or take any action to forestall the coming storm of destruction.

But the demon had surprised him by backing off and then escaping out the window. Even while doing so, however, Jake had felt the disturbing sensation of being able to decipher the demon's intentions regarding the two cops.

And those intentions were every bit as black and evil as the demon itself.

Jake could feel nothing more specific than that very general sense of pervading evil directed at the cops, but he *did* know the man and woman were a couple, and not just on the police force. In fact, he was pretty sure they were due to be married soon, or perhaps already were.

He'd heard his father discussing the inappropriateness of the chief of police having a relationship with one of his subordinates more that once. As head of the Paskagankee Town Council, the ultimate responsibility for determining the chief's future employment belonged to Van Beebe, and Jake had gotten the distinct impression that his father took the chief's living arrangements as a personal affront.

The point, though, was that Jake was aware of the chief and his female patrol officer's status as a couple, and if he was aware of that fact, the demon would be aware of it as well. And he could sense the demon even now planning something horrific regarding the chief and his fiancée, or wife, or whatever the hell she was.

And there was not a damned thing he could do to stop it.

Jake continued to move, tromping through the forest with no real destination in mind. It seemed like he'd spent most of his time in the damned forest since finding that book.

He had no idea what else to do, though. At least in the forest he couldn't hurt anyone. Jake was frightened and downcast and ashamed of himself for ever opening up the goddamned Pandora's Box of demonic possession. He wished he'd never found the leather-covered book with the bizarre drawings and symbols and conjurations.

He wished he'd never ventured inside the old falling-down barn in the first place.

But regrets were pointless, and it was impossible to turn back time, unless of course such a spell was included somewhere in the cursed book of conjurations. And if such a spell did exist it was irrelevant because Jake had left the book inside his desk drawer.

He supposed having the book in his possession was now irrelevant. The demon didn't need spells written on paper, it was a *fucking demon*.

Despair enveloped Jake like a blanket. *Like that black cloud enveloped me in the middle of the forest,* he thought.

And he still had no idea what to do.

So he kept walking.

16

Something was bothering Mike. Sharon would see it as plain as day and his distress was bothering her as she patrolled the streets of Paskagankee.

Normally closed-mouthed and stoic while on the job, her new husband was invariably warm and funny and loving during their off time together. But last night he'd barely spoken a word from the time they left the Beebe household until the moment they'd turned off their bedroom light.

Obviously there was plenty of reason for bleakness. Their little town had suffered another murder, apparently—again—with some kind of supernatural element involved. Sharon had recognized as much from the moment Marta Kuzinski admitted seeing glowing black eyes in Jake Beebe's face.

And that book.

Just looking at its cracked leather binding had turned her stomach last night. She didn't know how Mike was managing to hang onto the damned thing without losing his dinner.

But even given all the obvious reasons for gloom, Sharon knew Mike well enough to know that his bleak mood was due to more than the murder and surrounding weirdness. It was tied directly to the confrontation that had taken place inside Jake's bedroom. She was certain of that much; she just couldn't figure out the connection.

When Jake flipped out after opening his bedroom door, Sharon had been mostly screened by her husband's body and could see very little of what was taking place. And the whole encounter happened so quickly it was over in a matter of seconds.

After the kid fell or jumped out his bedroom window and Mike went streaking down the stairs, she'd been stunned into inaction by the peculiar symbols, drawings and letterings covering Jake's bedroom wall. She'd felt a lethargy that she couldn't really appreciate fully until Mike came back and steered her out of the bedroom.

She had snapped out of the weird trance immediately after leaving the room, but couldn't really recall much of anything that had happened during those chaotic few seconds.

Some cop you are.

From that point on, though, Mike had seemed different. Preoccupied somehow, or maybe even…scared. It felt almost sacrilegious to think it, given what the two of them had faced over the last couple of years. He'd seen some truly chilling stuff and never once showed signs of cracking. But she would be kidding herself if she didn't acknowledge that he'd seemed frightened on the drive home.

She sighed and pursed her lips. She'd been disappointed this morning when they got up and Mike told her he wanted her to spend the day on routine patrol. She'd been hoping to accompany him on what would surely be a long day spent driving from house to house running down possible leads on the Dunn murder. Everyone on the roster of staff and students they'd received from Sheldon Weems would have to be interviewed.

But it wasn't to be. He'd shaken his head and said, "I need you cruising Paskagankee. I've already talked to Gordie this morning, and there have been no Jake Beebe sightings. We need to find that kid, and unless he's stolen a car or borrowed one from a friend, he's on foot. And if he's on foot, he's still in the area."

She tried to hide her disappointment with a curt nod, but of course he saw right through it. He was too insightful and knew her too well to be fooled.

He smiled. "I'm sorry, babe. But I trust you more than I trust the rest of my officers combined. Plus you're a local, which means you know every back road and fire alley in and around this damned town. I want you to drive them all and see if you can turn up that needle in a haystack for us."

How could she argue, especially since he'd seemed so down?

As the morning turned into afternoon she of course remained in close contact with Mike via radio. The early interview results weren't encouraging, and he quickly seemed to resign himself to the realization that no new witnesses would be discovered. He wouldn't give up—quitting wasn't in his DNA and until a better lead developed he would continue moving forward with the interview process—but she could tell he already recognized it was pointless.

What he really wanted to be doing, she knew, was examining the book he'd taken from the Beebe house. Based on what Jake's hysterical sister had said last night she could understand why he would be so anxious to get a good look at it, but he was too much of a professional to make his subordinates to all the foot-pounding work of the investigation while he sat in his office reading a book.

He'd told her he intended to dig into the book tonight and she'd shuddered.

She didn't even want to be around the thing; it was creepy as hell and gave her the willies. But if it helped get them closer to solving the murder, she was all for *him* checking it out.

But after a day during which they'd both spun their wheels— Mike interviewed PHS staff members and students for more than nine hours without a single useable lead to show for his time, and Sharon had driven an entire shift on the outskirts and remote roads of Paskagankee without any sign of Jake Beebe—he ate a quick dinner and then disappeared into the spare bedroom they used as a den to begin examining the book.

Sharon had begun thinking of it as The Book, since it seemed clear—to her at least, and apparently to Mike as well—that the leather bound text represented the key to this whole tragedy.

She paced quietly in the living room, nursing a cup of tea, torn between the almost irresistible desire to be in the den with Mike examining the evidence, and her conviction that there was something very wrong with The Book, and it would be much better and healthier for her to stay as far away from the thing as possible. To have nothing to do with it.

She dithered for twenty minutes and then made up her mind. *Pull yourself together and be a cop, for Christ's sake,* she scolded herself and marched to the closed door of the den.

She was reaching for the knob when the door opened from the other side and Mike barreled through it. He rammed into her, nearly knocking her off her feet and sending her tea sloshing over the sides of the cup.

His hand shot out and steadied her. "Jesus," he said. "I'm sorry, I didn't expect you to be standing right outside the door. What the hell were you doing out here?"

Sharon took the opportunity the unexpected closeness had provided to lift up onto her toes and kiss him hard. His hand released her elbow and found its way to her butt, giving a quick squeeze and then wrapping around her waist as he pulled her closer and returned the kiss.

Finally they separated and Sharon swallowed hard. "Wow. What was the question again?"

Mike laughed. "Why were you standing so close to the door I nearly killed you just by leaving the room?"

"Oh, yeah, that." Sharon giggled. "Even though we're now an old married couple your kisses still take my breath away."

"I'm glad to hear it." He waggled his eyebrows mischievously. "But you still haven't answered my question."

"I was on my way into the den to join you."

"I thought the book creeped you out."

"It does. That's why it took me so long to get my courage up. But then I gave myself a stern talking-to and decided to act like a big girl instead of a little baby."

"Oh, I can testify to the fact that you're a big girl, all right. And thank you for coming to offer your support. But even after twenty minutes it's obvious I'm going to need some help deciphering the damned book. Half of it's written in some language I don't recognize, and even the half written in English is confusing as hell."

"Okay. So what do we do now?"

"We go find help."

"Well, yeah. Could you be a little more specific?"

Mike smiled. "I love how your nose wrinkles when you're concentrating. It's very sexy."

Sharon punched him in the upper arm. "Focus, lover boy."

"Oh. Yeah. Sorry. Let me turn it around on you. Who do we

know that's lived in town her whole life, knows everyone in the area, has access to historical documents going back centuries, and maybe most importantly, has a history of helping us?"

Now it was Sharon's turn to smile. "Rose Pellerin, of course."

"Bingo. I already called Rose and she's going to meet me at her shop in half an hour."

"I think you mean she's going to meet *us* in her shop in half an hour."

"I assumed you wouldn't want come. This whole discussion is going to be based on the book."

"You assumed wrong, Mister. I'm not letting you go off by yourself to see a single woman after sunset."

Mike laughed. Rose Pellerin was at least seventy years old and one of the sweetest people he'd met since moving to Paskagankee.

"Grab the keys then," he said, moving toward the front door.

"How come I have to drive?"

"Because," he said, "I'm old, as you never miss a chance to remind me."

17

Rose Pellerin's curio shop was located in a small downtown strip mall, if a village the size of Paskagankee could be said to have a "downtown."

Mike had asked Sharon about the shop once last year and been told *Needful Things* had been a part of the Paskagankee landscape for as long as she could remember. And that was a comment from someone who'd spent virtually her entire life in town, the only exception being her few months at the FBI Academy in Quantico.

They drove into the mall parking lot, the expanse of pavement empty with the exception of three vehicles clustered outside the sub shop adjacent to *Needful Things.* Sharon pulled the Explorer to a stop in front of the curio shop.

"I don't see Rose's car," she said as she killed the engine.

"She must have parked out back then," Mike answered. "The lights are on inside her shop and she said she'd meet me here. If there's one person I trust to keep her word in this town—"

Sharon looked sharply across the front seat, her eyes narrowed.

Mike grinned and continued. "With the exception of my beautiful wife, of course."

She smiled. "You're living dangerously, pal."

"It's what I do." Mike chuckled and stepped out of the car. "That one person—besides my lovely wife—would be Rose Pellerin. So let's go inside. I guarantee we didn't waste our time driving across town."

He reached back into the vehicle and removed a paper shopping bag from the front seat. Sharon had made him drop the book inside the bag and then seal it with a rubber band before leaving the house. "I don't want to look at that thing any more than I absolutely have to," she'd said with a look of grim disgust.

By the time he slammed the door closed, his wife had already moved to the *Needful Things* entrance and stepped inside.

* * *

Mike McMahon wasn't much for shopping, and with what little free time he had he definitely wasn't in the habit of hanging around Rose Pellerin's store.

To his eye, it looked as though all the items on display were exactly the same as they'd been the last time he was here, which was sometime late last spring. There were rows of greeting cards, scented candles, knickknacks, and stuffed animals placed alongside delicate-looking tables and chairs that he guessed must be antiques.

It struck Mike as the kind of place where a careless police chief could easily break expensive things by accident, and he picked his way carefully through the aisles toward the sound of female voices coming from the rear of the shop.

He rounded a corner and found Sharon and Rose locked in a hug. Rose was talking excitedly about the wedding, remarking on the beauty of the mountainside venue and what a shame it was the couple of honor had been forced to depart before the post-ceremony celebration had even begun.

"On the bright side," Rose said with an impish smile, "there was no shortage of toasts to a long and happy marriage."

"I'm not surprised," Mike said, "considering we had an open-bar reception. I shudder to think of the hit my wallet's going to take when the final bill comes in."

Rose finally released Sharon and turned her attention to Mike. She wrapped her arms around him and squeezed hard. *She might be in her seventies,* Mike thought, *but she's still one strong old lady.*

After a moment she let go. She stepped back and eyed Mike

and Sharon. "While it's wonderful to see you both, I have to admit it's a pleasure of the unexpected kind."

"You know we're always happy to see you," Sharon said.

"Likewise. But I'm confused. Michael told me on the phone that I may be able to help your investigation into the death of that teacher over at PHS, but I'm at a loss to imagine how."

"I really just need the input of someone with connections around town," Mike said.

"I'm flattered you thought of me, but I'm just an old lady."

"Not old," he said. "You're younger than a lot of people half your age, at least in all the ways that matter. But I need someone who's spent a lifetime in this town and who knows just about all its residents."

"And is an amateur Paskagankee historian to boot," Sharon added.

"Well," Rose said with a smile. "I don't know if I can justify the faith you two seem to have in me, but I'll do what I can. What do you need to know?"

"Is there anyone in Paskagankee that might have knowledge regarding..." Mike paused, suddenly embarrassed, "...what appears to be a book of...spells or incantations?" He finished the question hurriedly, not sure what sort of response to expect out of this stout, no-nonsense Yankee woman.

"Hm. Spells and incantations." She rubbed her chin and remained silent. Mike thought she might be questioning her decision to meet them this time of night in her shop.

"I know how ridiculous it sounds," he said.

She shook her head. "I'm not hesitating because you sound ridiculous. That's not it at all. I'm hesitating because it sounds..."

"Yes?" Mike and Sharon said, speaking simultaneously.

"It sounds like something I've heard before." She spoke slowly, deep in thought.

"Well," Sharon replied, "everyone's heard stories about books of magic, and about witchcraft and that sort of thing."

"That's not what I mean," Rose said. "What I'm saying is it sounds familiar to this area. It sounds like something Paskagankee has dealt with before."

18

Mike glanced at Sharon, surprised. He'd been prepared for any number of reactions from Rose Pellerin to their unexpected visit, but this one hadn't occurred to him. He supposed it should have, given his adopted hometown's bloody supernatural history.

Rose chuckled, enjoying his reaction. "Let's go into the back room, shall we?"

She disappeared through a door Mike remembered from the last time he was here. It was in the spring, when he learned the rich history of Paskagankee's roadside tavern, the Ridge Runner. He'd discovered then that Rose Pellerin possessed an impressive collection of back issues of the closest decent-sized city's newspaper, *The Portland Journal.*

Her collection went back not just decades, but centuries.

She'd come into the newspapers several years ago, when the Portland public library was undergoing massive renovations. Library officials had finished computerizing the collection and planned to destroy the originals in the name of saving space. Rose had been aghast at the thought of the rare artifacts' disappearance and had taken possession of them all.

Mike recalled Rose had stored the newspapers in airtight plastic bins stacked neatly in the rear storage area of *Needful Things.* He guessed that was why Rose was taking them into the back room.

He was right.

As with last spring's visit, Rose proceeded at her own pace. She set about making tea for everyone, not even asking whether they wanted any, just doing it. Once she'd served her guests, the elderly woman moved directly in front of the stacked bins and considered them silently, one arm crossed over her chest and the other resting on it, her hand stroking her chin thoughtfully. It was the same pose she'd taken in the front portion of her store.

As far as Mike could see, none of the bins were labeled. How she was trying to decide where to begin looking for the information she wanted was beyond him. But after a long moment of silence, Mike and Sharon sipping their tea and letting Rose concentrate, she turned and faced Mike head on.

She was grinning. "Well, are you going to stand there with your pinkie finger in the air like some metrosexual philosopher or are you going to help an old lady move some boxes?"

Sharon snorted and he elbowed her, jostling her tea, before setting his cup down. Then he stepped forward. "How can I help, ma'am?"

Rose winked at Sharon "Ma'am, he calls me. I haven't discovered many benefits to aging, but there are a few."

She reached up and squeezed Mike's shoulder affectionately. "I've spent the last few months reorganizing my collection. It's taken much longer than it really should, because every time I start working on my project, I end up spending most of my time checking out old newspaper stories."

"It must be fascinating reading historical accounts of the area," Sharon said.

"Oh, you have no idea, dear. Things have happened in northern Maine that would make the most outlandish novel you've ever read seem tame. Examining those ancient newspapers is how I know that the situation with the book of spells has had a bearing on tragedy in Paskagankee before.

"The problem," she continued, "is that since I've read so *many* stories over the course of several months, I can't quite recall in which time period the case I'm thinking of took place. I do know it was long ago, possibly right after the *Journal* began publishing the news."

"Centuries ago."

"Yes. As you may or may not know, our little newspaper was one of the first in the country to begin publishing on a regular schedule."

"I didn't know that," Sharon admitted.

"No wonder there are so damned many containers," Mike said. "It's going to take forever just to begin narrowing the search down."

Rose shook her head. "I don't think so. Since I'm relatively certain the case I read about took place a long time ago, let's start with the oldest issues. Take down those top two bins on the left, dear, and place them on the floor."

Mike did as asked, and then Rose lifted the top off one of the bins. Inside, the newspapers had been separated by year and placed carefully into clear plastic binders. Mike and Sharon stood side-by-side, gazing at a collected history of the local area that had been reported through the eyes of actual observers over the centuries, a history that was probably more complete and accurate than could be found in any book or university archive.

And the newspapers appeared remarkably well preserved. They were yellowed and brittle with age, but for the most part whole and fully readable.

Sharon whistled softly. "Look at the date on the top paper."

Mike bent and examined it. *Portland Journal* was printed across the top of the first newspaper under the clear plastic in a font that Mike didn't recognize but that looked ornate and somehow Victorian. Under the header was the date: *June 4, 1797.*

"Hooooly shit." The words slipped out before he realized what he was saying, and he immediately apologized. "I'm sorry about the language, Rose. It's just that I knew your collection was old, but I guess I didn't fully appreciate *how* old until seeing it in black and white."

She laughed. "No apology is necessary. My reaction was similar the first time I laid eyes on these treasures. It was exactly why I couldn't stand to see them destroyed."

"How should we do this?" Sharon asked. "How will we even know what we're looking for?"

"We each take a binder containing a year's worth of papers," Rose suggested, "and start digging through them. If I recall correctly, the story I'm referring to involved a massive fire to a Paskagankee home in which a number of people died. I believe it was front-page news, so we should be able to scan the years relatively quickly. Back in those days, the paper was only published once a week."

"So we just start scanning through each year."

"I can't think of any other way."

"Let's get started."

Mike carefully lifted three of the large binders out of the bin and handed one to each of the women, keeping the third for himself. They walked to a long workbench Rose had set up along one wall and began examining the written history of Paskagankee, Maine.

*   *   *

Mike had expected an hours-long search, with the most likely result being nothing. A dead end. But Rose had been a big help last spring and he was determined to give her the benefit of the doubt.

His guess that they would be scanning old newspapers until well past midnight with glazed and exhausted eyes was way off the mark. Twenty minutes after beginning their search, Sharon looked up excitedly and said, "I think I've found it!"

Mike and Rose stopped what they were doing and Rose bent over the *Journal* issue sitting face-up at Sharon's spot on the workbench. ARSON AND MURDER IN PASKAGANKEE, blared the headline, every bit as lurid as what one might expect out of a modern-day newspaper.

"Yes!" Rose said. "That's the story I'm thinking of. I'm pretty sure if you read the piece you'll find a reference to a book of spells, or witchcraft, or something of that nature. The tragedy involved the Beebe farmhouse, as I recall."

Mike's blood ran cold and he froze. He was aware of his mouth hanging open but he couldn't do a damned thing about it. "What did you just say?"

19

Rose glanced up at him in surprise. "The Beebe house. It burned, and murder was involved, as the headline states. Nearly the entire family was wiped out, if I remember the story correctly."

Mike felt Sharon staring a hole into the side of his head and he turned to meet her gaze. She had gone pale and looked exactly the way he felt.

Rose misinterpreted their shock as a lack of understanding. "You know, the Beebe family. Surely you recognize the name," she said. "Van Beebe is head of the Town Council. You must deal with him all the time, Michael."

"Yeah, I know Van," he said reflexively. His mind was whirring, his thoughts a jumbled mess, and he forced himself to slow down and think. He realized Rose was saying something else but he ignored it. "We need to see that story."

"Well, that's convenient," Rose answered. "Since that's why we're all here." She indicated the paper with a nod of her head. "Have at it."

Mike stepped away and shook his head. "Could one of you read it out loud? I need to think."

Rose glanced from Mike to Sharon and back again. "What's gotten you two so spooked? You look like you've seen a ghost, both of you."

"Yeah," Mike muttered. "Something like that."

Nobody said anything for a moment and then Rose began reading:

"One of the oldest area families was nearly wiped out Saturday, when Samuel Beebe of Paskagankee brutally murdered four relatives before setting fire to his home. The dead are identified as Dorothy and Thaddeus Beebe, parents of the killer, as well as his brothers, Michael and Wilmer. A third brother, Charles, somehow survived the vicious attack and currently lies near death in a Portland hospital.

"The only living witness, Charles Beebe, told authorities he was awakened in the middle of the night Saturday by the sound of screams coming from his brothers' bedrooms. When he arose to investigate, he says his brother Samuel entered and began slashing him with a large butcher knife.

"The victim says he fell to his floor, bleeding heavily, and lost consciousness as his brother left the room. Some time later he awoke to find the home burning out of control. Still bleeding from wounds to his arms and chest, Charles began crawling toward escape, managing to navigate the smoke-filled inferno on his hands and knees until reaching the ground floor. From there, he escaped the conflagration by shattering a first-floor window and crawling outdoors.

"In a puzzling twist, authorities say the perpetrator, Samuel Beebe, just thirteen years of age, traveled immediately to the local sheriff's office upon completing his murderous misdeed and confessed to the entire affair. Trusted sources tell the Journal the young man spun a bizarre tale in an attempt to justify his actions, a story involving demonic possession and a strange book of spells and incantations.

"The book in question was on the killer's person at the time of his arrest, and authorities immediately took possession of this critical piece of evidence. Sheriff Clete Wilson says the county will retain possession of the volume for the foreseeable future, determining it a danger to the community.

"When asked if the strange book bears out Beebe's claim of demonic possession, Wilson would say only that 'after a thorough examination, I have determined it would be in the community's best interest for this evidence to remain under lock and key inside my office safe.'

"In addition to admitting culpability for this horrific crime, young Samuel Beebe has begged to be put to death as soon as possible, 'before the demon returns and causes me to kill more people.'

"Beebe's execution by hanging has been scheduled for this coming Friday at sunset."

"There's more," Rose said, "but it's all background material on the Beebe family and their roots in the community. I can read it if you'd like me to, but I don't know that it's anything relevant to your current investigation."

Mike shook his head. "No, what you've already read gives me more than enough to think about, thank you." He looked at Sharon and her face was even paler than it had been before.

Rose glanced between Mike and Sharon. Even as distracted as Mike was, he could see that the look on her face was in equal measure concern and shrewd calculation.

"Wow," he said, trying to smile and knowing the best he could manage was a sick-looking grimace. "We didn't even come here for such a thorough history lesson. This has been quite the unexpected bonus."

"Although clearly an unpleasant one," Rose said. "But to your point: you told me when you arrived that you came to see me for a specific reason. You were hoping I could connect you with someone who could answer questions about witchcraft and a book of spells and incantations, correct?"

Mike nodded.

"That book the county sheriff took possession of more than two hundred years ago, the book that caused a thirteen-year-old boy to slaughter virtually his entire family..." Her voice trailed off but her eyes held Mike's steadily.

"What about it?" he said.

"That book has shown up again, hasn't it? It's somehow related to the murder of that young teacher at the high school, isn't it?"

"I'm sorry," Mike said, almost reflexively. "I can't comment on an ongoing investigation."

Rose nodded, her eyes sharp. "You don't have to. Helen Keller could read your body language, anyway."

Mike walked distractedly across the storeroom. He placed his ancient issue of the *Portland Journal* on top of the pile, aware of Rose Pellerin following his every move.

As he turned back toward her she said, "It's even worse than that, isn't it? But what could be worse than that old book of spells turning up and wreaking havoc—*again*—in Paskagankee?"

Her eyes widened and then she connected the dots. "Oh my

God. Now I understand your reaction when I mentioned the fact that the old *Journal* story involved the Beebe family. Unless I'm mistaken, there are Beebe kids of high school age right now. One of those children is involved in the teacher's murder. I'm right, aren't I?"

Mike ran his tongue across his lips. They felt dry and cracked. "Again," he said. "I can't comment on an ongoing investigation, I'm sorry."

"But if you see Jake Beebe wandering around outside your store," Sharon interrupted, "lock the doors immediately and call us, and do *not* approach him."

Mike nodded. "Yeah," he said. "That's damned good advice."

* * *

Rose Pellerin was able to give them a name, exactly as Mike had hoped.

She led the way back to the *Needful Things* showroom, leaving the dimly lit clutter of the storage area behind. The bright lights and colorful display objects out front did little to dispel the sense of pervading grimness that had settled over the group, but there was nothing to be gained by standing any longer out back, staring at each other with pale faces.

"His name is Brian Paquette and he's a Paskagankee resident," Rose said. "He's employed as a Professor of Occult History down at Bowdoin College in Brunswick."

"Professor of Occult History?" Sharon said. "Is there really such a thing?"

"Apparently so," Rose said. "And it sounds to me like he's exactly what you're looking for. Now, I must warn you I don't know him very well. In fact, I don't think anyone in town knows him very well. As far as I can tell, he keeps mostly to himself. He may not even want to talk to you."

Mike grimaced. "If he's interested in occult history, he'll talk once he gets a look at that book."

They moved toward the entrance and Mike said, "Thanks for

all your help, Rose. And, listen, about what Sharon said earlier…"

"You mean about steering clear of young Jake Beebe?"

"Yes, about that. There's no reason to believe your path will cross his. But he *is* missing, and he *is* a…person of interest… in our investigation. If you see him, do not engage him, do you understand?"

"Of course."

"Good. Because until I can get a handle on what's happening in Paskagankee, you want to be very careful."

"Yes, I gathered that already."

* * *

The ride home was a tense one.

Mike was in favor of going straight from *Needful Things* to the professor's house. "We can't afford to waste any time," he said. "Jake Beebe's still missing and the longer that remains the case, the more likely it becomes that someone else will die. Maybe someone already has and another body's going to turn up at any moment."

"I understand," Sharon said. "And I don't disagree. But if the professor is as antisocial as Rose claims," she argued, "he's not going to take well to being approached at night and without warning, even by a cop. Hell, maybe *especially* by a cop.

"And that's not even the biggest reason why you should be careful how you approach this guy," she added.

"Really. And what would the biggest reason be?"

"You even have to ask?" Sharon said. "Come on, Mr. Police Investigator, think about it. Weird supernatural stuff happening in town? Working on getting help from a college professor? Any of this ringing a bell?"

"Of course. Professor Dye." The UMaine Professor of Native American Studies had been instrumental in helping them stop a horrific killing spree in Paskagankee just two years earlier.

"Exactly. And the University of Maine and Bowdoin College aren't really that far away from each other. If this Brian Paquette was a friend of Professor Dye, or if he's even heard of the man and the fate he suffered while helping us, do you think he's going to be the least bit inclined to do anything for you?"

"Point taken. But if that's the case, maybe my best bet is to just show up and catch the guy by surprise."

"I don't think so. If you materialize on his doorstep after dark, waving some book of spells around like a lunatic, how do you expect the guy to react? How would *you* react?"

He had to admit she had a point.

"But if you call him and give him a little background on the case and then lay out the kind of information you're looking for, I think you'll have a much better chance of gaining his trust and the getting his assistance."

"Does it ever get tiring being the voice of reason and sanity?"

"Occasionally, but someone's got to do it."

20

Sharon wanted nothing more than to accompany Mike to see Professor Brian Paquette.

Mike had called the man the moment they arrived home from *Needful Things* last night, and the professor only hesitated briefly. It didn't take much description about the book to convince a professor of occult studies to agree to a meeting once he'd heard a little about its dark history and its potential relationship to a murder in their town. They'd set up a lunch date for today at a restaurant near the college.

But for the second day in a row, he squashed her desires.

"We still don't have a line on Jake Beebe," he said. "And while it's beginning to look more and more like he's left Paskagankee behind, I don't want to assume anything. The kid's dangerous and if there's even a slight chance he's still in the area, we have to make a concerted effort to get him into custody ASAP."

"Let me guess," she said. "You want me to beat the bushes looking for Jake again."

"I'm sorry, babe. I know it was your idea to set up the meeting with Paquette in advance, and I'd love to have you with me, but we just can't afford to devote two bodies to this interview, even if one of them is the sexiest I've ever seen."

"Flattery will get you everywhere," she said with a lascivious smile. She tried to hide her disappointment because she knew he was right about the importance of finding Jake Beebe.

She waggled a finger in his face. "Fine, I'll drive aimlessly around the outskirts of town if that's what you need me to do. But you'd better spill everything you find out from the egghead when we get home tonight."

"Deal," he said with a grin. "Of course, we might be too busy getting busy to do much talking."

"Promises, promises."

*   *   *

That had been at breakfast. They'd then traveled together to the police station.

Mike had told Sharon he was determined to put a solid three hours in behind a desk in the never-ending war against his own personal nemesis—paperwork—before leaving for Brunswick and his lunch date with Professor Paquette, and he seemed determined to keep his word.

Sharon pecked him on the cheek at the station, foregoing the erotic, tongue-down-the-throat, legs-wrapped-around-the-waist kiss she really wanted to give him. Reluctantly. Then she trudged to her Paskagankee Police SUV for what she was certain would be a second day spent spinning her wheels.

Perhaps literally, given the rough terrain surrounding the town. And her instincts were right on target the entire morning.

She cruised main roads and back roads. She bounced over unpaved thoroughfares that were little more than weed-choked parallel dirt tracks cut into field grass. She drove more fire lanes than she could count, including some in which she'd gotten brain-numbingly drunk and drugged-up during her lost teen years. She even patrolled the fire lane in which she'd been attacked by the undead Earl Manning and nearly lost her life.

She drove them all, certain she was wasting her time but determined to do her job to the best of her ability. She owed Mike that much.

About noon she decided it was time for a break and a bite to eat. She stopped the truck in the middle of one of those too-many-to-count fire roads somewhere behind the Beebe property and lifted her mini-cooler off the rear floor.

The vehicle idled quietly as Sharon placed her cooler on the passenger seat. A thin plume of exhaust swirled lazily into the air behind the Explorer and she considered killing the engine for a few minutes.

Decided against it. *It's too damned cold outside for that.*

There was no sunlight to warm things up because the day was overcast and grey. But even if the weather conditions had been perfect, the thick forest canopy would have served to filter out most of the sunshine long before it could reach the ground.

It was depressing. If Sharon hadn't seen so much worse in the woods surrounding her hometown, the murkiness might have been unsettling as well. But she had long-since gotten used to the quirks and oddities of life in Paskagankee, Maine.

So she unwrapped a sandwich and unscrewed a Thermos of coffee and began slowly munching as she listened to the sporadic bursts of radio traffic on the PPD frequency. Typically, day shifts in the sleepy town were slow for patrol officers and today was no exception.

Interviews were still being conducted with students and staff members at the high school, but more for the sake of thoroughness than the notion that a concrete lead might result. Mike had delegated the interview process to Harley Tanguay, with instructions to be immediately notified if Harley unearthed any significant information. Neither Mike nor Sharon considered it likely.

She lifted the plastic Thermos cover she was using as a coffee cup to her lips, pleased that even after four hours in the back of the truck, the drink was still hot and strong, almost hot enough to scald her lips. She savored it as it burned its way down her throat. The sensation was similar to the burn of whiskey she had once lived for, but different in the sense that a cup of coffee didn't hold the potential to destroy her life from the inside out like alcohol and drugs had.

Sandwich gone, she balled up the plastic wrap and tossed it into the cooler.

Capped the Thermos.

Lifted her lunch supplies off the front seat and swiveled onto her knees to drop everything again into the back of the Explorer.

And found herself face to face with Jake Beebe.

21

He stood inches away, on the other side of the Explorer's driver's door, bent at the waist and leering into the vehicle with a maniacal grin more appropriate to Hannibal Lecter than to a sixteen-year-old high school student.

Two things fired through Sharon's startled brain in rapid-fire succession:

How the hell did I not see him sneaking up on me?

And, *Holy shit, his eyes are glowing black.*

She released the lunch supplies and they clattered to the floor of the truck. Then she spun toward the front of the vehicle while reaching for her service weapon.

Jake Beebe—*or the demon inside him; it must be a demon because what I just saw was not of this earth*—returned to his full height. He reached out, lightning-quick, and yanked on the Explorer's door handle.

Sharon unsnapped the leather holster strap and grasped her weapon. The Explorer shook on its springs from the force of the Jake Beebe-thing pulling on the door, but its automatic locks had engaged hours ago and the locks held, even against the extreme force of Beebe's tugs.

Then the Beebe-thing spread its hands wide, like a priest offering absolution. It leaned back on its heels, and as Sharon began lifting the gun from her holster she could hear it chanting words she could not understand in a language she did not recognize, its voice guttural and menacing.

The gun pulled clear and she lifted it toward the murder suspect and out of nowhere came a piercing pain in her skull. It struck without warning, the worst and fastest headache she'd ever experienced, and the stinging pain shot through her brain like an ice-cream headache times one thousand, and she dropped her weapon and clapped both hands to the sides of her head in a fruitless attempt to shut out the pain, and then incredibly the agony began ramping up and she became dimly aware that she was moaning and she knew she was dying, she had to be dying because nobody could withstand this kind of relentless pain, it would cause her head to explode like a silly special effect from a Grade-B horror movie, except this was real, and she screamed from the pain, and she begged to die if that was what it would take to be released from the agony, and then she began slipping sideways in the front seat of the Explorer and as she crumpled numbly onto her side the darkness finally arrived.

And the darkness covered her like a blanket and took away the pain.

22

Mike wasn't particularly enthused about the prospect of driving to Bowdoin to meet with a man who lived right in Paskagankee. It was roughly a sixty-minute trip each way, which meant he would devote a significant chunk of the remainder of his day to a conversation that might well prove fruitless.

It seemed obvious to him that it would have made more sense to meet at the professor's home in town, or even at Sharon's house. But Mike hadn't wanted to push the man too hard and end up with no conversation at all. He was convinced the leather-bound book was that important.

So he'd agreed to the Bowdoin meeting without argument.

He eased into a parking spot down the street from the café at which they'd agreed to meet. Bowdoin was a college town, and even under northern Maine's overcast skies and mid-October chill, the sidewalks were filled with young adults strolling the area. A wide, grassy median strip separated the eastbound and westbound sides of Bowdoin's main thoroughfare, and on the grassy area Frisbees flew, sidewalk vendors hawked t-shirts and other items Mike could not discern from a distance, and a hot dog cart served a surprisingly large crowd of outdoor diners.

Mike stepped out of the cruiser and locked the door, stepping into the crowd on the sidewalk. The Bowdoin College campus was located no more than a half-mile away, which meant the downtown area tended to be filled with people during all but the worst winter weather conditions.

The café was called *Mister Moose*, and although Mike had never been here before, a hand-carved sign featuring gold-filigree lettering topped by a widely smiling moose told Mike he was in the right place. He slipped out of the crowd and through the door.

He was dressed in full uniform and while he'd never met Brian Paquette, he guessed the professor would have little trouble picking him out of the lunchtime crowd.

Assuming, of course, the man had already arrived. Maybe he'd been held up at work and wasn't even inside the restaurant yet.

Mike stood in the doorway, scanning the crowd. Tables of different sizes and shapes filled the interior, and as far as he could see, they were all occupied. Wait staff hurried from the kitchen to the dining area and back, the scene one of organized chaos.

From a small round table almost all the way toward the rear of the restaurant, a hand rose into the air in a tentative wave. A man climbed to his feet and gestured to Mike just as the hostess approached and said, "Table for one today?"

"I'm meeting someone," Mike answered. "And I think I just found him. I'll see myself to his table, thank you."

The harried hostess smiled distractedly and turned away without another word. Mike weaved between tables, dodging waitresses and waiters, and a moment later shook the hand of the man he hoped would help him get to the bottom of a young teacher's murder.

*   *   *

Mike vaguely recognized Professor Paquette, an unsurprising development considering the professor lived in Paskagankee and Mike had been chief of police now for nearly two years. The town was that small. They had undoubtedly passed each other at the post office or grocery store, perhaps nodding and smiling in polite acknowledgment but never actually having had occasion to speak.

Paquette looked younger than Mike would have expected for a full professor at a prestigious liberal arts college. Mike had never attended college, so his only real experience with the world of secondary education had been his relationship with Professor Kenneth Dye from the University of Maine at Orono.

Dye had been much older, a man beaten down by his past but committed to his principles. In the end those principles had cost him his life but saved the lives of many more.

The initial awkwardness of mutual introductions was cut short by the appearance of a young waitress, who took their lunch order and then disappeared into the kitchen.

Mike said, "Thank you for agreeing to meet with me today, especially given the short notice."

"It's not a problem," the young academician answered. He was tall and thin, with a head of unkempt but balding hair and a pair of black horn-rimmed glasses that seemed constantly to be sliding down his nose. "I heard about the death of that poor high school teacher and I'm happy to help in any way I can. Although I have to admit," he added with a semi-distracted smile Mike immediately associated with Professor Dye, "the prospect of seeing this mysterious book of spells with my own two eyes has certainly piqued my interest."

"I know your time is valuable, so I'll get right to the point." Mike unzipped the small leather folio in which he'd transported the book. He removed it and placed it on the table in front of the professor. "This is the item I told you about on the phone."

The man looked down and his jaw dropped. His face paled. It was as if someone had flipped a switch, immediately draining the blood from his skull. He had begun raising his water glass to his lips but he never quite made it. He lowered his arm and the glass thunked back down on the table, splashing water and soaking the white linen tablecloth.

He raised his eyes slowly to meet Mike's and said, "Where did you get this?"

"Later. Right now I want you to tell me about it."

"Do you have any idea what you have here?"

Mike spread his hands. "That's why I'm here, professor. Educate me."

Paquette breathed deeply. Cleared his throat. Seemed to realize he'd never taken his sip of water and did so, albeit with shaking hands.

Then he said, "What you have here is called a grimoire, Chief McMahon."

"Okay..."

"A grimoire could be considered a book of supernatural spells, but it's much more than that. Calling a grimoire a book of spells would be like saying Abraham Lincoln was a politician, or Jimi Hendrix a guitarist. Do you see my point?"

"I think so. A grimoire is a book of spells, but it's not just any book of spells, it's exceptional."

"Yes, although my comparison pales. A grimoire is a book filled with demonic conjurations, and any of the—"

"Whoa, professor, time out." Mike lifted his hand in a "stop" signal for emphasis. "Did you say demonic conjurations?"

"I did."

"I'm no expert on the English language, but isn't 'conjuration' another way of saying 'calling'?"

"Basically, yes."

"So what we have in front of you is an instruction manual for summoning demons."

"Exactly."

Mike blinked once and sat back in his chair. He guessed if someone had chosen this moment to hold a mirror in front of his face, it would be every bit as ghostly pale as the professor's had been just a moment ago.

Suddenly, everything was starting to make sense.

The transition of Jake Beebe's eyes from unexceptional to bizarre, glowing black orbs.

The boy's ability to crawl sideways down the sheer exterior wall of his house.

The fact that Lucie Dunn's killer smashed her head against a blackboard nearly seven feet off the classroom floor.

Mike closed his eyes. His guts had clenched in his belly and he tried to relax. When he failed, he reopened his eyes anyway to find the professor staring intently at the grimoire on the table.

"Please go on," Mike said, wishing to hell he could have said anything else.

The waitress returned with their food and placed it on the table. Salad without dressing for Paquette, cheeseburger and fries for Mike. Professor Paquette placed the book to the side and waited for the server to walk away before continuing to speak.

Then he did.

23

"You may have noticed a certain…look of surprise on my face," Professor Paquette said, "when you showed me your book."

"Oh, I noticed it, all right," Mike said. "Calling your reaction 'surprise' doesn't seem sufficient, particularly coming from someone who has made a career out of studying the occult. Seemed more to me like shock."

"Quite correct. And the reason for that shock is simple. The volume you brought here today is no ordinary grimoire."

"Is there even such a thing?"

Paquette smiled again. "Perhaps not to the uninitiated. But to those versed in the occult, yes. Purported grimoires are not particularly uncommon. They're not that difficult to get ahold of if you're determined to do so. But this volume here—" he nodded down at the table—"is different."

"I don't understand."

"There are many books out in the world that claim to offer the reader an instructions for accomplishing demonic conjuration, but this one is—."

"Why?"

"Excuse me?"

"Why would anyone want to conjure a demon, even assuming it was possible?"

"Oh, it's possible, Chief McMahon. I think you understand that already, otherwise you wouldn't be sitting here today. You just don't want to fully commit to the notion."

Mike thought about it for a moment. "Point taken. I guess. But my question stands. Why would anyone voluntarily summon a demon?"

"Demonic conjuration, if approached properly, can be accomplished in such a way as to render the demon essentially harmless. It offers the possibility of a supernatural 'helper,' if you will, affording the conjurer the opportunity to accomplish incredible things. They don't have to be negative things, either, since the demon would be bound, by the summoning spell, to fulfill the wishes of the conjurer."

Mike eyed the professor suspiciously. "I assume you're speaking hypothetically."

Paquette laughed. "If you're asking whether I've actually performed a summoning spell myself, the answer is no. But I *have* devoted my career to the study of the practice, which, again, is why you're here."

Mike nodded. "Okay. Fair enough. But just as I interrupted you, you were about to tell me why this particular grimoire is different from so many others."

"Yes. As I said, there is no shortage of purported grimoires floating around in the world, books that claim to offer a roadmap to demonic conjuration. But the genuine article is rare, as you might imagine. There are many more instances of imitations than of the real thing."

"Thank God for that," Mike muttered.

"Well, yes and no," Paquette said. "Sometimes partial summoning spells, or incorrectly translated spells, can be much more dangerous than complete and thorough ones."

"Is that what we're talking about here?"

"No, which is why I said this particular grimoire is the real deal, assuming of course it is authentic. There are only three known copies of this grimoire in the world—four now, I suppose. I'm going to ask again. How did this come to be in your possession, Chief?"

"I believe the prime suspect in the murder of PHS teacher Lucie Dunn was using this book."

"Oh, good Lord."

"Exactly. Let me ask you a question, professor. How difficult is it to perform one of these...demonic conjuration spells correctly?"

"Extremely difficult. I would say it's next to impossible to think a high-school-age student with little or no understanding of the occult could manage it."

"So, instead of the kid summoning a harmless demon determined to fulfill his wishes..."

Paquette nodded gravely. "If the boy was even off a little in his conjuration, it is entirely possible he summoned a demon alright, but rather than calling forth an essentially inert spirit, he may have unleashed an evil entity of nearly unlimited power."

"Is it possible the demon could...I'm not sure how to phrase this..."

"Possess the boy? Take over his body?"

Mike sighed. "I'm guessing I already know the answer, but humor me."

"It's more than possible. It's likely, in fact, if the boy was careless or inaccurate in performing the conjuration."

"The kid is sixteen. 'Careless' is pretty much the default setting for most sixteen year old boys."

"Then you have yourself a very serious problem, Chief."

"I'm starting to gather that."

"Do you happen to know how the boy came to be in possession of such a dangerous relic?"

"His sister said he found it in the family's barn, tucked away among other long-forgotten items."

"Hmm." Professor Paquette stroked his chin with one hand. Both men had stopped eating, their food forgotten on the table.

"That doesn't sound encouraging," Mike said, staring hard at the occult expert. "Shoot it to me straight, professor. What are you thinking?"

"Well, this particular grimoire is said to have unusual properties."

"More unusual than providing a recipe for any idiot to call forth a spirit from hell?"

"Unfortunately, yes."

"I'll bite. What's the unusual property?"

"In the case of each of the other three known copies of this grimoire, the tome has...attached itself to one party."

"Attached itself? What is that supposed to mean?"

"It means that one unfortunate family has been…cursed…with the presence of this book for generations. According to legend, it is impossible to separate the grimoire from its accursed owner. No matter the circumstance or the time that has elapsed, the book always finds its way back to that bloodline."

Mike thought about the chilling *Portland Journal* story Rose Pellerin had read aloud last night, centuries old but disturbingly similar to the current situation. He'd wondered at the time how a book secured by a sheriff determined to keep it out of the hands of innocents had found its way back to the Beebe barn more than two hundred years later.

The possibility that it could be tied to the family through some supernatural bungee cord seemed hard to swallow, but so did everything about this case: an evil demon summoned from the underworld by a foolish teenager, now free of its bonds and murdering innocents in northern Maine.

Mike shook his head and sighed heavily. "This wasn't exactly the way I had hoped our meeting would go, but I'm certainly learning a lot. Now for the sixty-four thousand dollar question."

"Let me guess. You want to know how to get rid of the demon."

"Bingo."

Professor Paquette pursed his lips. He started to say something and then snapped his mouth closed before pausing a moment, forehead wrinkled, and starting again. "Well, I'm not sure—"

That was when Mike's cell phone rang.

24

His first thought was to ignore the damned phone. He'd driven a long way to speak with this man, and he was finally getting some answers regarding the baffling murder, even if they *were* answers he would very much have preferred not to hear.

But one look at the phone's caller ID screen left him with little choice—it was the number of the Paskagankee Police Department.

Mike cursed under his breath. "I'm sorry, Professor, could you hold that thought? I have to take this, but I'll just be a moment and then we can continue."

"Of course." Paquette turned his attention to the grimoire. He had placed it upside-down on the table at the first approach of the waitress, and now he turned it over and began flipping idly through its ancient pages.

Mike punched the green "Answer" button and brought the phone to his head. "McMahon."

"Chief, this is Gordie. You need to get back to Paskagankee right away."

Mike furrowed his eyebrows. The dispatcher sounded distracted, upset and on the verge of tears. His tone was the antithesis of what Mike had come to expect from the decades-long veteran of the department.

"Gordie, I'm in the middle of a very important interview. You know that, we talked about it before I left the station not two hours ago."

"Something's happened, Chief. Something awful. Something… oh, God…"

"Spill it, Gordie, what's going on?"

"Chief, it's…it's…Sharon."

Mike felt his stomach drop. His body became instantly heavy, like it wanted to tip sideways off his chair and drop to the floor. He was filled with a bleak certainty that he knew what Gordie was about to say. What else could have gotten the man so upset?

He instinctively shoved the chair out with the backs of his calves and stood. "What about Sharon, Gordie? Tell me right now."

"Chief, she's…she's gone."

His blood turned to ice. "Gone? What do you mean, gone?"

"I tried to raise her a little while ago on the radio, you know, to keep tabs on her like you asked me to do, but there was no answer. I tried multiple times with no response and then tracked her via the cruiser's GPS unit. She was out on old Fire Road 17N."

"Okay. So?" Mike realized he'd started breathing heavily and forced himself to calm down until he could get to the bottom of this disturbing call. It wasn't easy. *Sharon is gone.*

"Well I sent Harley to check up on her, and when he got there…"

"What happened when he got there? Jesus Christ, Gordie, tell me what's going on or I swear this will be the last day you ever work for the town of Paskagankee."

"She's dead, Chief."

"Dead? What do you mean, dead? How could she be dead? What happened to her?"

"Harley got to the fire road within ten minutes. He says when he arrived she was laid out sideways across the front seat of her vehicle. She wasn't moving. He popped the locks and began assessing her condition, and she was unconscious and unresponsive. No pulse. No heartbeat. He attempted CPR and called for an ambulance, but…"

Mike had begun pacing behind the table as he listened to Gordie Rheaume describe the death—*Sharon is gone*—of his wife and lover. Other restaurant patrons were watching him warily and he didn't care. Professor Paquette's eyes were locked onto him and he didn't care. He could barely breathe and he didn't care about that, either.

"I don't understand," Mike heard himself say into the phone.

His voice sounded like someone else's. Someone who was frightened and lost. "She was alone inside a locked cruiser? How did she die? What injuries did she sustain? Tell me something that makes sense, goddammit!"

"There was no indication of any kind of injury, Chief. No bullet wounds, no stab wounds, no respiratory distress. No sign of a struggle. Nothing. She's just…"

Gone.

"Physically fit police officers in their mid twenties don't just keel over dead without obvious injuries, Gordie. That's ridiculous. Impossible. I'm not buying it."

"I'm sorry, Chief. I don't understand it, either. I'm just telling you what I know. I'm so sorry," he said again.

Mike realized the elderly dispatcher had begun to cry. That, more than anything the man had said, brought the significance—the reality—of his words home in a way nothing else could have.

His world was crashing down around him every bit as thoroughly as if *Mr. Moose's* roof had caved in.

Sharon is gone.

Sharon is gone.

Oh God, Sharon is gone.

"I'll be back in Paskagankee as soon as I can." He mumbled the words into the phone and could barely hear himself speak over the insistent buzzing coming from inside his head.

Sharon is gone.

"Chief, her remains are on the way to the medical examiner's office."

"I'll go straight there, then. Thanks, Gordie."

Rheaume said something else that Mike couldn't make out. He stabbed at the "End Call" button and took three tries before he could manage to disconnect.

"I-I've got to go," he heard himself say to Professor Paquette. "I've got to go."

He began stumbling toward *Mister Moose's* front door. Behind him, Paquette was saying something about him being in no condition to drive, and he had to agree with that assessment.

But it was irrelevant.

Everything was irrelevant.

He had to get to Sharon.

Sharon is gone.

25

Mike was driving by instinct, on autopilot, letting his eyes guide his hands on the steering wheel without the benefit of conscious thought.

There was too much else to occupy his tortured brain.

Sharon is gone.

This was his fault. He'd sent his wife out looking for a demonic entity, essentially acting as bait, telling her to scour the most remote areas of Paskagankee, to find and apprehend a young man who was no longer a young man at all, but a destructive mass of supernatural malevolence.

Of chaos.

Of evil.

Sharon is gone.

He dug his fingers into the wheel, gripping it with such force it seemed the damned thing would crumble in his hands. He glanced down and his knuckles were white, and he forced himself to loosen his grip and to breathe, although why he was worrying about something so trivial as breathing while Sharon lay dead en route to a date with the coroner was beyond him.

He was driving much too fast for a man whose vision was blurred by tears, but he didn't care. He blinked his eyes clear, more or less, swiped the salty evidence of regret off his cheeks and forced the accelerator even closer to the firewall. Siren blaring, blue lights flashing. Cars and trucks pulling hurriedly to the side of the road to allow the police cruiser to pass.

He had to get to Sharon.

Sharon is gone.

He had to get to his wife, to see her lifeless body lying on the gurney or perhaps the medical examiner's autopsy table, to torture his black spirit with the knowledge that he'd killed her himself, just as surely as if he'd put a gun to her head and pulled the trigger.

He came to a traffic signal, one of only a couple in the desolate stretch of mostly empty forested land between Bowdoin and Paskagankee, and began to slow. A line of three or four cars was stopped for the red light and as their drivers looked in their rear view mirrors and spotted the approaching cruiser the cars edged to the right, toward the side of the road.

Mike checked for oncoming traffic. There was none. He glanced quickly at both sides of the crossroad and could see no cars. He yanked the wheel left and hit the gas again and the Explorer roared through the intersection, reaching his previous speed in seconds.

And then he was through the intersection.

And then his phone rang.

Again.

26

He spat out a curse and glanced at the call screen, tearing his eyes from the road for a split-second.

It was Professor Paquette.

Ignore the call. You just saw him and you have more pressing matters to worry about right now.

The phone jangled, the sound somehow a pointed finger, a chanted indictment, an accusation of complicity in the death of his wife.

It rang twice, three times, and Mike knew one more ring would take the call to voice mail. That was exactly what he wanted to happen. But without knowing why, he reached down and plucked the damned phone out of his pocket, and before it could ring again he punched the green button and answered the call.

"This is not a good time, Professor."

"I know, Chief, and I'm sorry to...uh...disturb you. But you left the grimoire here upon your sudden departure, and—"

"I'm sorry about that. Uh, I'll make arrangements to have an officer drive down and pick it up later this afternoon." He wanted to scream at the professor, to tell him he didn't give a damn about the grimoire, that he didn't care if he never set eyes on it again, that his wife was dead and his world was crumbling before his eyes.

But of course Professor Paquette would have no reason to know what was wrong, and he was just trying to be helpful anyway. So Mike bit his tongue and made his offer to have the book retrieved, and then he shut his mouth and waited for the man to get the hell off the line.

But he didn't get off the line.

"No, Chief, you misunderstand. That's not why I called. I know this is a very bad time and I'm not sure exactly how to say this, but I feel it may be extremely important."

"Important? How important?"

"Life and death important, potentially."

Mike ran a hand through his hair and tried to control his building grief. "What is it, professor?"

"Well, I wasn't trying to eavesdrop, really, but I couldn't help but overhear your end of the phone conversation when you took the call just prior to leaving *Mr. Moose*."

"Then you know we're dealing with a very serious situation in Paskagankee and I really don't have time for other things at the moment."

"I know from your end of the conversation that someone is dead, presumably a police officer. I know the deceased officer is named Sharon. I also live in Paskagankee and am somewhat aware of local gossip."

"Meaning?"

"Meaning I know the chief of police is living with one of his officers, a young woman named Sharon."

Mike's eyes filled with tears—again—and again he swiped them away.

"We just got married a couple of days ago," he whispered.

"I'm so very sorry, chief," Professor Paquette said. "And I wouldn't interrupt at such a horrific moment if I didn't feel this call was of the utmost importance. Life and death, as I mentioned a moment ago."

"We've had more than our share of death, so go ahead. What is it?"

"Well, again, I wasn't trying to eavesdrop, but I got the very strong impression listening to you talk on the phone that your officer...uh, excuse me, your wife...was found unresponsive in her patrol unit, dead but with no sign of apparent injury or even of a struggle."

"That's what I was told, yes." He had to wipe more tears away and was aware he'd gradually begun increasing speed as he talked with Professor Paquette, until now the grey/green Great North

Woods were no more than a blur outside the Explorer.

"Well, as you spoke on the phone I flipped through the grimoire and have been scanning its pages since you left, and—"

"I already told you, professor, I'll have someone drive down and pick up the book."

"Oh, I'm not complaining about you forgetting the grimoire, Chief McMahon. Quite the opposite. I could very happily retain this rare artifact in my possession forever, or at least until it made its way back via the curse to the bloodline to which it is inexorably attached."

"So why are we talking about it again, given what you know about the…situation in Paskagankee?"

"Because, Chief, as I scanned the pages of the grimoire, I came upon one of the more esoteric conjurations contained in its pages, a spell that I believe may be directly related to your current situation."

"In English, please, Professor. As you might imagine, my deductive abilities aren't exactly at their best right now."

"Of course. In English, then: I believe your wife may not be dead at all, Chief McMahon."

27

Silence.

Mike had literally no idea how to respond.

Professor Paquette seemed to recognize his confusion and waited without speaking for Mike to absorb his words.

"Professor, one of my own officers, a man trained in CPR and emergency medical care, reported no detectable pulse or heartbeat. His diagnosis was confirmed by the ambulance crew, which arrived at the scene minutes later. No heartbeat and no pulse, Professor. I'm not sure there's any other way to interpret that information than that the patient is deceased."

"And maybe she is. Hell, *probably* she is. But don't you wish to explore *every possible avenue* before giving up hope?"

"Of course I do!" Mike exploded. "But how can there be hope?"

"Because contained inside the grimoire's pages is a conjuration designed to mimic the signs of death in a subject but leave that subject very much alive. And the spell could be cast from the outside, into a locked vehicle."

Mike's breath caught in his throat. "What are you saying?"

"I'm saying if this kind of spell exists in a grimoire, is it such a stretch to believe a demonic entity would have that ability as well?"

Mike realized he'd unconsciously taken his foot off the gas as he listened to the professor's impossible words. The Explorer was now creeping along Route 24 at a pace barely faster than a brisk jog. After the extreme speed of the last few minutes, the pace was disorienting.

Or maybe it was the news that Sharon might still be alive.

28

Sharon was paralyzed.

And she was afraid. She was more afraid than she'd ever been in her life. More terrified than when she was a teenage alcohol and drug abuser. More terrified even than when she lay on the floor of a filthy cabin with two broken arms and a concussion surrounded by corpses and human body parts, certain she was going to die a horrific death.

She was so afraid because she was fully, completely, utterly aware of her situation.

And her situation was dire.

When she'd lost consciousness from the excruciating pain in her skull, it had only been for the briefest of moments. The darkness fell and her eyes closed and her consciousness drifted away, but in a matter of a second, or maybe two, she'd reawakened.

The pain had vanished, and so had Jake Beebe. But she'd been paralyzed, unable to move so much as a single muscle. Unable to reach for her gun, which was poking her uncomfortably in the ribs.

Unable to sit up.

Unable even to blink, a sensation that was as disconcerting as anything she'd ever experienced.

She wasn't sure how long she lay in her cruiser, as helpless as a newborn baby, but eventually Harley appeared in her peripheral vision just outside the cruiser. He broke in and examined her and she'd wanted *so badly* to tell him she knew he was there, and she needed his help desperately, and to please not let her die like this.

But of course she hadn't been able to tell him anything of the sort. She hadn't been able to do or say anything. All she could do was lie there as he muttered "Holy shit, holy shit, holy shit," over and over while feeling for a pulse and a heartbeat.

She watched, again in her peripheral vision since she had no more ability to move her eyes than any other part of her body, as Harley backed out of her cruiser. He smacked the back of his head on her doorframe and swore harshly before calling for backup and an ambulance.

"Officer down," he'd said multiple times, a phrase Sharon had never heard other than in the movies, and his voice had been strained and frightened as he said it.

But as frightened as he obviously was, he couldn't possibly be as scared as she.

After calling for help, Harley slipped back inside Sharon's cruiser and began CPR, unaware her heart continued to beat and her lungs continued to move air, albeit very, very slowly.

Imperceptibly.

It was as if her body had fallen into a state of suspended animation.

A short time later the ambulance arrived and she thought things would get better but they got much, much worse. An EMT took over for Harley, performing the same attempt at lifesaving CPR but more smoothly and efficiently.

And just as fruitlessly.

The medical guy listened for a heartbeat and was unable to find one, even with his stethoscope. He checked for a pulse and couldn't find one of those, either.

The ambulance crew huddled with Harley for a short but intense conversation. One of the EMTs asked Harley how long the deceased had been lying in her cruiser, and how long he'd been working on her before their arrival.

The deceased. That was how they phrased it.

Harley answered that he had no idea how long she'd been there. "It may have been as long as an hour or more," he said reluctantly.

Then he told them he'd worked on her from the time he arrived on the scene until the time they'd shown up. "Maybe fifteen minutes," he said. "I called for the ambulance almost immediately."

And the lead EMT responded with words that chilled Sharon to the bone: "With no pulse and no respiration, we have no choice but to consider her deceased. She's gone. I'm sorry."

"No way. No fucking way," Harley responded. "She's not dead."

But his boots crunched on the hard ground and his voice faded and it was clear he was walking away from the cruiser and the ambulance and the EMTs. A moment later Sharon heard Harley's emotional call to Gordie at the station, telling him the ambulance crew had arrived on-scene and Sharon was dead and they were about to take her away.

Meanwhile, the EMTs were busy removing one of those fold-up aluminum gurneys from the back of their rig and trundling it over to the cruiser. Sharon couldn't see them doing it, but she could hear them clearly enough. And she'd been on the scene of enough fatal car wrecks and hiking accidents and hunting tragedies as a responding officer to have no trouble picturing in her mind the exact steps the crew was taking.

The gurney rattled over the uneven ground and she heard it roll to a stop next to her cruiser. A stiff, heavy flapping sound followed, like a large canvas flag billowing in a stiff breeze.

Sharon understood the significance of that sound, too. It was unmistakable. The blood that had gone cold in her veins turned to ice.

She willed herself to move, to shout, to scream, "I'm alive, I'm breathing, I'm still here!" but nothing happened, nothing at all, the words echoing around inside her panicked head but finding no escape.

Outside the cruiser, the EMTs worked methodically. One of them unzipped the body bag and placed it on the ground while the other began removing Sharon from the cruiser.

It was cramped inside the Explorer, hard for the man to get leverage even though Sharon was small and the EMT much larger. He ended up basically dragging her body across the bench seat until he could place one arm under her knees and the other under her shoulders.

He nearly dropped her as he pulled her clear of the vehicle and immediately Harley's agitated voice came from right next to her, telling the ambulance guy to be more careful.

"She's one of us," he said. "You'll treat her with respect or I'm gonna kick your ass right here and now." Harley's voice was jagged and rough and she could tell he'd been crying, and even amidst her crippling fear she felt a stab of gratitude.

She'd never been particularly close to Harley Tanguay. He was a few years older than she, and their personalities had never really meshed, and even though he'd never aired his grievances in public she knew he'd been one of the officers most miffed about her developing a relationship with the new chief of police shortly after Mike's arrival in town.

The EMT mumbled an apology, but nothing Harley could do or say would change what came next. The second EMT helped lift Sharon into the body bag, and then they zipped it closed and placed it on the gurney.

With her inside.

Seconds later they arrived at the ambulance, and Sharon felt herself being slid into the rear of the idling vehicle like a drawer being pushed into a bureau. The gurney's metallic legs folded up and she slid to a stop and of course she could see nothing. But she could hear the diesel engine rumbling, and the rear ambulance doors slamming closed, and the muffled sound of voices outside as the EMTs huddled with Harley Tanguay.

Then two more doors closed at the front of the ambulance and the vehicle began to move. Somehow the driver managed a K-turn on the narrow fire road, and then they were bumping and lurching toward the medical examiner's office.

And an autopsy table.

And there was nothing Sharon could do to let anyone know she was alive.

And she'd never been so fucking scared.

29

Nothing he'd heard in his telephone conversation with Professor Paquette changed Mike's destination. The conversation changed his entire outlook on life, that much was true—Sharon might still be alive!—but he still needed to get to Northern Maine Regional Hospital as soon as possible.

If anything, a speedy arrival was even more critical now than it had been before. Because in the case of a suspicious death, an autopsy would be performed by County Medical Examiner Jan Affeldt, and there could scarcely be a case that would qualify as *more* suspicious than a young police officer dying inside a locked patrol vehicle with no obvious sign of trauma.

And northern Maine differed from the much more heavily populated suburban Boston area Mike had spent the first fifteen years of his law enforcement career in one very significant way: suspicious deaths were rare up here, relatively speaking. That difference meant the investigative delays typical of such cases in Revere, Massachusetts were not usually an issue in Paskagankee, Maine.

In other words, depending upon his schedule, it was entirely possible—likely, even—that ME Affeldt could begin his autopsy on Sharon sooner rather than later. Mike had had a number of run-ins with the medical examiner in the past, some involving the man's reluctance to perform his duties in what Mike considered a timely manner, and it wouldn't surprise Mike if Affeldt jumped right on this case. It was even possible he would cut into Sharon

233

this afternoon, just to make a point to his law enforcement nemesis.

So after hanging up with Professor Paquette, Mike hit the gas again, driving with only slightly less desperation than he'd been doing when he knew his wife to be dead. It was still entirely possible she *was* dead, but he'd been given at least a small glimmer of hope, a tiny pinprick of light at the end of a very dark tunnel, and he was determined to hold onto that glimmer until every last bit of it was extinguished.

And, really, was it so hard to believe the professor's theory might be true?

With all Mike had seen and experienced since his arrival in Paskagankee, he could no longer dismiss things he'd previously *known* to be impossible. Too much water had passed beneath that particular bridge to go back to the world as it used to be.

Ultimately, of course, all the evidence of supernatural activity he'd seen in Paskagankee paled in the face of one fact: Mike believed the professor's theory that Sharon might still be alive because he *needed* to believe it. He *needed* that possibility to cling to, *needed* to think the life he'd just begun with his soul mate hadn't already ended with the abruptness of an inexplicable death.

Maybe Sharon Dupont—now Sharon McMahon—really was dead. Maybe even now she lay lifeless and cold atop a stainless steel autopsy table awaiting Dr. Jan Affeldt's scalpel. Maybe Mike would never again kiss her lips or squeeze her butt or watch her brush her silky hair before bed.

Maybe.

Probably.

But he'd been given the gift of a second scenario, and he would cling to that scenario until the last possible moment. He would cling to it like a drowning man hanging on to a floating life preserver, and he would do so until seeing the evidence of the unthinkable alternative with his own two eyes.

He had no choice.

It was the only way to have the slightest chance of maintaining his sanity.

30

Mike almost but not quite ignored Jan Affeldt's administrative assistant.

The older woman was seated at her desk, which had been placed in the antechamber adjacent to the doorway into Affeldt's office like a sentry's post. Her head was lowered in concentration as she read a report, her frosted hair hanging like a curtain, obscuring any sign of her face.

Mike closed the door firmly behind him and the woman didn't even look up. "Please have a seat," she said in a bureaucratic monotone that would have been the envy of any gatekeeper to any CEO of any Fortune 500 company. "Is the doctor expecting you?"

Mike didn't answer.

He didn't take a seat.

He positioned himself in front of the desk and said, "My name is Mike McMahon. I'm chief of the Paskagankee Police Department and I'm here regarding one of my officers who should have been brought in for autopsy within the past hour."

The woman finally raised her eyes from her reading material. "Please have a seat," she repeated steadfastly. Mike wouldn't have thought it possible, but her tone seemed even frostier than her hair.

"Is the doctor expecting you?" Her eyes were flinty and her expression hard.

And Mike had had enough. He stepped around her desk. Pushed open the door to Affeld's inner sanctum.

Behind him the gatekeeper sputtered, "What do you think you're doing? You can't go in there!"

He closed the door as the woman continued to protest, her words becoming muffled and insubstantial but continuing unabated. Dr. Affeldt seemed unperturbed by the unannounced visit and unsurprised to see Mike. He met Mike's gaze, eyebrows raised, but said nothing.

The office door opened and the flustered assistant stepped inside. In the same sentence she offered effusive apologies to Affeldt for the intrusion and threatened to call hospital security on the unscheduled visitor.

"That won't be necessary," Affeldt said. "I have a few minutes available before beginning the autopsy on Officer Dupont and I'm more than happy to speak with Chief McMahon, even if his arrival was unexpected and unprofessional."

Affeldt's administrative assistant retreated without another word, skewering Mike with a glare as she pulled the door closed.

"Let me guess," Affeldt said without standing, shaking Mike's hand or offering any sort of preamble. "You're here because you wish to convince me your case is so important you need me to bypass normal protocols and move on it immediately. As if I haven't heard *that* from you before."

"No," Mike said simply.

"Well, let me assure you," the medical examiner began before stopping in mid-sentence. His expression betrayed his surprise. "What did you just say?"

"I said I don't want you to move Officer Dupont's autopsy to the front of the line. In fact, I'm asking just the opposite. I don't want you to go near her with a scalpel yet."

"Is that so?" Affeldt said.

"Yes, that's so."

"Well, this an unexpected, albeit refreshing, change. Typically you seem to think the events in your little jurisdiction should trump everything else happening every*where* else."

Affeldt eyed Mike, hostility evident in his expression. "However," he continued, "it just so happens that there *are* no cases ahead of Officer Dupont's unfortunate demise at the moment. I have the time available on my schedule, so the autopsy will be performed this afternoon."

"I just told you I'd like you to hold off on that," Mike said. He returned Affeldt's hostile gaze with one of his own.

"And why would I do that?"

"Because she may not be dead."

The county medical examiner was a tall man with a thin face and a hawkish nose, and greyish skin tone that made him appear cadaverous at the best of times, of which this was not one. He sat back and stared at Mike, his hostile expression becoming instead one of incredulous disbelief.

"Excuse me?"

"I said I believe my officer may not be dead."

"I heard what you said, Chief McMahon, I'm just having trouble comprehending your words. Your own responding officer was unable to detect any signs of life in the victim. The ambulance crew that transported Officer Dupont to Northern Maine Regional had no better luck than your officer. And I personally examined the victim upon her arrival here less than forty-five minutes ago."

The ME stared unblinkingly at Mike before continuing. "She's dead, Chief McMahon. I'm sorry to say it, and please accept my condolences at losing your officer, but she is most assuredly dead. And I'm frankly surprised, given the lack of any apparent *cause* of death, that you're not here demanding I get to the bottom of the mystery ASAP, as you've done so often in the past."

"I want to see the body before the autopsy," Mike insisted. If Affeldt had already examined Sharon, trying to convince him she wasn't really dead would be pointless. His only hope was to get inside the autopsy lab before the man could slice her open from neck to navel.

Once inside the lab, it would then become necessary to find some way to delay the inevitable, to stall Affeldt's autopsy, but he would think of something. He had to.

First things first, though. He couldn't save Sharon until he was able to get to her. He was well familiar with the location of the lab in which Dr. Affeldt performed his autopsies, and had briefly considered going straight there, bypassing Affeldt's office entirely. But a lifetime of police work had meant a lifetime of adjudicating administrative disputes, and he knew things would proceed much more smoothly if he could operate with the approval of the man in charge.

Affelldt continued to stare at him, a quizzical look on his face. Finally he said, "Why?"

"Excuse me?"

"Why do you want to see Officer Dupont?"

"Maybe you're unaware," Mike said. "But I'm in a relationship with Officer Dupont. In fact, we were married this past weekend."

He suspected Affeldt knew all about his relationship with Sharon, but that the sadistic bastard wanted to put him through the wringer as some kind of sick payback for their previous run-ins. Fine. If that's the way he wanted to play it, Mike couldn't care less. His only goal was getting to Sharon.

"Is that so?"

"Yes, that's so. And I want to see my wife before the autopsy. Alone. Surely you don't intend to deny a grieving husband the chance to say goodbye to his wife."

"That's what funerals are for, Chief."

"I've just about had it, Doctor. Either you're going to allow me to see my wife before the autopsy, or my next move will be to call Melissa Mannheim at the *Portland Journal*. I'm sure her readers would be interested to learn how uncooperative you're being, not just with a grieving husband, but with a law enforcement officer making a legitimate request."

Affeldt smiled blandly. "While I don't appreciate being threatened," he said, "and while I seriously doubt there's anything your precious newspaper reporter could write that would endanger my standing as county medical examiner, I will of course allow you the opportunity to spend a few minutes with your deceased wife, Chief."

His eyes narrowed and he glared at Mike from behind his desk before continuing. "A *very* few minutes. And as far as delaying the autopsy because you seem to have some hare-brained notion your dead wife is somehow alive, you can forget it. *I* do the scheduling in this department, not some hick cop. The autopsy will proceed as scheduled."

31

The stillness of the autopsy lab was the worst, much worse even than riding to the hospital in the back of an ambulance while zipped into a body bag.

The relentless silence.

The coolness of the lab table Sharon was unable to feel on her skin but that she knew she should.

The chemical odor she *could* smell, a scent that couldn't quite overcome the stench of blood and bodily fluids and decaying flesh.

The knowledge that she was soon to be sliced open from breastbone to pubic bone, laid bare before the medical examiner. He would assume he was determining her cause of death but would unwittingly *become* her cause of death.

She knew it was happening soon because Dr. Affeldt had already done a cursory examination, muttering under his breath as he poked and prodded about the utter lack of apparent injury to a young and healthy woman. He'd dictated a few notes into a microphone suspended from the ceiling, and while doing so had mentioned his desire to complete the autopsy today.

This afternoon.

Within the hour.

Then he'd departed the lab, along with his assistant, and the silence had once again descended.

And Sharon was left, paralyzed and alone, with only her silent terror for company.

32

Mike texted directions from the visitor parking lot to the autopsy lab to Professor Paquette the moment he left Dr. Affeldt's office. The professor should be arriving at Northern Maine Regional soon, and Mike didn't want him drawing any more attention to himself than was absolutely necessary.

A stranger asking directions to the morgue would not accomplish that goal. If hospital administrators were to learn a professor of the occult from Bowdoin College was not just inside their facility but sniffing around dead people, Mike was pretty sure that would draw the wrong sort of attention.

And quickly.

He approached the lab's frosted-glass doorway and pressed a blue button next to the door. A muffled buzzer sounded from inside, and after a momentary delay a voice floated out of a tinny speaker mounted on the wall. "Yes?"

Mike had done this song and dance many times, and he lifted his badge, displaying it to a CCTV camera positioned above the door.

"Chief Mike McMahon," he said into the speaker. "I've been approved for entry by ME Jan Affeldt." As he spoke, he felt a presence approaching from the left, and he glanced up to see Professor Paquette hurrying down the hallway with an equipment bag slung over one shoulder.

The buzzing of the lock coincided with Paquette's arrival, and as the automatic door swung open both men stepped inside. Mike led the way to a reception desk, behind which a youngish-looking bearded man dressed in blue scrubs regarded them suspiciously. Mike had seen the man before and he nodded a greeting, flashing a smile in an effort to ward off what he knew was coming.

It didn't work.

The man nodded at Professor Paquette and said, "Who's this?"

"An expert I've enlisted from Bowdoin College down in Brunswick. His name is Professor Brian Paquette and he's here to assist me in an investigation."

Paquette stuck his hand out and the lab technician took it reluctantly. He squinted at the equipment bag and said, "An expert in what, camping?"

Paquette chuckled and started to answer and Mike cut him off. "He's working with me on a case regarding a missing teen up in Paskagankee."

"Uh…okay. So why are you here and not in Paskagankee?"

Mike was beginning to lose what little patience he had left. All he cared about was getting into the lab to see Sharon.

"It's related to the case," he said firmly. And gruffly. "We've been cleared into the lab and that's where we're going."

He pushed past the man and stalked toward the lab door.

"Wait a second," the tech said. "That's not true."

Mike turned and spread his hands impatiently. "What's not true?"

"Affeldt cleared *you* to enter," he said. "The doctor didn't say anything about any Bowdoin professor."

"Then that's his mistake," Mike shot back. "Call him and clear it up. In the meantime, we have work to do." He entered the lab with Paquette on his heels as the technician reached for a phone hanging on the wall.

The swinging doors closed behind them and Paquette said, "How much time do we have? It seems pretty obvious that guy Affeldt knows nothing about me, and I assume he'll tell Mr. Gatekeeper out there exactly that."

Mike shook his head. "I don't know, but probably not much. Affeldt and I have a history and it's not a good one. He's not likely to cut me much slack beyond what he's already done, so you'd better get started."

"Where is she?"

Mike took a good look around the autopsy lab for the first time since their hurried entrance and his heart broke. His mouth dried up and he struggled to breathe and he nodded at the three stainless steel autopsy tables located in the center of the large room.

His wife lay still and silent on the middle one. She was clothed in her uniform, and for that Mike was grateful. He'd been afraid they would find her naked in preparation for the upcoming autopsy, a standard and obviously necessary part of the procedure, but one that under the circumstance seemed a gross violation.

Apparently, though, the technician hadn't yet gotten to that point in the prep process.

Mike approached the table and reached for Sharon's hand, dimly aware of Professor Paquette dropping his equipment bag onto the table next to Sharon's and then unzipping it and beginning to remove various items, including the grimoire. He knew he should be helping the professor, or at least offering his assistance, but he felt numb and ineffectual, slow, like he was wading through chest-deep water.

He knew exactly the reason for the semi-paralysis, although knowing the reason did nothing to alleviate the pain. He'd seen dozens of bodies lying on dozens of autopsy tables exactly like this one over the course of his career, and had felt confident that he was as prepared to deal with whatever he might find in here as he could be.

But none of those dozens of bodies had ever been the woman he loved. None had been the woman he undressed at night, the woman whose hair he stroked while she lay with her head in his lap watching television, the woman whose hopes and dreams and fears he'd shared in the three a.m. darkness of their bedroom.

Seeing her here was like getting kicked in the stomach by a mule. It was worse. It was the emotional equivalent of having his limbs removed, one by one, with a rusty saw and no anesthesia. He'd never felt anything this intense, this unrelenting, this...desolate.

He reached for one of her hands and took it in his. It was cool, lifeless, and he instantly understood how Harley, the ambulance crew and even Dr. Affeldt himself had been so readily fooled into thinking she was dead.

Unless…

He tore his eyes away from Sharon and turned toward Professor Paquette. "Are you sure she's really alive?"

"No," he said simply, without slowing his preparations. "I'm not sure of anything. I'm taking a leap of faith, here, Chief McMahon, that the things inside this book," he nodded in the direction of the grimoire, which he'd placed face-up next to the equipment bag on the autopsy table, "the things I've spent my entire academic career studying, are, in fact, real, and not just the millennia-old products of philosophers with decidedly dark personalities."

Now the professor stopped what he was doing and met Mike's eyes. His gaze was direct and penetrating.

"And I suggest you do the same."

33

None of what Professor Paquette was doing seemed to make much sense to Mike.

He removed a package of colored chalk from his bag, tore it open, and, working quickly, drew a red circle around Sharon. He then fashioned a pentagram, converging all of the lines toward the center of the circle, where Sharon lay still and cold atop the autopsy table.

Then he removed a compass from the equipment bag and gazed at it intently before drawing the cardinal compass points—N, E, S, and W—next to four of the pentagram points. That done, Paquette knelt and drew four bizarre animals similar to the disturbing renderings Mike had seen inside the pages of the grimoire.

Within three minutes the circle, the pentagram and the related drawings were complete.

Mike didn't think he'd ever seen anyone work so fast. It was like watching a talented street artist. He shook his head in amazement. "How the hell were you able to draw those freakish animals from memory?"

"A lifetime of study, remember?" Paquette muttered as he tossed the chalk aside. He stood and lifted a large butcher knife from the bag and in an act that appeared ceremonial, dragged the tip around the outer edge of the circle, and then in a similar fashion traced the outline of the pentagram in the interior.

He replaced the knife in the equipment bag and withdrew a series of tapered candles, each maybe four inches in height and set in identical brass candleholders. The holders were ornate and had been polished to a brilliant amber glow. The professor moved around the circle, placing the candles at more or less equidistant locations along its circumference.

Then he fumbled in his pocket for a lighter. He flicked it on and touched it to each candle before extinguishing the lighter and dropping it back into his pocket.

It had still been no more than five minutes since Mike and Professor Paquette entered the autopsy lab, but Mike could feel the time running out, and Sharon was no closer to showing any signs of life than she had been upon their entrance.

For the first time since beginning his preparations for the satanic ritual to come, the professor stepped back and consulted the grimoire. He buried his head in the text for what felt to Mike like an eternity, and then lifted his eyes from the book and began to speak.

The professor spread his arms wide, chanting words that sounded vaguely prayer-like. Some of the words were in English and some were not, and then it sounded like Paquette repeated a series of names, none of which Mike had ever heard before and all of which carried a definite Old Testament feel.

The temperature inside the autopsy lab was dropping. It had started out cool and now the lab began to feel like the inside of a restaurant freezer. Mike glanced down at his arms and saw they were covered in goose bumps.

And the candles were changing. Their flames lengthened, flickering wildly, as though a stiff breeze had begun blowing, which was ridiculous because the lab was buried deep inside the hospital and featured no exterior windows. The yellow of the flames darkened and began to turn red, in seconds becoming the deep crimson of arterial flow.

Professor Paquette continued to chant and his voice deepened, his tone intensifying, becoming insistent. He reminded Mike of a particularly dedicated preacher.

The flames climbed higher and higher, reaching for the ceiling, turning an even deeper shade of red. Mike had clutched Sharon's hand the moment the professor's ritual started, and throughout it her touch remained cool and unresponsive.

But now, as the man's words reached a fever pitch, he felt a finger twitch.

It wasn't much, and for the briefest of moments Mike thought he might have imagined it.

Then it twitched again, and that twitch was followed by another, as a different finger pressed lightly against Mike's palm, and then a shudder rippled through Sharon's body and her eyelids fluttered, and Mike felt a rush of the most intense emotion he'd ever experienced.

And the lab doors burst open.

Medical Examiner Jan Affeldt rushed into the room and then skidded to a stop. He froze, a look of shocked disbelief etched onto his features.

Then he screamed, "Just what in the holy hell is going on here?"

Professor Paquette stopped chanting, his concentration broken, and Sharon's hand and eyelids fell instantly still.

Mike placed Sharon's hand gently onto her belly and stepped around the now-guttering candle flames and out of the circular pentagram. He stabbed a finger into Professor Paquette's chest and said, "No matter what happens here, you keep going, do you understand me?"

The professor nodded and resumed his strange chanting, and instantly the blood-red flames leapt once again toward the ceiling.

Mike approached the medical examiner, who seemed to have recovered, if only slightly, from his shock.

Affeldt looked from Professor Paquette to Sharon on the autopsy table, to Mike and then back to Paquette. "Whatever you think you're doing, I insist you stop it right now!"

"We're almost done," Mike said. He reached for the ME's elbow to lead him out of the lab, and Affeldt yanked it out of Mike's grasp.

"You're going to prison," Affeldt said. His face was red and furious with righteous indignation, and as he spoke, spittle sprayed into the air and dripped down his chin. "Both of you are going to jail for a long goddamned time, I'll make sure of it. And if it's the last thing I do, you'll never work in law enforcement again."

"Just wait a minute, Doctor, and—"

"I will *not* wait a minute. I will not wait even another *second.* Do you hear me, Chief McMahon? I'm calling hospital security and the state police, and *you're* going straight to jail."

Affeldt began backing away from Mike, edging toward the lab's swinging double doors. Then he stopped, frozen in place for the second time in less than a minute as he stared unblinkingly across the lab. His face had turned sickly pale and he looked as though he might be sick.

Mike followed his gaze and his heart soared.

Sharon Dupont was climbing off the autopsy table.

34

She looked none the worse for wear.

She looked every bit as vital and healthy as she had standing in their kitchen this morning.

She looked like herself.

The ambulance crew had left the top few buttons of her uniform shirt unfastened after working on her, or perhaps it had been Dr. Affeldt earlier this afternoon, and now she self-consciously buttoned her blouse as she crossed the lab toward Mike and Dr. Affeldt.

Professor Paquette had gone silent. He leaned against the second autopsy table, sweaty and shaking. He looked exhausted.

The flames were no longer crimson-colored and spiking several feet in the air. They'd returned to the typical length and coloring expected of four-inch tapered candle wax, and now Paquette staggered forward and began extinguishing them, then picking them up and dropping them into his bag.

Sharon reached Mike and he wrapped his arms around her, and she was warm and alive and shaking like a leaf.

"I knew you'd save me," she said into his chest. "I knew you'd save me. I knew you'd come. " She kept repeating the words like one of Paquette's mantras and Mike squeezed his wife so hard he began to fear he might crack a rib.

He eased off a little and she shook her head violently.

"Harder," she said. "I need to feel your arms around me."

Mike knew he was experiencing a moment that would be

burned indelibly into his memory for the rest of his life. He'd lost his wife and gotten her back, and he never wanted to let go of her again.

From next to him came Dr. Jan Affeldt's shaking voice. "You stop what you're doing," the medical examiner said, pointing in the direction of Professor Paquette.

The professor ignored him and continued to retrieve candles and drop them into his bag.

"Leave everything where it is, that's all evidence!"

Paquette ignored him again.

"I'm calling the police," Affeldt said, turning his attention to Mike. "You're leaving this hospital in handcuffs, all of you."

Mike spun on his heels. "I *am* the police."

"I'm talking about the state police," Affeldt spat. *"Real* police. Police that will take…whatever just went on here seriously."

The medical examiner took a step toward the door.

"You might want to think twice about that, Doctor."

The ME stopped. Turned slowly. He glared at Mike with unreserved hatred. "What the *hell* are you talking about?"

"Sure, the professor and I will go to jail. Maybe. For a short time. But if you call the state police, guess what happens then?"

Affeldt stared.

Opened his mouth.

Closed it.

"When the staties get here," Mike said, "I'll start talking, and once that happens you'll lose everything. Your career will be gone in the blink of an eye. You'll never practice medicine again."

Affeldt's face flushed crimson. It rivaled the deep red of the candles just a few moments ago. He stepped toward Mike, his entire body shaking with fury.

"I'll lose my career? How in the hell do you figure that? *You're* the ones who came in here and desecrated this hospital with… whatever abomination went on. How could any of that reflect on *me?"*

"You're not thinking clearly, Doctor. You're too upset about the breach in hospital protocol to consider the big picture."

"Oh, really? Please, fill me in then. What's the big picture?"

"You told me yourself back in your office that you pronounced

Officer Dupont officially dead upon her arrival at Northern Maine Regional. Well, take a good look at her and tell me, as a trained medical professional. She look dead to you?"

Affedlt blinked twice, as if only now beginning to understand the implications of Mike's words. "But…she *was* dead. No heartbeat, no pulse. She wasn't breathing. No vitals. She was dead," he repeated firmly, as if to convince himself.

Mike leaned in and lowered his voice, speaking slowly for emphasis. "If you call the state police in here, or insist on prosecuting the professor and I for a relatively minor crime—I'm here to tell you the most you'll ever see stick is a charge of malicious mischief, with a suspended sentence for each of us—I'll start talking, and I won't stop until your career is in ruins. I'll go straight to the press and the Maine Medical Licensing Board. Would you like to guess what I'll tell them, Doctor?"

Mike held Affeldt's contemptuous gaze and waited for him to answer.

The man remained silent, so Mike continued. "I'll lay it all out for everyone, how you pronounced an obviously healthy woman dead. I'll emphasize that our only purpose in coming to this hospital was to prevent that obviously healthy woman, *the one you pronounced dead*, from being carved up in an unnecessary autopsy by our very own county medical examiner."

The lab had fallen deathly silent. Even Professor Paquette had stopped his cleanup efforts and was watching to see what would happen next.

"So you go right ahead and call the staties in here," Mike said. "And while you're at it, you can start doing a little outreach to local factories and warehouses, maybe set up a few job interviews, since you'll soon be unemployed and disgraced."

Affeldt had curled his hands into fists as Mike spoke, and he stood shaking with rage but still not speaking.

"Or," Mike said. "You can take the path of least resistance. Turn around and walk out of here and go back to your office. Allow us a few more minutes to finish cleaning the lab and getting the hell out of here, and nobody ever has to know about this little… incident. We certainly aren't about to tell anyone, isn't that right?"

Mike nodded in the direction of Sharon and Professor Paquette, both of whom shook their heads solemnly in response.

"That's not feasible," Affeldt said slowly, speaking through gritted teeth. "The ambulance crew knew the patient was dead. Hell, your own officer knew she was dead."

"Don't worry about my officer," Mike said. "I'll handle him. And as far as the EMTs go, use your imagination. Hell, with a little effort you can come out of this debacle looking like a hero."

"How in the world could that even be possible?"

"Think about it," Mike said. He was starting to believe they might actually get out of this. It was clear Affeldt wanted a way out, he was just too upset to find it.

"You were up in your office, reviewing Officer Dupont's situation. Something was bothering you about the case. Something didn't seem right, so you decided to take a second look. You examined the patient again and discovered that not only was Officer Dupont alive, you were able to revive her. Hell, you probably haven't had time to file the death certificate yet, so all you have to do is destroy it and no one ever has to know you pronounced her dead in the first place."

Affeldt continued to stare at Mike with anger and hatred, but now those emotions shared space with something else: thoughtful consideration.

"I'm no doctor," Mike continued, "but I'm sure you can come up with some medical scenario to explain the situation that will be plausible but also nonspecific enough that no one can really challenge it. Whatever you decide to say will be backed up by Officer Dupont without question."

Affeldt glanced at Sharon, who nodded. "Absolutely."

"That still doesn't solve the problem of the ambulance crew," Affeldt said quietly.

"Again, use your imagination. You're one of the most powerful men in this hospital. Throw your weight around a little, let the EMTs believe they made a mistake. Tell them Officer Dupont's heartbeat had slowed dramatically but that you were able to detect it with extra effort, and they should have been able to as well."

This time Affeldt actually nodded, and Mike knew he had him.

"Just don't go overboard," Mike said. "Don't punish the EMT crew, or we *will* speak out."

Affeldt sighed. He shook his head as some of his officious bureaucratic manner seemed to return. 'I don't know what went on in here this afternoon," he said, "and I don't want to know. I just want to be done with the lot of you."

The ME glanced at his watch and said, "You have fifteen minutes to finish up and get the hell out of here. I don't ever want to see any of you in my hospital again."

35

"How did you know you could bring her back?" Mike asked Professor Paquette.

They'd finished picking up the professor's supplies and then washed the chalk off the lab's ceramic tile floor, working quickly. Ten minutes after Mike's tense conversation with Doctor Affeldt, they had cleared out of Northern Maine Regional Hospital and hit the road.

Aside from an extremely suspicious look thrown at them by the lab tech they'd seen on the way in, no one seemed to pay them any attention.

Now they were seated at a roadside coffee shop halfway between Portland and Paskagankee. Coffee seemed an odd choice, given the nerve-wracking situation they'd all just been through, but a steaming cup sat on the table in front of each of them, and they sipped as they talked.

"I didn't," the professor admitted. "As you know, I wasn't even certain my theory was correct. For all I knew, Officer Dupont really *was* dead, and the cause of her death would become clear upon completion of the autopsy. But given the things I'd overheard during your phone call, the moment I saw the related item in the grimoire I knew I had to relay my suspicions to you."

"Thank God you did," Sharon said. "But what did the demon do to me, and how were you able to reverse it?"

Professor Paquette thought about it for a moment. "After Chief McMahon—"

"Mike, please," Mike interrupted.

"Excuse me?"

"I have a hard and fast rule. I insist that anyone who saves me or, in this case, the woman I love, from certain death call me by my first name."

The professor grinned. "Fair enough," he said. "After Mike received the phone call about your…death, I continued to flip through the pages of the grimoire. When I did, I came upon a section of the book devoted to what's called 'Illusionist Experiments.' Included among those experiments was one designed to make a live person appear dead. I made the obvious connection and called Chief Mc…uh, I mean I made the connection and called Mike."

"Thank God," Sharon said again.

"The problem," Paquette continued, "was that even if my theory was right, I had no idea whether I could reverse the spell using the grimoire."

"Why not?"

"It probably goes without saying that a grimoire is written for human use. Its sole purpose is to call forth demonic entities from the spirit world. Unfortunately, the young man who found this book did exactly that. Except he did so improperly, unleashing a demon now willing and able to spread its evil."

"I still don't follow," Mike said.

"Once set loose in the world, the demon needs no grimoire to cause chaos. It possesses its own awesome power, which it used to cast the illusionist spell on you. My concern was that such a spell cast by a demon might not be reversible using the griomoire's conjurations."

"So we lucked out."

"Exactly."

"But that begs another question," Mike said. "Why would the demon bother to make Sharon *appear* dead, when it seems patently obvious it could simply have killed her and made her *be* dead for real?"

"I think I can answer that one," Sharon said, her voice still shaky. "If the demon's goal is to cause pain and misery, if it gets off on tormenting human beings, then what it did to me makes perfect sense."

"Not to me," Mike said.

Even Professor Paquette looked mystified, his forehead wrinkled and his mouth drawn into a frown.

"Think about it." Sharon's voice sounded a little stronger. "Even though I appeared dead, to the ambulance crew and even to a medical professional with decades of experience like Doctor Affeldt, I was fully aware of everything going on around me. From the moment Jake Beebe—or rather, the demon inside Jake—cast the spell, to the moment I regained the ability to move and sat up on the autopsy table at Northern Maine Regional, I could hear every word spoken around me."

"Wait a minute." Mike stared at her in horror. "You were conscious?"

"Yes. I heard the ambulance crew discussing how long I may have been lying deceased inside my cruiser before Harley's arrival. I heard Dr. Affeldt declare me dead when we got to the hospital. I heard Affeldt tell his assistant to prep my body for autopsy. I heard it all."

"Oh my God," Mike said. His heart broke for his wife's suffering. "Your level of terror must have been off the charts. Lying on the autopsy table, helpless and alone, knowing at any moment Doctor Affeldt could enter the lab with a scalpel..."

"But I wasn't alone," she said quietly. "You were with me the entire time. And I won't try to make you believe I wasn't terrified, but I also knew in my heart that you'd come for me. I knew you'd figure something out. I just knew."

There was no way to respond. Mike wasn't about to tell her that it was nothing more than the sheerest form of random luck that had saved her, that if he'd been anywhere other than with Professor Paquette when the call had come in to his cell phone, she would even now be getting sliced open by the county medical examiner.

They stared at each other. Mike had felt the blood drain from his face as Sharon described her situation, and he felt once again washed-out and ill thinking about how close he'd come to losing her.

"You're right," Professor Paquette said. "It all makes perfect sense now, why the demon would have done this instead of just killing you."

Mike forced his mind back to the coffee shop. "I'm not at my best right now, and I'm sorry but I still don't get it. Explain it to me."

"I think we can all agree the demon's goal is to inflict pain and suffering, correct?"

"That's putting it mildly," Mike said drily.

"And given the entity's obsession with torturing and causing that pain and suffering, what better way to accomplish that goal than to force its victim to live through the horror of knowing exactly the kind of agony that's coming?"

"And being able to do nothing to stop it," Sharon said, eyes wide and lips trembling.

"I see what you mean. But it's even worse than that," Mike said.

"What could possibly be worse?"

"The demon is evolving, adjusting its tactics to fit the reality of its situation."

"I don't follow," Sharon said.

"Well." Mike spoke slowly, puzzling it out it his head. "There's no indication the first victim, Lucie Dunn, was anything other than the unfortunate recipient of a violent attack. She was battered and beaten, yes. Brutally so. But the blood loss she sustained from having her head smashed against the blackboard, over and over, as awful as that is, gives the appearance of being nothing more than an act of extreme, uncontrolled rage."

"It was the exact opposite of the attack on me," Sharon said.

Professor Paquette nodded. "I see what you mean. The demon is refining its strategies."

For the first time since getting the call that Lucie Dunn had been killed at the high school, Mike truly began to realize the level of depravity they were facing.

He sipped his coffee. It tasted bitter against his tongue and sour in his stomach. When he set the cup down on the table it rattled loudly.

He looked from Sharon to Professor Paquette. Nobody seemed inclined to speak, so he said what everyone was thinking.

"And we have no idea where the demon is."

"Or how to stop it when we find it," Sharon finished.

36

"Are you sure you don't need to be checked out by a doctor?" Mike said.

The group had parted ways following thirty minutes spent discussing their situation at the roadside diner. The professor climbed into his Prius and turned east toward Bowdoin, while Mike and Sharon headed northwest to Paskagankee in his cruiser.

The nearly overwhelming sense of elation and relief Mike felt at discovering his wife alive and apparently none the worse for wear was offset by the realization of just how dire the situation was regarding Jake Beebe and the demonic spirit inhabiting his body.

The demon could be anywhere.

It could be wreaking havoc on an innocent victim right this very moment.

And even the expert who'd devoted his entire academic career to studying exactly this kind of scenario had just admitted he was clueless how to stop the carnage.

Professor Paquette had asked to retain the grimoire for a few days in order to study its pages in an effort to find something—anything—that might allow them to combat the demon, and Mike had readily agreed, despite the book's status as evidence in a criminal case. According to law enforcement protocol, the grimoire should be secured in an evidence locker at the Paskagankee Police station.

This wasn't a typical law enforcement case, however, and it wasn't going to be solved—if it even *could* be solved—via the usual law enforcement protocols. They needed to think outside the box, and Mike readily agreed to the professor's request, asking only that Paquette contact him immediately should he find anything useable inside the grimoire's pages.

But even as dire as the situation was, the focus of Mike's attention at the moment was his wife. The demon stalking Paskagankee would have to take a backseat to ensuring Sharon really was healthy and safe.

She'd ignored his question the first time he asked it so he tried again. "Sharon," he said sharply.

He waited. After a moment she turned and looked at him and only then did he continue. "I don't know the medical consequences of being, for all intents and purposes, dead for several hours, but it's hard to imagine your system would be unaffected by the trauma. I think you need to see a doctor."

"I feel fine," she said. "Seriously, I feel one hundred percent. Never better."

Mike couldn't quite hold her gaze, given the fact he was navigating the Explorer over the twisting backwoods route to Paskagankee, but he knew his skepticism must have been showing because she grinned and lifted her hand in the traditional three-finger Girl Scout salute.

"I swear," she said. "I'd tell you if I felt like something was wrong. Honestly. But the last thing I want to do right now is go back to the guy who was minutes away from slicing me open and cracking my ribcage apart like a turkey leg at Thanksgiving dinner."

"It doesn't have to be Affeldt," Mike said. "In fact, considering what we just did to the poor guy, it's probably best if we don't have anything to do with him for awhile."

"Or forever."

"Or forever. Although, given what I've seen of life in Paskagankee, I doubt we're done with the county medical examiner. But the point is you could always see a different doctor. You know, just for a quick tuneup, make sure your engine is running smoothly."

"My engine's just fine. I'll rev it up tonight and prove it to you. In the meantime, what I really want is to get back to work. I figure I owe the taxpayers an afternoon's worth of work since I spent the second half of today's shift lying down on the job."

Mike sighed. Trying to get Sharon Dupont...or McMahon... or whatever the hell they were going to call her now that they were married...to do anything she didn't want to do was like trying to wrestle a mountain lion barehanded: you knew it was going to be impossible to begin with and the end results were worse than you expected.

He sighed again and Sharon laughed. "Jeez," she said. "Maybe *you're* the one who needs a doctor."

"You're not the only one who almost died today," Mike said softly. "I can face anything, including a rogue demon, with you by my side. But if I had to do it alone I'd be lost, babe. Don't ever do that to me again."

She reached across the seat and took his hand and he squeezed hard.

"Dude," she gasped. "If you break my fingers you'll just force me to kick your ass one-handed, and imagine how embarrassing *that* would be to explain to everybody at the station."

"Sorry about that," he said. He eased off on his grip bet didn't let go. "Promise me you'll tell me immediately if you start to feel sick or strange in any way."

He expected a wise-ass remark, something about her feeling something strange right now—him.

But she surprised him. She hesitated a moment and then nodded. "I promise."

Mike wheeled the Explorer into the police station lot, still uncertain of the next steps to take in the search for Jake Beebe. Obviously, single-person police patrols were now out of the question. The problem was he had no way of knowing whether a pair of officers per cruiser would be any more capable of defending themselves against the powers of a demon than Sharon had been.

But paired patrols might at least give the second officer a chance to radio for help while the first was being subdued by the demon. Unless of course the damned entity could immobilize more than one person at the same time.

Christ, he thought. *What a mess.*

Mike eased the cruiser to a stop in front of the station. He and Sharon exited the vehicle, both lost in their own thoughts, and he blinked in surprise at the sudden slamming of a car door in the parking lot. He hadn't noticed anyone driving in behind them.

He glanced back to see Julie Beebe hurrying toward them. Her hair was mussed and her appearance haggard, like someone who hadn't been sleeping well. He supposed that was probably the case, given what she knew—and what else she must suspect—about her twin brother.

Mike stopped and turned, and Sharon turned with him. They waited and a moment later the girl had caught up to them. She held a wool hat, fingering it distractedly. Mike doubted she even realized she was doing it.

"I'm sorry to bother you," she said, "but I didn't know who else to talk to."

"How long have you been sitting in the parking lot?" Mike said.

"Not too long. I called the station to speak with you and the man told me you had been out but would be back soon. So I decided just to drive here and wait."

"You should have gone inside. The officers on duty would have handled any problem for you."

The girl took a deep, shuddering breath and then blew it out. "After what happened at my house the other night, I really felt like I should speak with you two specifically."

"You understand we've been prohibited by your father from speaking to you without him present."

"I don't care about that."

"But we have to care about it," Mike said. "We have no choice."

"What if it was an emergency?"

Mike smiled thinly. He liked this girl. "An emergency situation changes everything."

"Fine. Then consider this an emergency."

"What's going on?" Sharon asked.

Julie started to speak and then stopped. Took a deep breath and blew it out.

"Is it your brother?" Sharon asked. "Have you seen him? Has he contacted you?"

Another deep breath.

"Not exactly," she said in a tone that made Mike immediately question the response.

"Let's get you inside," he said. "We can talk about whatever you need to tell us in my office."

37

Gordie Rheaume was still inside the station house chatting with night dispatcher Rob Cornell following shift change. A couple of officers were hanging around as well. All four sets of eyes tracked Mike and Sharon as they crossed the room with a teenage girl, moving toward Mike's office.

In a way, the appearance of Julie Beebe outside the station had worked to their advantage—for now, at least—because her presence prevented the men from rushing forward and demanding an explanation for Sharon Dupont's miraculous resurrection from the dead at Northern Maine Regional Hospital. Mike had discovered long ago that cops were every bit as prone to gossip and rumor mongering as any other group of people.

The small group filed into Mike's office, nobody speaking, and he closed the door behind them. Mike placed three seats in a semicircle in front of his desk. He settled into one and waited for Julie and Sharon to take the other two. He wasn't about to sit behind his desk; the last thing he wanted was to intimidate the teen when she was already plainly shaken.

"Okay," he said. "What can we do for you, Julie? You say you haven't been in contact with your brother, but I'm not entirely sure I believe you. We're here to help you in any way we can, but in order to do that we need to know what's going on."

"Thank you," she said. "I didn't know where else to turn. Even after seeing all that strange stuff Jake carved into the walls of his room, my parents don't believe Jake killed anyone or is any real trouble. They think he's just acting out, looking for attention and that he's being harassed by the police. They don't want to see the situation as it is, and they definitely don't want to hear anything about a book of spells, or about magic, or anything like that."

Mike wasn't surprised. He'd dealt with the town council and its leader, Van Beebe, for more than two years now. He'd found Beebe to be competent in his own way, but officious and brusque, unwilling to consider views outside his own narrow experience.

She shook her head. "Maybe this was a mistake."

She started to climb to her feet and Mike raised his hands in what he hoped was a placating manner. "Please, Julie, sit down. If your instinct was to come to us, then I don't see how you could be making a mistake. Talk to us for a couple of minutes, and if you still feel uncomfortable after that you can get up and leave then. We'll even have an officer accompany you so we know you arrive home safely."

She hesitated and then retook her seat. Reluctantly.

"Start at the beginning," Mike said, "and take your time. Just tell us what brought you here and we'll figure out how to deal with it."

"You won't believe me if I tell you."

Mike shared a quick glance with Sharon and then said, "You might be surprised. I've seen a lot of things most people wouldn't believe since moving here, Julie."

She pursed her lips and then blurted out, "Okay fine. Yes, I've been communicating with Jake."

"So you've seen him?"

"No. Um…not exactly."

"What does that mean?"

"He's been coming to me in my dreams, Chief McMahon. He's been talking to me while I sleep. And he's terrified."

38

"He's been speaking to you in your dreams?" Mike sat back and scratched his head. He'd thought he was prepared to hear anything, but this was…unexpected.

Sharon nodded. "It's the twin thing," she said.

"What does that mean?" Mike asked.

She ignored him and leaned toward Julie. "I've heard about the invisible bond shared by twins. You've always been close to Jake, haven't you? I mean, closer than typical brothers and sisters."

"I suppose," Julie said. "Although I've never had anything to compare my relationship with Jake to, so it's always just felt normal to me. But even if that was the case, what's been happening since Jake disappeared is much…deeper…than that."

"He speaks to you in your dreams," Mike prompted. He wanted to refocus her, see where she was going with this bizarre conversation.

"Yes. It started the night Jake disappeared after falling out his bedroom window. The dream I had was hyper-realistic, although it was also very simple."

"Simple?"

"Yes. It consisted of nothing more than Jake's voice coming into my head and talking to me. That was it."

"Okay. And what was he saying?"

"He…" She took another deep breath and blew it out. It was obvious she was trying to work up the courage to continue.

"He said he's been…possessed. He said he was fooling around

267

with that stupid spell book, and that he took things too far, or something went wrong or whatever, and...and...a demon has taken over his body."

Mike glanced again at Sharon. It was a visceral reaction. Everything Julie was telling them fit perfectly with what they'd learned from Professor Paquette about the material contained inside the grimoire.

Julie saw the look pass between them and misunderstood. She said, "I knew you wouldn't believe me. I knew this was a mist—"

"No," Sharon interrupted. "It's not that we don't believe you. In fact, the reality is just the opposite. We *do* believe you. What you're telling us, Julie, is consistent with what we've learned so far in our investigation."

She left out the part about her terrifying face-to-face confrontation with the demon controlling Jake's body. It wasn't anything the boy's sister needed to hear.

"Please continue," she said.

"Well, that was the extent of the dream the first night. I woke up in a cold sweat, my heart racing. It took me forever to get back to sleep, but once I did I slept the rest of the night without hearing from Jake again, or even dreaming at all."

"But Jake returned the next night."

Julie nodded. "Oh yes. And he's come back every night since. He says he's tried to control the demon, to expel it from his body, but that it's too powerful. He says that for much of the time he's in control of himself, that the demon goes away, or recedes, or something, but that every time he thinks it's gone and tries to go for help, the demon regains control of his body and won't allow it."

Julie had started shaking. She stared at the floor and sniffled, and Sharon took her hand protectively. She held Julie's one hand between both of hers and waited quietly for the girl to continue.

After a long moment, she did. "Jake says he watched the demon kill Miss Dunn, and that it was horrible, and that he's sorry he ever messed around with the book of spells. He says he doesn't know what to do. He says he's afraid, and he needs help, and he *doesn't know what to do.*"

"Why didn't you come to us right away with this, Julie?'

"I thought I was going crazy that first night. Jake was gone and my parents were angry and upset and I was afraid and…I guess I didn't believe it was real. Like I said before, I thought I had had a really vivid dream or something. When Jake came back the next night I knew I wasn't dreaming, or rather that I *was* dreaming, but that Jake really was speaking to me. I didn't know what to do. I didn't think anybody would believe a story as crazy as mine."

"Trust me," Mike said. "You're not crazy. And I'm glad you came here today."

"Is there something you can do? Can you help Jake?"

"I don't know yet, but—"

"Has Jake ever come to you when you were awake? Like, say, at night before you've fallen asleep?" Sharon released Julie's hand and leaned back in her chair, staring intently at the girl.

"Um…yeah, I guess maybe, like when I was almost asleep but kind of in-between."

Mike squinted at Sharon. "What are you thinking?"

"I'm not sure yet. But, Julie, you said Jake told you that every time he tries to get help the demon wakes up, or jumps back into his body or whatever, and prevents him from doing so, correct?"

"That's what he told me, yes."

"And yet the demon doesn't seem to realize Jake can contact you while you sleep."

Julie shrugged. "Um, I guess not. Does that matter?"

"Maybe. Because if he was able to communicate with you while you were still awake, then theoretically it's a telepathic channel that could perhaps be reversed."

"I don't know. Maybe. Why?"

Sharon tucked a stray hair behind her ear and then nibbled on her lip. It was a subconscious act Mike had come to recognize, a sign that indicated either extreme stress or focused concentration.

Her forehead wrinkled and she stared out the window behind Mike's desk. He knew she wasn't seeing anything.

Eventually she said, "Here's what I'm thinking. If we can contact Jake and communicate with him via back channels, so to speak, maybe we can get him out of this mess."

"Really? How?" Julie said the words but they comprised an exact mirror of Mike's own thoughts.

"I'm still not sure," Sharon admitted. "Do you think you can try something for me?"

"If it will help Jake, of course I will."

"I want you to close your eyes and try to relax. Push all your worries about Jake away if you can and clear your mind."

"I'll try," she said. "But why are we doing this?"

"We're going to try to contact your brother."

39

Mike stood and circled his office, lowering the blinds lining the glass walls one by one until they'd all come down. Only Rob Cornell remained of the group that had been present in the station a little while ago, but Mike wanted to create a darkened cocoon in which to help the nervous girl relax.

Julie had closed her eyes at Sharon's suggestion, and as far as Mike could see she hadn't opened them since. Her posture, previously rigid and tense, gradually loosened and her breathing slowed and became drawn-out and regular. After ten minutes he almost thought she might have fallen asleep.

Only then did Sharon speak. "How are you feeling, Julie?"

"I'm fine," she said. The tone of her voice was lower and calmer than it had been while describing her frightening situation with Jake, but she was obviously conscious.

"Good," Sharon said. "Now, I want you to reach out with your mind to Jake. Send a feeler out and see if you can get him to respond to you. It doesn't even have to be with words. You're using your mind, not speaking verbally, so it can be a mental picture or even something as simple as a feeling that might get his attention."

"I'll...I'll try."

Silence again. Night was falling outside and with the lights off and the blinds drawn in the office the illumination was murky and insubstantial.

Five minutes passed with no activity and no talking.

Nothing.

Mike drew in a breath to ask Sharon—quietly—how long she planned to give Julie before conceding the experiment had failed, but before he could get the words out Julie stirred in her chair.

"It's working."

"You're in contact with him?" Sharon's voice was low and relaxed, belying the excitement Mike knew she must be feeling.

"I think so. Yes. Yes, I'm in contact with him."

"Ask him—"

"He's so afraid. Oh gosh, he's so afraid and so sorry for what happened to Miss Dunn. He's cold and tired and hungry and he says he knows he's doomed. He...oh God..."

Julie began crying, quiet little sobs that sounded vaguely like hiccups.

Sharon reached for Julie's hand again and grasped it lightly. "What is it, honey?"

"Jake says...he says he knows he's going to die, he knows there's nothing anyone can do to save him, he knows he's going to die and he just hopes he doesn't take anyone else with him when he goes."

Mike watched as Sharon squeezed the distraught girl's hand. "Is he still there, Julie?"

"Yes."

"Ask him how certain he is that the demon is unaware of his ability to communicate with you."

Silence fell over the room again as Mike and Sharon shared a dark glance.

"He says he has no way of knowing. He assumes the demon is unaware, because he figures the demon would stop him from communicating with me if it knew, just as it's put a stop to the rest of Jake's attempts to get help."

"Tell Jake to hang in there. Tell him there are people working very hard to save him, and that those people aren't about to give up on him. Can you do that?"

Julie nodded as tears continued to roll down her face.

"He says...he says to stay away. He says if anyone tries to come near him, he knows the demon will take over and the outcome will be bloody and messy and deadly and he won't be able to stop it."

Sharon had edged gradually closer to Julie until her face was just inches away from the girl's. Now she eased back in her chair but the expression on her face remained intense.

She thought hard and then said, "I know Jake says he's been unable to stop the demon from wreaking havoc when it takes over his body. But this is important: ask Jake if he's been able to make any headway at all when he tries to interfere with the demon's activities."

More silence and more shaky sobs as the terrified teen communicated telepathically with her brother. "He says he can tell it takes effort for the demon to keep him under control when Jake puts up a fight, but in the end the spirit is just too strong. He's always able to keep Jake trapped inside his body. Jake says that fighting the demon in that way is physically, mentally and psychically exhausting."

"Okay Julie, you're doing great, and so is Jake. Just one more question for now: when Jake fights for control of his body, approximately how long is he able to engage the demon? How long can he distract the demon if he puts everything he has into the effort?"

Just like that it all clicked and Mike knew what Sharon was thinking. He'd been mystified as to where she might be going with her line of questioning.

But now that he understood, he almost wished he didn't.

A moment later Julie answered. "Jake says he's never gone as far as he probably can, because he's afraid of losing himself in the effort. He's afraid if he exhausts himself too greatly, he won't be able to recover and will be gone forever. But even if he gives that kind of effort, he thinks he can last no longer than maybe thirty seconds against the strength of the demon's will."

Julie had grown steadily more upset as the bizarre interview proceeded, and now she was crying heavily. Her face was flushed and her body tense and rigid, much as it had been when she first walked into the police station. It was well past time to wrap things up, if only for the girl's mental wellbeing.

Apparently Sharon agreed, because she said, "That's all for now, honey. Please tell Jake to hang tough. Tell him we're not giving up on him and are going to do everything we can to save him."

A moment later Julie opened her streaming eyes and looked from Sharon to Mike. "I'm never going to see my brother again alive, am I?"

"Did you tell him what I asked you to, about us not giving up on him?" Sharon said gently.

"Yes, but—"

"I wasn't lying to him, Julie, and I'm not going to lie to you now. He's in big trouble, as is everyone in Paskagankee until we can get this situation resolved. But your ability to communicate with Jake, *without the demon's apparent knowledge,* is huge. It might be the only advantage we have in this situation. But if we can exploit it, maybe this story can still have a happy ending."

Julie kept her eyes on Sharon as she spoke, but Mike could see the girl didn't really buy what Sharon was selling. She wanted to, but she couldn't quite bring herself to do it.

But she didn't argue the point.

She appeared drained, sapped to the point of exhaustion.

Mike said, "Let's get you home. You're in no condition to drive, so I'll take you in my cruiser and Sharon will drive your car. We'll be in touch very soon once we decide how to proceed, but for now you need to rest. And if Jake comes to you in your dreams, or outside your dreams for that matter, try to remain positive and let us know immediately that you've spoken with him again."

With that, the trio exited the office and snaked their way through the station. Mike could feel Gordie's hungry eyes on them with every step.

He ignored the dispatcher and kept a firm grip on the shaky girl's elbow for support.

40

"You don't truly believe we can defeat this demon and save Jake Beebe, do you?" Sharon spoke the words almost causally as she brushed her hair at her mirrored vanity table in the corner of their bedroom.

It was a bedtime routine she'd maintained since the very first night he'd spent with her—and undoubtedly well before—and Mike suspected the act was as much a method of relieving stress as it was a grooming technique. He didn't care what her reasons were. The act was languid and sensual, and he loved watching her do it.

He considered her question as he lay on their bed, his back supported by a pillow propped against the headboard. He'd been asking himself the same thing ever since dropping Julie off at her home earlier in the evening. The girl had begged Mike to stop at the end of their long driveway and allow her to drive her car onto the property herself.

After the ugly confrontation with Van Beebe, and his demand the police not speak with either of his children without his permission, Mike had reluctantly agreed to her request. She was still shaky and stressed, but he'd kept a close eye on her until she'd parked the car and walked into the house. Only then did he and Sharon drive away.

And he'd been considering the very issue Sharon had just brought up ever since.

"I don't know," he admitted. "But I do know we can't allow a homicidal demon to continue to roam Paskagankee inside a human body. We have no choice but to try."

Sharon nodded. "I thought that was what you'd say. What do you think of Professor Paquette's plan?"

"I don't know what to think of that, either." He chuckled drily. "I wish I had more definitive answers for you, but even by Paskagankee standards, this isn't exactly a typical law enforcement problem. We're in uncharted territory here. Hell, we're *way past* uncharted territory."

"I can't argue with you on that one." She continued to brush her hair, the well-rehearsed movements smooth and almost hypnotic.

"But I'll tell you this," he said. "Paquette's plan is all we have, and as much as I hate involving him in what's liable to go south and end up being a massive shit-storm, I also know we don't have a choice in that, either. We need someone with experience in the area of demonology, and he's our guy."

Sharon continued to brush her hair and Mike continued to watch. He'd tried counting the brush strokes before and had always given up before she finished, distracted by her beauty every time. Once, way back at the beginning of their relationship, he'd asked her how many brush strokes she used every night and she'd smiled.

"I have no idea," she said. "I do it until it's time to stop."

"How do you know when it's time to stop?"

Another smile. "I can just feel it."

He'd said, "Come over here and feel this," and the subject had faded to insignificance.

Now she apparently decided it was time to stop, because she placed her brush—a pearl-handled antique handed down from her grandmother—carefully on the table and padded to their bed. She slipped under the covers and laid her head on Mike's chest and he ran his fingers through the silky, freshly brushed jet-black hair.

"I don't want you to go tomorrow," he said quietly.

She lifted her head off his chest and looked up at him, mystified. "What are you talking about? Why not?"

"This isn't a situation where we need massive show of force. I think the supernatural element of this case renders numbers irrelevant."

"I don't understand."

He continued to stroke her hair. "It's not like we're dealing with an armed desperado ready to shoot his way out of the situation. Jake wants to be saved. Everything is going to come down to whether or not we can execute the plan. If we can, the only people who need to be there are me and Professor Paquette."

He paused.

Cleared his throat.

"And if we can't, then superior numbers are not going to matter. If we can't, the only result of having more people at the scene will be greater carnage. I won't have that on my conscience."

"You're not going to bring along any backup at all, are you?"

He shook his head. "Nope. Like I just said, there's no reason to."

"And this decree from on high includes me?"

He'd expected resistance, which was why he had avoided bringing the subject up until now.

But he had to laugh at her response. "I *am* in charge, you know. What you call a 'decree from on high,' most people would refer to as a command decision."

"Well, your command decision sucks. I've been involved in this case since the beginning, remember? The murder of Lucie Dunn, in addition to being a horrendous and brutal act, disrupted my wedding day and eliminated my honeymoon. I want to make this demon pay for that, if for nothing else."

"It didn't eliminate our honeymoon, it just delayed it. We're still going to have one, don't worry."

"You know what I mean, Mike. I'm as invested in this case as you are. I'm probably *more* invested in it than you. That son of a bitch tried to make me suffer through my own autopsy, aware and afraid and unable to scream, even as Doctor Affeldt sliced me open from stem to stern."

"Exactly," Mike agreed. "That's my point. You've been through one hell of an ordeal. Who knows what kind of lingering effects there may be from that illusionist spell?"

"Don't give me that," she snapped. "There are no lingering effects. I feel just fine. And I fully acknowledge that you're in charge. If you feel the best way to attack this situation is not to include other members of the department as backup, I understand.

But I *will* be by your side tomorrow when we take down this demon. I *will* be in it until the end, no matter the outcome."

Her eyes flashed and anger had compressed her lips into a thin, bloodless line. One of the things that had attracted Mike to Sharon from the very beginning was her intensity, her refusal to surrender to victimhood no matter the situation.

She projected the air of vulnerability common to those who'd suffered great anguish and loss, who had seen and done terrible things they could never take back, and he supposed she always would. But for all her petite size and delicate features, she was one tough young woman. He suspected that if there were a test to determine such things, he would discover she was tougher than he, in most of the ways that mattered.

He knew she'd made up her mind about tomorrow.

He knew she wasn't going to back down.

He was now torn between the desire to protect his wife and the knowledge he may need someone like her if (*when*) things started to slide sideways tomorrow. And the recognition she would show up anyway, with or without his permission.

He sighed, and the hint of a smile tugged at the corners of her mouth.

He cleared his throat and the smile widened.

"Fine," he said tightly. "You can come. But you'll damned well follow orders once we're there. I've almost lost you too many times already. I'm not taking the chance of losing you tomorrow."

"Of course," she said. "Follow orders. What else would I do?"

Mike bit back the response that tried to leap out of his mouth. He had a sudden premonition of chaos and disaster and death, of blood and tragedy, but he said nothing as a wave of darkness and fear washed over him.

But he never stopped stroking that silky black hair.

41

It was a relatively simple plan, but there were still too many moving parts for Mike McMahon's taste.

The fact that the whole thing hinged on the participation of two civilians—one of them a teenager—was particularly troubling. But he'd thought long and hard in an attempt to come up with a decent alternative and finally given up.

There wasn't one.

The four principal parties in the desperate attempt to save Jake Beebe—Mike, Sharon, Julie and Professor Brian Paquette—had spent a good two hours yesterday huddled around a small table at the same anonymous roadside diner Mike, Sharon and the professor had stopped at after saving Sharon from the autopsy knife.

They spent a fair amount of money on coffee, hot chocolate and pie during their planning session, so Mike doubted the diner's owner objected to their lengthy stay.

On the other hand, he didn't much care.

If their meeting of the minds accomplished nothing else, it reinforced how difficult their challenge was going to be.

The first thing Mike insisted on was that Julie's participation take place with her positioned safely out of harm's way in her bedroom.

"You've already proven," he said, "that it's not necessary for you to be physically close to your brother in order to communicate with him. So there's no reason for you to be on-site when we put this plan in motion." He nearly slipped up and called it "this debacle," but stopped himself just in time.

Julie hemmed and hawed. "I want to be there to help Jake. If there's anything I can do to defeat the demon, I'm going to do it. This is my brother we're talking about."

"I understand how you feel, but no. You're not going to be anywhere near the demon. If things go south, I do NOT want you in the line of fire."

The young girl opened her mouth to argue but before she could, Sharon said, "You already have the most important job of any of us, Julie. You're the one who's going to help Jake distract the entity while we do our thing. We can't risk something happening to you before we're able to complete the job, because that would then put the rest of us at additional risk, and I know that's the last thing you would want."

Mike almost shook his head in amazement. Every time he thought he'd seen the depths of his beautiful wife's capacity for empathy and intelligence, she surprised him once again. With three simple sentences she reminded Julie Beebe of her importance to the cause of saving her brother, and also phrased the reminder in such a way that virtually eliminated any further argument. Because what could Julie now say?

It turned out she could now say nothing. Her disappointment was obvious but she agreed to remain out of danger. And that was all Mike cared about.

The remainder of the meeting consisted of the three adults hammering out details, most of which were of the hypothetical variety because the sad fact was that they had no idea what they would really face tomorrow. Even Professor Paquette, the expert in the group, freely admitted his knowledge was vast but hypothetical.

It wasn't a reassuring thought, but Mike appreciated the man's honesty and told him so. "Nothing will get us killed faster than a false sense of security."

"Well then," the professor replied, "we should live forever, because I have absolutely no sense of security, false or otherwise."

The statement was met with tense laughter, and Mike decided it was as good a time as any to bring the meeting to a close.

"Tomorrow morning," he said. "Early. Agreed?"

The other three nodded and mumbled their assent.

They said their goodbyes and went their separate ways, Professor Paquette back to Bowdoin College, Julie Beebe back to her isolated farmhouse on the outskirts of Paskagankee, and Mike and Sharon to her little home west of downtown.

Seeing their faces as they walked out of the restaurant, Mike couldn't help but think all four people were doing their best to maintain a strong front for their partners' sakes, but inside were likely convinced they might be facing a death sentence tomorrow.

If so, he certainly couldn't argue the point.

*   *   *

On the ride home, Mike caught Sharon regarding him carefully. Her face was drawn and her eyes narrowed. Even handicapped by having to keep his eyes on the road, it would have been impossible to miss her intense gaze. He tried to ignore it but eventually the curiosity became too much to bear.

He glanced across the seat and spread his hands. "What?"

"There's something you're not telling me."

"Why would you think that?"

"Really? You have to ask? Maybe you've forgotten, since it's been damned near a whole week since the wedding, but I love you."

"Okay. Well, I love you too, but I'm not making the connection between that point and our current conversation."

"I've loved you from practically the first time we met, and—"

"Ditto."

Sharon smiled. "Thank you. And I know. But in my case, loving you means spending every free moment watching you, learning your every mood, every worry, every concern. I know when you're being straight with me and I know when you're not. And right now, you're not."

"I would never lie to you."

"I know that. But I wasn't talking about lying. You have a habit of trying to protect me from things you believe might hurt me. And I think right now you're keeping something from me. I want to know what it is."

Mike sighed and shook his head, then he laughed. "I was married to my first wife for a hell of a lot longer than we've been together, and she never came close to knowing me the way you do. It's amazing."

"Don't change the subject, either. What are you not telling me?"

"Jesus, you're relentless, you know that?"

"Spill it."

"Okay, okay, you win. Here's the thing. I know we've settled on a game plan for dealing with the demon, and I believe Professor Paquette knows what he's doing, to the extent it's possible to know."

"But…"

"But no matter what else happens, when we come face-to-face with the evil inside Jake Beebe, I have to ensure the situation ends right then and there. That entity cannot be allowed to hurt or kill anyone else."

"Meaning what exactly?"

"Meaning I intend to stick to the plan and give the professor every opportunity to prove himself right, but if it seems like things are going sideways, well…"

In his peripheral vision, Mike could see Sharon's eyes widen. "You're going to shoot him, aren't you?"

"No," Mike said firmly. "No. I am not going to shoot an unarmed teenage boy. I most certainly am not."

"Unless you have to."

"Yes. Unless I absolutely have to. But it's my responsibility to protect Julie and Professor Paquette, not to mention everyone else in this town. And if we throw everything we have at the demon and come up on the losing end of the confrontation, I don't want to think about the havoc that entity will wreak on this town, the people it will kill and the damage it will cause."

He looked across the front seat to see his wife staring at him, her concern evident.

"I won't have that on my conscience, Sharon. I can't. This has got to end tomorrow, one way or the other," he said quietly. "If I kill the demon's host, it will have no alternative but to go back to Hell where it belongs."

"But Jake Beebe is an innocent kid. Unbelievably careless, yes. Monumentally stupid, sure. But stupid doesn't equal evil."

"I agree."

"And you're going to kill him."

"I sure as hell hope not."

"But if you have to…"

"If I have to, yes."

"You won't pull the trigger on an innocent boy, Mike. You can't. You don't have it in you."

His hands were shaking and he gripped the wheel tightly so Sharon wouldn't notice. Her face had gone ashen and Mike could feel her eyes boring holes in the side of his head.

"I hope we don't have to find out," was all he could think of to say.

42

The morning was overcast and drizzly, typical of late fall in extreme northern Maine. Mike's breath was steaming out of his mouth and then dissipating slowly, as was Sharon's and Professor Paquette's as they approached the ancient barn at the extreme rear of the Beebe property.

The professor had driven to Sharon's house, arriving at six a.m. as instructed and parking his car in her driveway. Then the three of them took a Paskagankee PD cruiser to the point along Route 24 that placed them on a more or less direct path through the thick forest to the barn.

Then they started hiking.

It was a quiet walk, partly due to the inhospitable terrain. It was imperative they maintain constant awareness of their surroundings or risk tripping over a fallen branch or stepping in a hole or on an exposed tree root and twisting an ankle. Or worse.

Mostly, though, the silence was due to the little group's consciousness—unspoken but unanimously agreed upon—that they were facing an entity many times more powerful than themselves, an entity possessed of limitless evil. And that the end result of their efforts this morning might not just be terror, but pain and suffering and eventually death.

They snaked through the forest single-file, Mike in the lead, checking the GPS coordinates constantly to ensure they remained on course. Professor Paquette followed, with Sharon bringing up the rear. Twigs snapping underfoot and the occasional muffled sniffle or cough were the only sounds as they plodded through the damp forest.

When Julie revealed during their midday meeting yesterday that Jake had been hiding inside the family's crumbling barn, Mike had been initially surprised and then angry with himself it hadn't occurred to him to search the damned thing. Paskagankee was so vast there were an almost unlimited number of places someone who didn't want to be found could hide, but it made perfect sense a sixteen-year-old would try to stay close to home if he were confused and afraid.

Mike had been so concerned about the grimoire and the supernatural aspect of this case, he'd allowed himself to be distracted from basic search protocol, and that knowledge ate away at him even as they picked their way through the underbrush.

The sun was a distant rumor, locked away behind a steel-gray overcast curtain as they approached the Beebes' back fields and their old barn. The property had long-since stopped being a working farm and the fields were fallow and overgrown with weeds and trees.

But the barn was visible in the distance, looming out of the mist like a bad omen. Mike raised his hand and the group came to a stop, far enough from the opening in the forest to avoid being seen—he hoped—should a demonic spirit happen to look in their direction from the barn, but close enough to permit surveillance on the structure.

Due to the unreliable nature of cell communication throughout Paskagankee, Mike hadn't wanted to rely on phones for the plan's execution. He'd tested the cell connection yesterday and the call had gone through, but he still wasn't convinced the results would be the same when they mattered most.

"I'll try to call you tomorrow morning around 6:45," he told Julie. "But if you don't hear from me at that time, you should assume the cell signal isn't working. In that case, I want you to put the plan in motion at exactly seven a.m., because barring some event totally outside our control, we *will* be at the barn and ready to go at that time."

Now he checked his phone and discovered, somewhat to his surprise, that there was a signal. He pressed the button to call Julie and nodded approvingly as she picked up on the first ring.

"Hello?" she said hesitantly.

"Good morning, Julie," Mike said, speaking in a voice barely above a whisper. "How did you sleep last night?"

"Non-existently," she said. Her voice was tight and fearful.

Mike wanted to put her at ease, if that was even possible, so he said, "Join the club." He put as much confidence as he could muster into his voice and continued, "This will all be over soon and you'll have your brother back."

"I know," she said.

"Good. Are you ready to go?"

"As ready as I'll ever be, I suppose. I just want to save Jake and get this over with."

"That's what we all want, Julie. Are you relaxed enough to contact your brother?"

"I hope so...I-I think so, yes."

"Excellent. We're going to approach the barn now, so I want you to start reaching out to Jake. I'm going to keep the phone line open, and when you and Jake are ready for us to enter, you let me know."

"Okay. Good luck, Chief McMahon."

"Thank you, Julie. And it's Mike."

"Good luck, Mike."

He removed an earpiece from his pocket and plugged it into a jack on the bottom of his phone. Then he placed the earpiece into his left ear and slipped the phone into his breast pocket.

Breathed deeply.

Turned to Sharon and Professor Paquette and said, "Let's get this show on the road."

43

There wasn't much to the plan. Julie would enter her twin brother's consciousness and together they would fight to expel the demon from Jake's body.

Professor Paquette theorized that the supernatural connection the two shared as twins would allow Julie to add her own psychic energy to Jake's, and that the combination might be strong enough to force the demon out of its human shell and back into the ether.

But that wasn't the extent of the plan.

Even the professor admitted his theory was based on little besides an educated guess predicated on years of research, plus a healthy dose of wishful thinking. However, even if he was wrong about the dual forces being enough to evict the demon, Paquette believed strongly that the psychic energy the entity would be forced to expend in order to protect itself from Jake and Julie would leave it susceptible to an outside attack.

An exorcism.

To be performed by Professor Paquette.

"Even a demon isn't all-powerful," he'd said. "It's a supernatural being capable of nearly limitless evil, yes, but it is *not* a god, and thus there are limits to what it can do. It very well may not be capable of fighting a three-front war, so if I'm able to time the ritual so that the demon is forced to battle Jake and Julie on one hand, and you and Sharon on the other, all while I'm performing the exorcism, I believe we can be successful."

Mike had held the professor's gaze a long time before answering.

The man looked sincere and earnest and it was clear he was fully committed to his words.

"You believe," Mike had said. "Which means you don't know."

"I'll grant you that point. As I've mentioned before, this is uncharted territory for all of us. But think about it from a perspective you're an expert in: law enforcement. Isn't it easier to take down a suspect if he's surrounded first? If you come at him from multiple angles?"

Mike had been forced to agree with the professor's thinking, and the fact of the matter was that he had no better plan. No other plan at all. So they'd run with Professor Paquette's idea.

Now they broke cover, approaching the barn in a straight line once leaving the protection of the forest and its heavy vegetation. The distance from trees to structure was approximately eighty feet, and without much beyond the occasional scrub brush to shield them from view, Mike had decided their best bet was to take the most direct route to the barn and cross the open area as quickly as possible.

Nobody spoke. The ground was mostly frozen, hard and crunchy. Mike concentrated on avoiding twigs and brittle leaves, on finding the quietest spots upon which to step, trusting Paquette and Sharon to follow in his footsteps precisely.

In less than ninety seconds they sidled up to the barn's rear wall and paused for a moment to catch their breath. Then they moved to the corner and edged along the side wall, ducking low to pass beneath a series of filthy windows placed every ten feet or so along the length of the barn.

Mike had just reached the front corner when Julie's breathy voice came through his earpiece.

"We're ready," she said, her terror clear.

"Good girl," Mike answered. "Start now, and good luck."

"You too," came the reply, and then the voice was gone.

Mike turned to his partners and nodded once.

Then he spun on his heel and rounded the corner.

44

From the moment deep in the Paskagankee forest when the demon first materialized out of thin air, Jake had known he was losing himself. The thing had begun taking over not just his body but his spirit as well, the process as inevitable as death, until he was now no longer sure where Jake Beebe ended and the limitless evil of the demonic spirit began.

Was no longer sure he wanted to know.

Things had started out slowly as the ancient demon felt its way around inside Jake, flexing its muscles and testing its limits, becoming accustomed to life in the modern world. But as the days passed and the demon became stronger and more confident, the progression accelerated.

Jake had initially reached out to Julie in her dreams almost without realizing he was doing so. Their psychic, "twin" connection had always been strong despite their sibling bickering, which had eventually driven them apart on a conscious level.

Subconsciously, though, they had remained linked: Julie would find herself upset for no particular reason, only to find out later that Jake had been getting reamed out by a teacher for failing to complete a homework assignment on time. Starting at puberty, Jake began to feel off sometimes physically, tired and mopey, several days each month without any idea of the cause, only figuring out much later that he was suffering as his sister did with the onset of her menstrual period.

The psychic link was something they both understood, if

rarely discussed. They'd never lived any other way, so to them it was normal, and the notion that Jake would connect with Julie in her dreams after being taken over by a malevolent spirit was not particularly surprising.

Quite the opposite, in fact. It made perfect sense.

For Jake, confused and terrified and alone, the visits were a reassuring slice of normalcy and a glimpse back into a life that was no longer his, a few moments of comfort amidst chaos and confusion and upheaval and fear.

He'd been as certain as he could be that the demon was unaware he'd reached out to his sister. No one had ever known about the connection between Jake and Julie—even *they* were barely conscious of it themselves most of the time—and with so much else to worry about, Jake simply took it for granted that his forays into Julie's consciousness were their own little secret.

It was only in the last twenty-four hours or so that he'd become aware of how wrong that assumption had been. The demon was well aware of Jake and Julie's ability to communicate. Not only was it aware of their psychic ability, it had *been* aware since the very beginning.

As Jake began to absorb the demon into his own consciousness, his understanding of the demon's knowledge and power—and limitless evil—necessarily grew. The demon never *told* Jake it had been aware he was communicating with his sister; it didn't have to. As the spirit and the flesh melded, Jake simply knew.

And that was the most terrifying aspect of the entire terrifying scenario.

Because even as Jake lost himself to the demon that possessed him, he continued to feel an overwhelming need to protect his twin. To save Julie even if he could not save himself.

When she came to him this morning, pushing her way into his consciousness, he thrashed against the psychic restraints imposed on him by the demon, flailed against them and screamed psychically in a desperate attempt to warn her that her friends—the people putting their lives on the line to save Jake—were walking into a trap.

To warn her that the demon had allowed Jake to communicate with Julie intentionally, for the sole purpose of luring them into that trap.

To warn her that unless they called off their rescue attempt they were doomed, that the demon knew they were coming and was ready for them, that it would toy with them like a cat toying with a mouse, torturing it and playing sadistic games with it until finally tiring of those games and devouring it whole.

Jake fought and screamed with all his dwindling sense of self and his psychic energy to *push* a warning into Julie's brain, so that she would contact her friends and call them off, or at the very least so that she would leave the Beebe house and save herself, that she would hit the road south and escape and never return to the haunted village of Paskagankee.

But his efforts had been fruitless. Pointless. The demon shut down the psychic link, effortlessly and completely, ending Jake's feeble attempt at heroism, or redemption, or whatever the hell it was, before it had ever even started.

And in the process, the spirit cackled inside Jake's head, ridiculing him for his weakness and filling his fevered brain with visions of torture and mutilation and rape and domination and blood, oh so very much fucking blood, crushing his resolve once and for all, leaving no doubt as to Jake's powerlessness, the demonic malevolence within him growing all the time.

The spirit capered inside Jake's skull, reminding him that it had been invited into Jake's body and spirit by Jake himself, that without Jake's foolish interest in forbidden things, he would still be a normal teenage boy whose only concerns were somehow trying to pass Algebra, and whether he'd have any luck getting into Tina McCaffrey's pants Friday night.

Jake fought as long as he could, continuing his attempts to warn Julie even after realizing those efforts were pointless. His struggles grew weaker and less effective, which was like saying twenty-five degrees below zero was colder than twenty below: it was true, but what the hell difference did it make?

Finally he surrendered to inevitability, giving up even as the demon continued to mock him for his impotence.

There was no hope.

He was doomed.

Julie's friends were doomed.

The town of Paskagankee was doomed.

45

The barn had been built centuries ago and featured a pair of entrances in the front.

One massive door consisted of a wooden half-wall hanging via iron wheels from a track bolted to the roof support beams. When rolled open the door was sufficiently large to allow access for horses, cattle and hay wagons. A normal-sized door had been built into the much larger wheeled door to permit the farmer entry and exit without having to roll open the large one.

Mike paused in front of the smaller door.

He lifted his weapon and held it in two hands, then leaned his shoulder against the rotting wood and shoved hard, expecting resistance. The door swung open easily and he stumbled into the barn, nearly dropping to his knees but somehow managing to stay upright.

He scanned the barn, gun lowered but ready, his gaze moving quickly left to right, alert for any sign of trouble as he edged forward. Behind him, Sharon and Professor Paquette crowded through the door. He knew Sharon's weapon would be drawn as well.

The barn's interior was murky and grey as the light from the overcast morning struggled to penetrate the grimy windows. Ancient farm implements lined rotting walls, rusted and unusable, as piles of decades-old—perhaps centuries-old—junk were scattered randomly around the gigantic space.

Mike continued to move forward. The barn appeared empty

and desolate and his initial thought was that they'd been snookered. The information Julie had gleaned from her brother must have been wrong. There was no sign Jake had ever been here, much less that he was here now.

Two more cautious paces and then Mike froze. He stopped so quickly he was jostled from behind by Sharon or Professor Paquette and pushed forward another half step.

He ignored them. Raised his weapon instinctively and tilted his head in focused concentration.

Because someone was singing.

The sound was barely audible, something almost sensed rather than heard. A childlike, angelic voice floated through the barn's musty air, sweet and innocent and melodic, the sound like a wind chime jingling musically in a soft summer breeze.

Mike couldn't make out the words but the tune sounded oddly familiar. A gospel song, or a hymn, something he'd heard decades ago sitting on his mother's lap inside the Revere Presbyterian Church:

"A beggar blind sat by the way...
They sought to still his cry
Heeded not, yet cried the more
Lest Jesus should pass by..."

The voice began to change as the singing continued. The sweetness melted away, the childish innocence disappearing and the tone becoming jangled and harsh, the tune menacing.

Portentous.

A chill ran down Mike's spine and his breath caught in his throat. He'd begun to lower his weapon but now he raised it to eye level and said, "Paskagankee Police. Stop right where you are."

Jake Beebe stood on the far side of the barn, barely visible through the gloom and the clutter. His arms were raised in what may or may not have been an intentional depiction of Christ on the cross.

And he was singing.

And he was smiling widely.

The teen took one step forward and then a second.

Mike sighted down the barrel of his weapon. "I said freeze. I'm not going to warn you again. Do not take one more step."

Jake's grin widened.

He said, "Welcome to your worst nightmare."

46

The demon inside Jake took another step forward and flicked its right wrist as if backhanding an invisible victim across the face.

Instantly Mike's gun was yanked from his grip by an invisible but powerful force. It sailed backward across the barn, struck the floor and skittered to a stop against the door they'd stepped through just seconds before. Sharon's astonished gasp told him her weapon had suffered the same fate.

"Did you like my little ditty? It's an obscure tune from the nineteenth century that I selected just for you, Chief McMahon." The voice was low and scratchy and somehow otherworldly, and it was obvious Jake Beebe wasn't speaking at all.

It was the demon, ancient and evil and mocking.

"Don't move," Mike repeated, "and let's work through this."

The demon ignored him. "I chose this particular song," it said in that otherworldly bass, "because I wanted to emphasize to you that your desperate cries for help will not be heeded. Not by that fraud Jesus, and not by anyone else.

"You're screwed, Chief McMahon, in case you're having trouble following."

Things had fallen apart faster than Mike would have imagined possible. So he did the only thing he could think of: engage the enemy. Keep it talking. Try to distract it long enough for Professor Paquette to do his thing.

Assuming his thing would even matter.

"Let the boy have his body back," Mike said. "Let him have his body back and take mine instead."

From behind him Sharon hissed, "What the hell are you doing?"

He wasn't sure. The possibility of offering a trade hadn't come up at any point in their strategy sessions, nor while Mike and Sharon discussed the issue at home.

But he had to do something. Maybe the proposed trade would gain the interest of the demon long enough to allow the professor the time he needed. Or maybe it wouldn't, but the spirit would accept the trade and at least the boy would be saved.

It was a spur-of-the-moment decision that seemed like the best option out of a whole bunch of bad ones.

So he said it, half expecting to be instantly filled with malevolent energy, half expecting a cackle of ridicule from the demon.

Neither expectation was realized. The demon ignored him entirely.

Instead it said something unexpected: "Psychic communication is a funny thing, don't you agree?"

Mike blinked in surprise but tried to react quickly.

"Is that so?" he said. "What's funny about it?"

Behind him, Professor Paquette had finally begun mumbling, speaking words Mike could barely hear and could not understand, and he knew the man was trying to begin the exorcism ritual.

Meanwhile the demon was speaking. "You seem to think human twins possess some mystical supernatural ability to communicate, but your little 'plan' had a flaw from the beginning, one you didn't consider. It should have been obvious to anyone with half a brain, even a brain as limited as your pathetic human one."

Sweat rolled down the back of Mike's neck, even in the damp chill of the barn. The thing inside Jake continued to move slowly forward, advancing without the slightest indication of fear or concern.

Mike breathed deeply and tried again. "Well, a blind man could see you're itching to fill us in, so why don't you go ahead and get it over with. What's the flaw we should have considered?"

"You still don't know?"

"Humor me. Pretend I'm as stupid as you think I am."

The grin widened even further, spreading across the boy's face until Mike thought it might just split open. "Why, it's simple. You should have considered that a supernatural being would possess far more expertise in the field of supernatural communication than a few simple humans ever could."

The demon had now crossed half the distance between the rear barn wall and Mike. A sensation of pressure, of rising static electricity, began to build with the entity's approach, and Mike felt sluggish and ineffectual. Something was happening to him, something the demon was *making* happen, and he knew he had to take action soon or it would be too late. He would be rendered immobile and helpless simply by the force of the entity's approach.

Behind him, Professor Paquette continued to mumble, desperately working the exorcism Mike knew without a shred of doubt was doomed to failure. He wracked his brain for a response, anything that might slow things down, but before he could come up with one the demon spoke again, that bizarre and terrifying rumble emanating from deep inside the chest of a sixteen-year-old boy.

"Oh, by the way, there's something else you should know," the demon said.

"And what's that?"

"I've been here on earth before, and I've waited a *very* long time to return. Practically an eternity, at least as you measure the passage of time. Now that I've finally made it back, I'm not about to go anywhere. And your feeble attempt at exorcism, as weak and laughable as it is, makes me…"

It took another step forward.

"Extremely…"

Another step.

"Angry."

It flicked its wrist exactly as it had done before, and Professor Paquette screamed in anguish. The grimoire he'd been holding tumbled to the floor and then so did the professor, and he rolled around in agony in the filth, hands clapped to the sides of his head, his screams for mercy spiking into incoherence and then fading to desperate moans.

"I've been aware of your sorry attempt to corral me and send me back to the place you call Hell from the very beginning. I must say I'm disappointed in your efforts. I expected a bit more of a challenge than…whatever this is."

It flicked its wrist again and again Professor Paquette screamed loudly. Then he began sobbing, mumbling something that sounded more like a plea for his life than any kind of exorcism ritual. The exorcism seemed to have disappeared from Paquette's to-do list and Mike didn't think it would be returning any time soon.

"The question now becomes," the demon said, it's voice lowering even further until it was nothing more than a malignant otherworldly growl, "what the *hell* do I do with you? With the emphasis on *hell*."

Mike debated sprinting for his weapon but knew he would never make it. He would suffer the same fate as Professor Paquette—or worse—long before he reached his gun.

"There's something else you should have considered," the demon said.

"Oh, really? You just have all the answers, don't you?"

Rumbling laughter. "I have a hell of a lot more than you. Of course, that's not saying much."

"Okay, I'll bite. What else should I have considered?"

"This: why would I allow poor, confused Jake to retreat to this foul-smelling hiding place and simply wait for you three heroes to save the day when I could have gone anywhere inside his body and done as much damage as I wanted? It wasn't like *you* were going to stop me."

Mike had actually considered that very question. But he'd been so focused on stopping the demon that he hadn't given it the attention it deserved. Obviously that had been a mistake, as had apparently everything else about this ill-conceived rescue mission.

The demon regarded Mike through Jake's eyes. They appeared simultaneously amused and menacing.

"The answer," it said, "although perhaps even you have figured it out by now, is that there *was* a reason to stay here and wait. The answer is that I *wanted* you three to charge in here determined to save the young lad who is—trust me on this—far beyond 'saving' at this point. The answer is that even seventy-two hours of time spent cooped up in this hell-hole—see what I did there?—is worthwhile if it ends with the chance to torture and then eliminate you three sad little savior-wannabes."

"Why us? What sets us apart from anyone else in this town?"

Mike asked the question partly to keep the demon talking, but also partly out of a sincere desire to hear the answer. "Why would an ancient supernatural entity care so much about destroying three random people?"

The shell of Jake Beebe shrugged. "Why *not* you? What better place to start whittling down the population of Paskagankee than with the people who forced me from a nice, warm comfortable bedroom into…this?" The demon opened Jake's hands like a game-show hostess revealing a prize as it indicated the decrepit barn.

"But you haven't started with us. You already murdered an innocent young woman."

"Details," the demon said dismissively. "That teacher simply got in the way while I was still getting my feet on the ground, so to speak. Her death was nothing more than the byproduct of my unfamiliarity with this world in the centuries since I was here last.

"But I am nothing if not a fast learner." An ugly leer erupted on Jake Beebe's face. "As far as I'm concerned, the real fun starts right here, right now."

"But what about—"

"I know what you're trying to do," the demon interrupted. "And it won't work. You're out of time. Let's get the party started, as the boy who was kind enough to serve as my host might say."

"I don't think—"

Mike choked on his words as the demon flicked its wrist again. The air pressure rose dramatically and he found himself flying through the air as his gun had done moments earlier. He struck the wall and crumpled helplessly to the floor, groggy and injured.

But he was still conscious, and bile rushed up his throat and into his mouth as the demon loomed over Sharon.

She had fallen to the floor next to Professor Paquette and lay moaning, hands pressed to her head, exactly as the professor was still doing. Mike couldn't hear her from across the barn but he knew she was doing so.

The demon turned its head toward Mike.

And winked.

And Mike knew Sharon was about to die, this time for real.

47

The demon extended Jake's hand horizontally over the floor. As it did, an ancient wood-handled farm implement flew upward from the floor where it lay nestled in decades-old straw. It was an old-fashioned iron-tined rake, menacing and lethal-looking, and it whipped into Jake's downturned palm with a loud *thwap*, as if drawn by magic.

Which, of course, it was.

Black magic.

Demonic magic.

Mike shook his head savagely in a futile attempt to clear his thoughts after smashing the back of his skull on a support beam. He shoved hard against the dirt-covered floor, his only thought to bolt to his feet and rush the demon. He would tackle it before it could plunge the foot-long tines through Sharon's prone body, and after that he would figure things out as he went and hope for the best.

But try as he might he couldn't break the demon's spell. He'd been immobilized; it was as if an invisible weight had dropped onto him, a weight that was impossible to cast aside.

He spit a curse and tried to shout a warning to his wife, to tell her to roll away toward the door, to kick at the legs of the boy whose body had been taken over, to do *something* to give herself the chance at a few more seconds of life and the opportunity to continue the fight. But all that came out was a strangled, guttural cry that was useless from this distance even at getting Sharon's attention, never mind helping her survive.

The demon leered down at Sharon, its bizarrely wide smile clear to Mike even from across the barn and through eyes watering and blurred and a skull pounding from a likely concussion.

The entity knew it was in control.

It had always been in control.

It hefted the ancient farm tool slowly, almost casually, drawing out the moment. It could sense Mike's agony and wanted to prolong his suffering; that much would have been obvious even if the demon hadn't told him so specifically.

"KILL ME!" Mike finally shouted through a force of will greater than anything he'd even had to summon. The words exploded up though his chest and out his mouth and echoed across the cavernous barn.

The demon had raised the rake high above its head in advance of plunging it into Sharon's helpless body, but now it turned and locked eyes with Mike. The rake hung suspended like the word of Damocles, but it hadn't dropped yet, which meant Sharon was still alive, which meant Mike had—finally, and undoubtedly temporarily—done something right.

"Excuse me?" the demon said, the absurd smile still pasted onto its face. The words came out soft, almost effeminate, a jarring contrast to the gravelly rasp the entity had effected up until now.

"I said kill me instead. Come over here and use the rake on me." The words came out marginally easier, but speaking was still a struggle. Rising from the floor remained every bit as impossible as it had been before.

"Oh, I shall. But, you see, it's not an either/or situation. Why traipse all the way over to that side of the barn and kill you, only to have to return here to finish off your sweet, juicy wife?"

"You don't have to move. Reverse whatever spell you used to send me flying over here. Use it again to pull me over there and kill me. Just spare Sharon and Professor Paquette."

Jake's arms remained stretched above his head, the rake rocksteady in his hands. In the grip of a normal teenage boy, the rake would have been shaking by now from the effort required to keep his arms so fully extended, but the demon held it effortlessly aloft. Mike guessed the spirit could hold it there for the rest of eternity if it so chose.

The smile grew even larger. "You still do not seem to understand. No one will be spared. You will die. Your sweet, juicy wife will die. The *professor*"—the demon spat the word *professor* out like a profanity—"who tried to exorcise me will die. Then I will move out of this disgusting barn and begin cutting a bloody swath through this miserable, God-forsaken town before wandering south and repeating the process in town after town, village after village, an endless succession of victims to be dispensed with."

"But you can't—"

"I can and I will!" The voice changed again, now strident and angry, like a petulant child after being sent to bed in the middle of his favorite cartoon. "I've waited centuries for this, and I'm going to enjoy every...

"Last...

"Second of it!"

"No!" Mike shouted, but it was too late. The demon turned away and raised the rake even higher over Sharon's body, then it pivoted at the waist and thrust downward and

48

A gunshot roared from behind Mike.

It was followed in rapid succession by another, and then a third, three staccato reports coming from the barn door.

He flinched and then watched, stunned, as all three slugs struck Jake's body.

The demon stumbled backward, shifting its attention from its victim to the door in stunned surprise as the rake fell from its hands and clattered to the floor next to Sharon.

A fourth shot and the demon fell, collapsing to the rotting wooden floorboards as blood began to soak Jake's filthy clothing. Even from a distance Mike could see a crimson flood soaking a t-shirt that had once been white but was now a grimy, greasy gray.

He craned his neck and looked behind him. Julie Beebe stood silhouetted in the open doorway, outlined starkly against the drizzly grey of the overcast morning. She held Mike's service weapon in a two-handed shooter's grip but her hands were shaking so badly he was concerned she might squeeze the trigger again and hit Sharon by accident.

His concern became moot as she dropped the gun and sank to her knees on the floor. She buried her face in her hands and began sobbing; deep, wrenching cries punctuated with, "Jake oh God I've killed Jake oh God Jake is gone."

From across the barn came a faraway buzzing noise, the sound of a million angry, swarming bees.

Mike turned back toward Jake and the strange buzzing sound.

The boy lay flat on his back and unmoving a few feet from Sharon and Professor Paquette.

Mike watched, transfixed, as a cloud of what looked like black smoke burst from Jake's body. The cloud came not from Jake's nose or mouth but from *everywhere*, seeping through his skin and his clothing and then coming together in a dense formation and floating above his motionless form.

The buzzing noise was much louder now, like a freight train roaring into an enclosed tunnel. It was the sound of anger, of fury, of impotent rage, and Mike knew he was hearing and seeing the demonic spirit, expelled in death from Jake's body in a way Mike had been unable to accomplish while the boy lived.

The angry buzzing continued to build, increasing in volume and intensity, and then the cloud began to rotate in place, still suspended over the body of its apparently dead host. In seconds it was spinning like a tornado, the darkness whirling and all Mike could think of was how much it reminded him of a swarm of furious bees.

Then the cloud began to move. It slid toward Sharon, slowly and menacingly. She'd removed her hands from her head and pushed herself up into a sitting position. She rubbed her eyes in confusion with her dirty hands and then froze, gaping as the angry demonic cloud approached.

The cloud began circling Sharon and Professor Paquette, whose torture had apparently also ended with Jake's death. The cloud swirled ever faster, enveloping the two in its ominous blackness but seemingly unable to inflict any damage on them.

Mike's heart hammered in his chest. He was certain the demon was searching in desperation for a new vessel to inhabit. The professor had said a demonic entity must be invited in before it could take over a body, but the professor had also admitted multiple times that his knowledge was theoretical, and as Mike contemplated the awful possibility of his beautiful wife suffering from demonic possession his stomach flip-flopped and his blood froze.

The darkness whirled and spun, its anger and evil intent evident. The buzzing noise continued as the black dervish roared around Sharon and Professor Paquette. The cloud was coal-black and dense, and Mike could see nothing of its interior, where he knew two potential victims huddled back-to-back, frozen in fear.

Mike tried to rise again and this time when he shoved upward from the floor he discovered he could. The death of the host had apparently not just expelled the demon but also rendered all of its previous spells inert. Mike was relieved but still fearful.

He kept a sharp eye on the black cloud as he hurried to Julie. She remained on her knees and continued to sob deeply but had removed her hands from her face and was staring in shock at the black cloud. Mike wrapped an arm around the girl's shoulder and squeezed tightly.

Then he picked his gun up off the floor and returned it to its holster. Shooting at the demon would do nothing in terms of stopping it and would likely serve only to kill or injure Sharon or the professor. His heart continued to race but his terror began to recede at the dawning realization the demonic entity was now helpless, its obvious fury notwithstanding.

He left Julie and began moving toward the demon, unsure of exactly what the hell he intended to accomplish but determined to come to the aid of his wife. Before he'd covered half the distance toward the cloud, it rose above Sharon and Professor Paquette and hovered. It gathered itself into a tightly spinning angry black swarm and raced directly at Mike.

He stood his ground, shaking from adrenaline and, he had to admit, terror, but determined not to flinch against a foe he was somewhat—but not entirely—certain could not harm him.

The cloud was on him in an instant, pulling itself apart and swirling around him, exactly as it had done to Sharon and the professor. It twisted and pulsed and inside the deafening roar Mike could hear the sound of suffering and torment, the cries of long-dead victims whose misery lived on, echoing down the ages in a grim reminder of a fate he and Sharon and Professor Paquette had narrowly avoided.

Then the demon was gone. It rose above Mike and came together one last time in a malevolent black swarm before racing past Julie and out the still-open barn door. Mike hurried outside and watched as the cloud circled over the fallow farmland and then vanished, sinking straight into the ground and disappearing.

Instantly the bee-swarm noise ended, cut off in mid-roar at the exact moment the cloud ceased to exist. In its place was a ringing in Mike's ears that could not quite blot out the sound of Julie's anguished cries.

He returned into the barn to see Sharon hurrying toward the door. She'd started brushing dirt and the grime off her clothing but given up when it became clear her efforts were doomed to failure. She half-walked and half-trotted to Julie and helped her to her feet.

The girl stared unblinkingly in the direction of her brother's body even as she rose. Sharon wrapped an arm around Julie's shoulder, much as Mike had done moments earlier, and then gently but firmly turned her away from Jake. They walked side-by-side past Mike, out the door, and toward the Beebe farmhouse a quarter-mile away.

Mike crossed the barn and met Professor Paquette stumbling in the opposite direction. He was blinking rapidly, as if trying to recover from a blow to the head. His gait was slow and awkward.

"I'm so sorry," the professor mumbled. "I don't know what happened. One second I was working the exorcism ritual and the next I was flat on my back and I barely knew who the hell I was. It felt like a rusty railroad spike was being driven into my skull and I couldn't concentrate on anything but the immense pain."

"Don't apologize," Mike answered. "This whole thing was a set-up from the get-go. The demon knew everything we were doing and was just waiting for us to get here so it could take us down. You never stood a snowball's chance in hell of completing that ritual."

He pursed his lips and said, "In fact, *I* owe *you* an apology for getting you into this mess. To say you're lucky to have survived would be the understatement of the century."

Paquette chuckled weakly and continued toward the exit. "We can continue our mutual apology tour later. Right now I need a hot shower and a the biggest cup of coffee I can find."

"I'll second the motion on the coffee," Mike said, "but as far as a shower goes, for me it's going to have to wait. I've got a lot to do, and the first thing item on the list is to check poor Jake for signs of life."

"You won't find any," the professor said with a tone of grim certainty.

"How can you be so sure? Julie shot him four times but people have survived more gunshot wounds than that. It's rare, I'll admit, but it happens."

"I'm certain Jake's dead because if he weren't, the demon would still be inside him and *we'd* be dead instead. The only way to get that spirit out of a human host—short of exorcism, which was a massive failure—is by killing that host. I'm sorry, Chief, but Jake's gone."

Mike nodded and turned wearily toward the body of Jake Beebe, still sprawled motionlessly on its back in the center of the barn.

"That's basically what I thought," he said. "But I still have to be sure."

49

Mike lay against the headboard watching his wife brush her hair in the nightly ritual that had become one of his favorite parts of their day.

And this day had been a long one. They hadn't talked much since arriving home, maintaining an exhausted silence.

Finally, almost out of nowhere, Sharon said, "What's going to happen to Julie?"

Mike shook his head. "Nothing, at least not in a legal sense."

"Meaning what?"

"Take away the supernatural aspect of the case—which we're going to have to do, for obvious reasons—and the shooting of Jake is legally justified. Not counting Julie herself, there are three reliable witnesses who've testified to the fact that Jake was about to kill you when Julie shot him."

"But if you take away the supernatural aspect it looks really bad for us. How did a sixteen-year-old boy disarm two trained police officers and disable all three of us to the point we had to be rescued by the boy's teenage sister?"

"I know it looks bad," Mike acknowledged, "and in my case I just don't care. I don't like that people will question *your* law enforcement skills, but the reality is most of the scrutiny will be on me, and I'm fine with that."

"I'm not fine with it."

"It comes with the territory, babe. Anyway, here's how the story plays out: we suspected Jake was hiding out in the barn, we went in there to check it out, and we were taken by surprise. He knocked us down with the rake, we lost our guns when we fell, and then Julie came along and took action when she saw her brother about to turn you into a human shish kebob."

Sharon never stopped brushing as she considered Mike's words. "Sounds pretty thin," she finally said, "even if all three of our stories match up."

"That's because it is pretty thin. But in lieu of any evidence to the contrary—and there won't be any because that's exactly what happened, again, minus the supernatural stuff—the D.A. won't have any choice but to rule the shooting justifiable homicide. I spoke with him at length after you, me and Professor Paquette were interviewed separately, and he told me at that time that unless new evidence turns up his intention is not to file charges.

"And Julie's obvious grief also didn't hurt her standing with D.A. Pierce, either," he added after a moment's consideration. "He told me he doesn't think he's ever seen someone so shattered."

"She was inconsolable as I was walking her back to her house," Sharon said.

"How did she happen to show up at the barn, anyway? She saved all our asses, but I had stressed to her over and over that she was to stay safe and sound inside her bedroom. She was not to leave that house."

Sharon put her brush down and turned to face Mike, and his heart skipped a beat as it always did at the sight of her. God, but she was beautiful.

"That was the first question I asked her when I tried to take her mind off what had just happened."

"What did she say?"

"She told me that Jake 'turned off' while she was in the middle of this morning's psychic conversation."

"Turned off? What's that supposed to mean?"

"She said it was like someone hanging up a phone in the middle of a conversation. He was there, and engaging her, as she told him we were about to enter the barn, but then he just disappeared. She said that was so completely unlike him, especially given how terrified he was of the demon inhabiting his body, that she knew something was wrong. So she left her bedroom and ran to the barn."

They fell silent again, staring at each other as each relived the horror of the day.

Then Mike said, "Does she understand her brother was already gone by the time she shot him? Does she realize it wasn't really Jake she killed at all, that he'd been fully absorbed by the demon before we ever arrived at the barn this morning?"

"She knows," Sharon said softly. "In fact, I didn't have to make that point to her at all. It was exactly what *she* told *me*. She said she knew her brother had disappeared. She said she wasn't grieving because she shot the vessel that contained the demon. The reality was just the opposite. She knew Jake would not have wanted to go on with a demon inside him, wreaking havoc and killing innocent people."

"She's grieving his loss."

"Yes. But also hers. She's grieving for the twin brother who'll never grow up and get married, never have children and a career and a happy life. She's grieving for what they've both lost."

Sharon had begun to cry, and Mike realized he was close to doing the same.

"You need to let go of this for awhile," he said. "Stop worrying and stop fretting. It's not healthy."

"I'm not sure that's possible. Not right now, not while everything is still so fresh and so raw."

Mike regarded his wife from across the room. "You think too much, you know that?"

"Yeah," she said. "I do know it. And I hate it sometimes."

"Come over here," he said, patting the bed with his hand.

She stood and padded across the room and then slipped under the covers, snuggling against him.

Neither talked. There didn't seem to anything else to say.

They held each other, and Mike stroked Sharon's hair, and eventually they both fell asleep.

50

Sharon was preoccupied. It was obvious to Mike she was miles away.

Something was bothering her, over and above nearly being skewered inside a crumbling barn yesterday and then seeing a teenage girl shoot her twin brother to death. From the moment she woke up her mouth was drawn down into a tight slash, her forehead wrinkled in concentration.

She was chewing on something relentlessly, but he couldn't put his finger on what that something might be.

They ate a quick breakfast and gulped down a cup of coffee each. Then they were out the door and into the Explorer for the drive to work, during which Sharon was as quiet and preoccupied as she'd been since awakening.

They made it almost all the way to the station before Mike's curiosity got the best of him.

"Okay, what is it?" he said as they pulled into the station parking lot.

"What is what?"

"Come on babe, don't give me the innocent act. You're so far inside your own head it's lucky I was able to find you this morning. What's bothering you?"

They climbed out of the truck and slammed the doors and began walking toward the station's entrance.

She said, "Okay you're right, something's…bothering me."

"Tell me."

She sighed deeply. When she continued, her voice was reedy and brittle. "This is over for now, but it's not really over. It's never really going to be over."

"I don't follow. We weren't able to save Jake, and that's a tragedy. But the demon is history, driven back to hell or whatever fiery pit it crawled out of."

"Yeah, I know."

"But…"

"But this is all going to happen again."

"The hell it is," Mike said firmly.

"No, really. Professor Paquette said the grimoire is cursed, right? Or, rather, that the Beebe bloodline is cursed, and that the book will eventually find its way back to them."

"No way. Not gonna happen."

"How can you say that when Paquette says differently? He's the expert."

"I can say it because I'm going to destroy the goddamned thing, that's how."

"Destroy the grimoire?"

"Damn right. As a general rule I'm philosophically opposed to burning books no matter their content, but in this case I'll make an exception. I've placed it inside the evidence storage locker for safekeeping until the investigation into Jake Beebe's death is complete. After that I'm taking it out, tossing it into a fifty-five gallon metal drum, dousing it with gasoline and dropping a match on it. And then I'm going to watch it burn with my own two eyes until there's nothing left but a pile of smoking ashes."

"But the evidence locker…"

"I know what you're thinking," Mike said, "and for once in my life I'm way ahead of you."

"Is that so?" Sharon made an effort to smile. Even upset and preoccupied as she was, the smile transformed her face into something stunning.

"Yep, it's so. You're thinking that Gordie and Rob and every officer on the force can get inside the evidence locker. You're thinking that's way too much traffic. You're thinking something's going to happen and the book's going to disappear, am I right?"

"That's about the size of it, yes."

"Well, you can stop worrying. I've removed the storage locker key from the station and I'm personally going to hold onto it until I've destroyed that book. The only way anyone's getting in there for the foreseeable future is with an escort from me. The grimoire has ruined its last life."

Sharon stopped walking and looked up at him. "You're a good man, you know that?"

"I'm a lucky man. I almost lost you yesterday. *Again.* I'm getting damned tired of that and I'll do whatever I have to do in order to make sure yesterday was the last time it ever happens."

"I'm sure that's all true, but I know you better. I know it's more than just me you're worried about. The boy who died yesterday morning was nothing more than a typical teenager, stupid and foolish but basically harmless. He certainly didn't deserve to lose his life for his foolishness. I think you're every bit as committed to ensuring Paskagankee never loses any more innocent lives to the grimoire as you are to ensuring I survive."

They'd opened the door and entered the station, and now Mike regarded his wife closely as they crossed the lobby. "You're still not convinced this thing is over, are you?"

"I'm sorry, it's just…"

"Come with me," Mike said and led her down the hallway to the evidence locker. It was nothing more than a large storage room, similar in design to a janitor's closet, only instead of cleaning materials the room contained rows of metal shelving upon which had been placed items logged into the facility. Guns, knives, computer hard drives, bloodstained clothing; any lawfully seized evidence relating to criminal activity was stored here pending resolution of the case to which the evidence pertained. The locker was accessible through one secure metal door, with no windows or any other form of access.

"I know what the evidence locker looks like," she protested. "I've been in and out of here a thousand times."

"Humor me," Mike answered. "Sometimes we need to see things with our own two eyes to make them real in our heads. You'll feel better once you get a look at that damned book sitting on a shelf awaiting a lit match."

She rolled her eyes but didn't argue.

"Look," Mike said. He fished around inside his pocket until his hand emerged holding a key attached to a white plastic fob.

He held it up for her examination and said, "This is the only key for the evidence locker and, as you know, it's usually stored in the safe behind the dispatcher's desk. From now until the grimoire is a nothing but a bad memory, this key will stay in *my* possession, and anyone with business in the storage locker will be accompanied by *me*."

He slid the key into the lock and turned it, then pushed open the heavy metal door. "Couldn't be any more secure than this, don't you agree?"

"You're quite the showman. P.T. Barnum had nothing on Mike McMahon."

"Do you agree it's secure or not, wiseass?"

Despite her obvious lingering concern, Sharon chuckled. "Fine. Yes, Mr. Barnum, I agree it's secure."

"Small victories," he said as he took her hand. "Follow me."

They wound their way through the shelves until Mike stopped midway down the third row.

"Now, take a look at the damned grimoire and tell me if you don't...think..." His voice trailed off and he released Sharon's hand.

He took a step back.

Glanced back along the route they'd just walked.

Looked from the empty spot on the shelf to her face and then back again to the shelf.

"Please tell me you've forgotten where you put it," she whispered.

"I don't understand," he said. "I tagged the book and put it here last night. *Right in this spot.* Then I marched straight out of the room and locked the door. I haven't spoken to anyone besides you since that moment and I've had the key with me ever since."

"Professor Paquette was right. He's been right about everything so far and he was right about the grimoire."

"But the damned book is solid and real. How the hell could it disappear out of a locked room?"

"Maybe it fell off the shelf and into your pocket while you were—"

"Come on Sharon, you saw that book. It was thick and heavy,

there's no way it could have dropped into my pocket—even if I had a pocket big enough, which I don't—without me feeling the weight of it and noticing immediately."

"Maybe there's a second key to the evidence locker, a key we don't know about."

"Even if that were true, why would anyone on the force come in here and remove the book?" Mike shook his head. "I'm not buying it."

"It's demonic, Mike. Maybe it actually did move itself. Maybe it actually vaporized, or dissolved itself somehow, only to come together on the other side of these walls."

He stared at her. "It's just a book, Sharon."

"I know how it sounds," she protested. "But it's not 'just a book.' That's the whole point. If it was 'just a book,' you wouldn't be talking about dousing it with gasoline and immolating it. If it was 'just a book,' I wouldn't have felt a sense of revulsion deep enough to become physically ill just from looking at it. It's not 'just a book,' and you know it. It's a demonic relic, and who knows *what* sorts of powers it possesses?"

He shook his head and ran a hand through his hair and tried to decide what to do next.

He couldn't think of a single thing.

EPILOGUE

AUGUST 28, 2029

Julie Compton sipped her coffee at the kitchen table, idly thumbing through a magazine as she listened to the sound of her twin sons playing in their bedroom. The eight-year-olds were boisterous, with boundless energy and an infectious curiosity about the world that never failed to brighten her mood.

For a long time after Jake's death inside that horrible barn twelve years ago, Julie doubted she would ever find pleasure again. In anything. Just getting through each day was exhausting, and putting one foot in front of the other was often the most she could manage.

She finished high school because it was expected and attended college because doing so got her out of Paskagankee. Actually getting an education was irrelevant to the equation, because what was the point of learning when you already knew everything that mattered? Julie was a killer who had ended her own brother's life and that was all that she would ever be.

The couple of seconds it had taken to squeeze off four shots were all that would ever matter.

That moment in time would define her forever, at least in her own mind.

But a funny thing happened while she was zombie-walking through life down at the University of Maine. Somehow, against all odds, she met someone.

A young man who saw through the shock and the pain and the self-loathing, and who seemed to think she might be a person with a little value after all. A young man who was sweet to her, and patient, and smart and handsome to boot.

Eventually friendship turned into a date, and then one date turned into several, and by graduation Julie Beebe had become Mrs. Phil Compton and was pregnant with twins.

And while Phil put up an argument about Julie's suggestion to name the twins John and Jake if they were boys—"You do realize 'Jake' is a slang version of 'John,' right?" "I realize it, I just don't care."—she knew all along the argument was mostly for appearance's sake.

Phil was by then well aware of her tragic personal history, and more importantly, Phil was utterly, completely and insanely in love with her. He was perfectly content to name the boys whatever made her happy. Jake and John was what would make her happy, so Jake and John was what they were named upon their birth, three months after graduation.

The intervening years had served to dull the pain of losing her brother.

Somewhat.

While a day never went by that she didn't think of him, most of the time she was too busy raising a pair of human perpetual motion machines to do much more than think back wistfully to a time when her twin had been present in the world. She knew she would never get over losing him, particularly in the horrifying way it had happened, but at long last she could truly say she had moved on with her life.

And she knew in all honesty that was what her brother would have wanted.

Sometimes she even felt something akin to true happiness. Not always, and even then not for very long. But sometimes, and that was good enough.

Then there were the other times, when the boys' roughhousing went a little overboard, or the play swordfights got a little too rough, or the volume of their voices escalated a little above what she was willing to accept, and she was forced to dampen their youthful enthusiasm.

Even then, she almost always did it with a smile, because along with Phil, those two little boys were the only things that kept her tethered to her sanity. And really, what was a little commotion and chaos compared to the joy of watching your flesh and blood grow into beautiful little human beings before your very eyes?

She sipped her coffee and scanned her magazine and eventually decided it was time to check on the boys.

Not because it had gotten too loud in their bedroom.

Just the opposite, in fact.

Things had gone completely silent in there, and long experience had taught her that where her twin boys were concerned, too little noise was almost never a good thing. It was usually worse than too much.

She smiled to herself and stood up and refilled her coffee mug. Then she moved soundlessly across the kitchen floor, fresh coffee clutched in one hand.

She paused a moment at their bedroom door to note its current status—closed, which it was not supposed to be unless someone was sleeping—before turning the knob and stepping into the room.

The boys huddled together at their shared desk on the far side of the room, kneeling shoulder-to-shoulder on chairs as they examined something they'd placed on the surface of the desk. They jumped in guilty surprise at the sound of their mom's sudden, unexpected arrival, and turned around to face her so quickly it was clear something was up.

Something she probably wouldn't like.

Not that the closed door hadn't already delivered that particular message, loud and clear.

"What's going on in here, boys?" she said, eyebrows raised and the smile still lingering, if a little less broad now than when she'd left the kitchen. But how could she *not* smile, even when it was obvious her kids were sneaking around? Every time she looked at her sons, their striking resemblance to her long-dead twin brother was reinforced.

The boys looked down at the desk and then back up at each other before returning their attention to Julie. The motion was so synchronized it was almost as if they'd spent hours choreographing and then practicing it.

The twin thing, Julie thought. *I wonder if this was what Jake and I looked like?*

The familiar wave of grief rolled through her and then disappeared, and without missing a beat she said, "Out with it, dudes. What are you looking at in here with the door closed?"

She hoped eight years old was still too young to be looking at porn, but who could say for sure? That day wasn't far off, and she hated its approach, and the loss of innocence it signaled, almost as much as she hated how much she still missed Jake.

The boys did their choreographed look into each other's eyes again, and then John said, "This is sooo cool, Mom!"

Jake nodded in solemn agreement and it became immediately apparent it wasn't a porn magazine on the desk, if those relics from a more innocent age even still existed. Little boys might be excited about looking at women's naked bodies, but there was no way in the world *her* little boys would be so transparent about their excitement with their mom standing in their doorway, of that she was sure.

"Yeah," Jake said. "We found this yesterday while we were playing in the basement and it's just about the coolest thing in the whole world!"

And the alarm bells began going off in her head.

Julie couldn't quite put her finger on what it was about that statement that so bothered her, but it had the unsettling ring of familiarity and carried with it a sense of subliminal dread that made her stomach drop and her head swim.

"We've been reading it since last night," John said, "and it's kinda hard to understand but sooo cool!"

"You already said that," Julie answered, surprised at how well she'd been able to enunciate, given the fact her lips had turned numb and her tongue felt like it had swollen to twice its normal size.

"We both want to be scientists when we grow up, so we're going to try some of these experiments as soon as we can! Maybe today, if it ever stops raining."

She swallowed heavily. *This can't be happening.*

Oh, it's happening. You're not even that surprised. In the back of your mind you knew it would happen, you just didn't know when.

You've been waiting twelve long years for exactly this to happen. Don't even try to tell yourself you haven't.

"Jake and John Compton. Show me what you're looking at, right now."

The boys exchanged their choreographed look into each other's eyes for the third time. It was no longer amusing.

"It's just a book, Mom."

Jake lifted the volume off the desk and held it up for her inspection, leather cover facing outward toward Julie.

"Look how weird and cool the cover is, Mom! Check it out!"

The coffee mug slipped from her nerveless fingers and landed on her bare foot before smashing into a million pieces on the floor.

She didn't feel the bone bruise the mug gave her big toe.

She didn't feel the burn the hot coffee made on her bare feet.

She didn't feel anything.

All she could do was stare at the grimoire as her world crashed down around her.

Again.

Mike and Sharon and the citizens of Paskagankee will return soon in their fifth supernatural thriller. To be the first to learn about new releases, and for the opportunity to win free ebooks, signed copies of print books, and other swag, take a moment to sign up for Allan Leverone's email newsletter at AllanLeverone.com.

Reader reviews are hugely important to authors looking to set their work apart from the competition. If you have a moment to spare, please consider taking a moment to leave a brief, honest review of Grimoire at Amazon, Goodreads or your favorite review site, and thank you!

About the author

Allan Leverone is the *New York Times* and *USA Today* bestselling author of nearly twenty novels, as well as a 2012 Derringer Award winner for excellence in short mystery fiction and a 2011 Pushcart Prize nominee. He lives in Londonderry, New Hampshire with his wife Sue, and has three grown children and two beautiful grand-children. He loves to hear from readers and other authors; connect on Facebook, Twitter @AllanLeverone, and at AllanLeverone.com

Also by Allan Leverone

Dark Fiction

Paskagankee
Revenant
Wellspring
Mr. Midnight
After Midnight
Covenant
Linger: Mark of the Beast (Co-written with Edward Fallon)

Thrillers

The Lonely Mile
Final Vector
Parallax View: A Tracie Tanner Thriller
All Enemies: A Tracie Tanner Thriller
The Omega Connection: A Tracie Tanner Thriller
The Hitler Deception: A Tracie Tanner Thriller
The Kremlyov Infection: A Tracie Tanner Thriller
The Organization: A Jack Sheridan Pulp Thriller
Trigger Warning: A Jack Sheridan Pulp Thriller

Novellas

The Becoming
Flight 12: A Kristin Cunningham Thriller

Story Collections

Postcards from the Apocalypse
Letters from the Asylum
Uncle Brick and the Four Novelettes
The Tracie Tanner Collection: Three Complete Thriller Novels

www.ingramcontent.com/pod-product-compliance
Lightning Source LLC
Chambersburg PA
CBHW070627260626

47161CB00007B/2609